LORD OF DESTRUCTION!

They had named him Grand *Strahteegos* of Southern Ehleenohee for life in recognition of his proven military genius and long and honorable service. The Council had been sure he would keep the kingdom safe and the army strong, and guard against the many enemies at the borders until the High-Lord Milo's forces succeeded in conquering the barbarians and ending their deadly raids.

But no one had foreseen that an insidious madness would transform Grand *Strahteegos* Pahvlos into an enemy far more dangerous than any invader. And time was fast running out for Milo and his secret agents to save this new Confederation kingdom, driven to the brink of civil war by a madman's cruel decrees. . . .

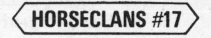

MADMAN'S ARMY

ROBERT ADAMS

A SIGNET BOOK

NEW AMERICAN LIBRARY

PUBLISHED BY
THE NEW AMERICAN LIBRARY
OF CANADA LIMITED

NAL BOOKS ARE AVAILABLE AT QUANTITY DISCOUNTS
WHEN USED TO PROMOTE PRODUCTS OR SERVICES. FOR
INFORMATION PLEASE WRITE TO PREMIUM MARKETING
DIVISION, NEW AMERICAN LIBRARY, 1633 BROADWAY, NEW
YORK, NEW YORK 10019.

First Printing, September, 1987

2 3 4 5 6 7 8 9

SIGNET TRADEMARK REG U S PAT OFF AND FOREIGN COUNTRIES
REGISTERED TRADEMARK — MARCA REGISTRADA
HECHO EN WINNIPEG, CANADA

SIGNET, SIGNET CLASSIC, MENTOR, ONYX, PLUME, MERIDIAN
AND NAL BOOKS are published in Canada by The New American
Library of Canada, Limited, 81 Mack Avenue, Scarborough,
Ontario, Canada M1L 1M8
PRINTED IN CANADA
COVER PRINTED IN U.S.A.

For Alessandro Ferrero, M.D.,
for David and Susan Crippen,
and for all the fine folk at Swamp Con.

Prologue

The old, white-haired, newly dead man lay face down upon the floor tiles, the ornate and bejeweled hilt of a dress-dagger jutting up from his back. Beside the body stood the man who had just killed him, a bared saber in one hand.

"It had to be done," he said, his voice sad, regretful. "There was never a warrior and leader of warriors I respected more, but his stubborn, senile sadism was tearing the army apart at the seams, and with it our Council and our future, as well."

Of the score or so of other men in that chamber, some nodded in agreement, most just stood, staring in shock of the suddenness of the fatal deed, and one burst out bitterly, "*Murderer*! Back-stabbing murderer! It's you deserve to be dead, and if I had a sword . . ."

The tall, saturnine man with the saber stepped off to one side, waving his hand toward a rack of swords and a table on which lay an assortment of dirks and daggers, saying, "Come up and choose a sword, then, my lord Vikos, and I'll meet you here and now, or later, ahorse or afoot."

The shorter, slighter, balding man began to push through the crowd, grim resolution on his shaven face, but near the forefront of the group, he was grabbed by both biceps and shaken mercilessly by a broader, more massive, greying man, who half-shouted, "Now, dammit, Vikos—*Vikos*! Blast your arse, listen to me! Portos was right, can't you see that, man? Yes, I know

7

Strahteegos Pahvlos once spared you, saved your life, but that Pahvlos wasn't the one we've been having to deal with of late. It was a simple choice: the life of an old, stubborn, selfish man or the lives of who can ever know just how many of us, of our people. And he's dead now, thank God. How can you killing Portos or Portos killing you alter the situation, hey? May God damn you for a stubborn fool!" He shook his prey again, harder, hard enough to cause the witness to unconsciously wince. "Come to your senses, Vikos."

A man even more massively built than the shaker touched his thick arm with a huge hand, rumbling in a bass voice, "Stop it, Grahvos. Keep it up and you'll snap his neck or his spine, and we don't need two deaths here today, do we?"

With a deep sigh, Grahvos nodded. "You're right, of course, Bahos. I just couldn't see a duel to add to everything else."

The bigger man took the released Vikos and eased him into an empty chair off his wobbly legs, where he just sat, breathing hard and dabbing with tremulous hands at his bleeding nose, while using the tip of his sore, bitten tongue to take inventory of the teeth in his jaws.

A younger version of Grahvos said, "My lords, please resume your places at the table. This Council meeting has not yet been adjourned, and now there is even more business to consider, weigh and decide. Lord Portos, that includes you, please; put your saber back on the rack . . . and the other sword, too."

"Sweet Christ!" yelped one of the men, "Grand *Strahteegos Thoheeks* Pahvlos lies knifed and dead by the door and you insist on business as usual, Mahvros? You must have ice water in your veins, not blood, like the rest of us."

"Not at all, man," said another. "He's simply practical rather than as emotional as some I might name here."

The first man bristled, but before he could do more than open his mouth, the man next to him, another thick, solid specimen, growled, "Enough of this, all of you. You heard our chairman. Take your places, unless you want Lord Grahvos and Lord Bahos and me going around and shaking each of you, in turn." To the chairman, he said, "Mahvros, you're bleeding like a stuck pig. It wasn't enough to get that dirk out of your shoulder, man, it needs at least bandaging. Here, let me, I own some small experience at such tasks. Want to give me a hand, Tomos?"

As soon as *Thoheeks* Sitheeros and Sub-*strahteegos Thoheeks* Tomos Gonsalos had completed their work and resumed their places, the chairman—his left arm now in a sling and his shoulder swathed in linen strips torn from his shirt and that of his two benefactors— spoke, saying, "All right, let's try to make this short and sweet, get as much as possible done in as short as possible a time, lest pain and blood loss pitch me down on the floor, too.

"We stand in need of another field commander, now. I'd recommend Tomos Gonsalos save for two reasons. Number one, of course, is that he is not one of us, but from Karaleenos; number two is that he is doing a superlative job in his current position and, were we to appoint him field commander, I cannot think of any man who could replace him, who could run his present command anywhere nearly as well.

"Therefore, I suggest that Captain *Thoheeks* Grahvos take on that command either permanently or at least until we weigh out the remaining officers and find a better commander."

All eyes turned to the greying nobleman seated near the chairman. He shrugged. "I'll take over, but only if there is a firm understanding that it *is* purely temporary, and that I will own the authority to groom candidates for the permanent posting. There are two men I can think of right now who would most likely make us excellent *strahteegohee*." He did not think it just then politic to mention that one of the prime men he thought of was the very man who just had slain the previous *strahteegos*, Captain *Thoheeks* Portos, Sub-*strahteegos* of Cavalry.

Mahvros nodded. "I thank you, Acting-*Strahteegos* Grahvos, on behalf of Council and . . ."

"Wait a minute, now," yelped one of the younger of the men ranged about the long table. "Council must vote. When do we vote?"

"You don't, Lord Pennendos," snapped Mahvros peevishly, gritting his teeth against the pain of his pierced shoulder. "When it comes to a final, permanent appointment, *then* Council votes. Something like this does not require the votes of the full Council, only a half plus one. Stop trying to start up a controversy. If you have nothing better with which to occupy yourself, you can search out claimants to the now-vacant *thoheekseeahn* of our recently deceased *Thoheeks* Pahvlos."

Thoheeks Sitheeros sighed and shook his head. "I suppose we can't hope that the word won't spread that we murdered the old bastard, in here . . . ?"

"Of course that word will be disseminated," agreed Grahvos. "There're just too many big, loud, flapping mouths for it to be otherwise . . . not a few of them presently in this room, amongst us."

"And what answer can we give to such calumnies?" demanded *Thoheeks* Neekos, a man built along the lines of *Thoheeks* Vikos but about the age of *Thoheeks* Grahvos.

"The truth," replied the chairman, Mahvros. "The old fool went out of his head completely, threatened us all with a sword from off the rack, put a dirk into my shoulder and was put down for it—treated the only way you can treat mad dogs or murderously mad men.

Most who've had any dealings with him of late will believe it, and that means almost all of the army. Those few who choose to not believe will likely be the born troublemaker types, anyway."

"Who votes his two proxies, now?" rumbled *Thoheeks* Bahos. "Someone will have to, and a proxy for his own, too, until we find and confirm another claimant to that *thoheekseeahn*."

Mahvros wrinkled up his brows. "Yes, there's that problem. To the best of my knowledge, his only living relative is *Thoheeks* Ahramos of Kahlkos . . . and that's one of the proxies he was voting."

"Well, then," mused *Thoheeks* Grahvos, "where there are no relatives, then I suppose friends will have to suffice. Let Lord Vikos vote the three proxies. Is that amenable, Vikos?"

The slighter man nodded, stiffly, cautiously, but still the movement set his nose to bleeding once more.

Captain *Thoheeks* Ptimnos frowned and rubbed absently at the patch covering the empty socket that once had held his right eye. "We may well have more than merely a little trouble with his lover, you know. He announced some time back that he was going to make the young man his legal heir."

"Utterly ridiculous on the face of it!" snorted Captain *Thoheeks* Portos, derisively. "He may be pretty as a girl and he may or may not be pleasant in bed, but he still is only the third son of a *vahrohnos* and in no way suitable to rule lands and regard the welfare of peoples. It's but another evidence of senility . . . if he even meant it at all, of course. In their cups or in the throes of pleasure, men are apt to make promises they would not otherwise make. When I get back to camp, I'll seek out young Ilios and have some words with him. As I recall, he intimidates easily. With Pahvlos dead, now, he just may decide that he's had enough of army life and hie himself home and out of our hair."

On a lighter note, *Thoheeks* Sitheeros said, with a wide grin, "Why don't you take him on yourself, Portos? Couldn't you use a bedwarmer?"

"Don't tempt me," the saturnine officer grinned back. "As I said, he's pretty as a girl. But unfortunately, he can't give me increase, and I don't want my house to die with me. Why don't you find me a fair, well-dowered little wife like you found for Tomos, eh?"

"You, a *kath'ahrohs* of pure Ehleen heritage, would marry a mere barbarian?" said Sitheeros, mockingly.

Portos chuckled. "For a large enough dowry, my friend, I'd marry one of your cow elephants."

Everyone save Vikos laughed; he was afraid to do so lest his nose again begin to drip blood, but he did venture a smile. Mahvros, holding his breath against his pain, still uttered no rebukes for the time being wasted in frivolous chatter, for he would far rather hear the Council jesting and laughing than snarling and hurling insults and edged weapons at each other.

Far and far to the northeast of the city wherein the *thoheeksee* sat in council, a mounted column crossed the shallow Kuzawahtchee River that served as border between the Kingdom of Karaleenos and the onetime kingdom to the south. Once across the river, they began to make camp, unloading felt yurts from off high-wheeled carts.

They were mostly men of slight, wiry, flat-muscled build, having hair of various shades of blond or red and eyes that were mostly blue or grey or green. They wore baggy trousers tucked into the tops of felt-and-leather boots, embroidered shirts that were full in the body but tight in the sleeves, plus armor that was mostly mixtures of cour boulli, mail, scale and plate, much of it gaudily painted or enameled. Their helmets bore plumes, feathers, horsehair crests or whatever else suited individual fancies, and the saddles of their horses were works of art—heavy tooled and dyed leather, inset and fitted with hooks, rings, buckles, decorations and plates of steel, brass, silver, gold and pewter.

Their weapons, however, were almost uniform in character, at least. Every man bore a cased hornbow—short, recurved and reflex, handmade of orangewood or elm, cowhorn and sinew, with arm-tips of antler or bone and bowstrings of waxed silk—and two dozens of arrows for it. Each also was armed with a saber, a target of leather-covered lindenwood, a spear or lance six to eight feet long, a war-axe, a heavy dirk and one or more other knives and daggers of varying sizes and purposes.

Someone unfamiliar with them might well have thought them a military unit, possibly mercenary cavalry, but they were not, not strictly. They were of the race called Horseclansmen. For hundreds of years, the forebears of these men had, with their herds and their families, roved the prairies and plains far to the west called the Sea of Grasses. Then, less than a hundred years before, above ten thousand of them—men, women and children, with all they possessed—had crossed some thousand or more miles of territory—fighting where they had to fight, moving peaceably elsewhere—and at least one range of mountains to invade and conquer that Ehleen land called Kehnooryos Ehlahs. They all would have been happy with that land alone, but with that land they also had inherited enemies on every border who would not let the new overlords live in peace, and therefore the past seventy years had been a time of almost constant border wars for the Horseclansmen, their new vassals and the mercenaries they had had to hire on, even as had the native ruling dynasty which had preceded them and been paramount in the land before their victorious incursion.

First, it had been war on the northern and north-western borders. The upshot of their victory over these enemies had been acquisition of them first as allies, then as vassals. The next war had been all along the southern border, with the Kingdom of Karaleenos. After driving the invading Karaleenohee back, twice, only to see them invade again each following year, the army of Kehnooryos Ehlahs and its dependent states had followed the beaten-off invaders back across the border and taken the fight into Karaleenos itself, driving the king out of his own capital and slowly conquering chunk after chunk of his kingdom, trouncing every Karaleenos army they could bring to battle and killing no less than two succeeding kings in two of those battles.

Meanwhile, along the western border of Kehnooryos Ehlahs, warfare against the mountain tribes had never really ceased for all of the four hundred plus years since the Ehleenohee had invaded the land from the Eastern Sea, once called Atlantic, nor did it cease with the change of overlords from Ehleenohee to Horse-clansmen. It was not, had never been, the formal warfare of the northern or southerly borders, but it was no less bloody, vicious and brutal, for all its informality.

Another drive against the battered army of Kara-leenos, fighting now under a new-crowned young king, Zenos XII, had come to grips with him and it just south of the Lumbuh River bridge and so badly mauled it that another immediate battle would have been out of the question. However, Demetrios, one of the High Lords of Kehnooryos Ehlahs, had been knocked from off the bridge and drowned in the battle's prologue; therefore, a truce had been struck and the other High Lord—Milo Morai, a Horseclans chief—had been summoned by gallopers. He had brought with him reinforcements and the High Lady Aldora Pahpahs of

Linsee, widow of Demetrios, who had cordially hated her husband for his homosexuality.

Milo had treated his beaten foemen with magnanimity, and it was as well that he had, for he shortly had received word from his capital that the Lord of the Pirate Isles—one Alexandros, himself a *kath'-ahrohs* or Ehleen purebred of the old stock—had sailed in with word that the new-crowned High King Zastros of the Kingdom of Southern Ehleenohee was even then preparing to lead a host of upwards of a half million warriors across Karaleenos' southern border, with the avowed purpose of bringing all of the eastern coast under his sway.

When Milo had convinced his sometime enemy King Zenos of the mutual threat and joined the two armies, he had sent messengers far and wide to sound the tocsin, even while striking shaky alliances with hill chiefs and swamp-dwellers to attempt to slow the advance of the huge army of Zastros and interdict its lines of supply insofar as possible.

Help had, indeed, come. Not only from his own lands and those of King Zenos, either, but from far to the north—the Kingdom of Harzburk, the Kingdom of Pitzburk, the Aristocratic Republic of Eeree on the shore of the Great Inland Sea, all had sent noble knights and a horde of mercenaries. Upon learning just why units of the army of Kehnooryos Ehlahs were being withdrawn, warband after warband of mountain tribes had descended from their fastnesses to try selling their services to their ancient enemies.

What had finally occurred at the environs of that bridge over the Lumbuh River had been almost in the nature of an anticlimax. Starved of supplies and near mutiny upon its arrival, the monstrous force had tried but once to cross the heavily-fortified bridge, been driven back in rout, and then had simply hunkered down in low, unhealthy riverside camps to sicken and die of fever, fluxes, wounds, starvation and the nightly attacks of Horseclansmen, swampers and river-borne pirates.

At last, certain of the higher nobility—the *thoheeksee* or dukes—of Zastros' kingdom had had enough and sent a herald to the High Lord by night, offering certain things if they were allowed to march their remaining forces back south, out of Karaleenos and into their own lands in peace.

The High Lord had agreed; however, he had done more than that. He had announced to the herald the imminent merger of his lands with the Kingdom of Karaleenos and the Grand Duchy of Kuhmbuhluhn, the resultant state to be called the Confederation of Eastern Peoples, and he offered the sometime Southern Kingdom a equal place in this state. Upon their acceptance of this astounding offer and the delivery of signed and sealed oaths from every noble landholder still alive and with the army that Zastros had led north, the High Lord had also agreed to send to the fledgling Council of Consolidated *Thoheekseeahnee* of the Southern Ehleenohee a sub-*strahteegos* commanding a force of troops about which a new army to enforce the will of Council might be formed.

He had sent one of the relatives of King Zenos, Sub-*strahteegos Thoheeks* Tomos Gonsalos, with a regiment of mercenary pikemen, a squadron of heavy lancers and a squadron-size of Horseclansmen, this group including a cow elephant captured from Zastros' force during the single attack on the bridge.

The pike regiment and the heavy lancers still were there, but most of the original contingent of Horseclansmen had followed Chief Pawl Vawn of Vawn, their leader, back to Kehnooryos Ehlahs, feeling like him that five and more years separated from wives and families was enough and more than enough.

Most of the unit now going into camp just to the

south of the Kuzawahtchee River was replacement
for that earlier-sent force of Horseclansmen. The bulk
of this present lot were of Clans Skaht and Baikuh,
and were led by Chief Hwahlt Skaht of Skaht, along
with subchiefs from both clans. In addition to these
larger contingents, however, there were quite a few
young, wanderlusting warriors from some dozen other
clans who had heard from Chief Pawl of the vast
opportunities available in the far-southerly lands for
young men of their race, who were greatly respected
by the ruling *thoheeksee* of the onetime Southern Kingdom of Ehleenohee.

Squatting between the chief of Skaht and the senior
sub-chief of Baikuh, all three of them watching the
establishment of the night's camp, while chewing at
stalks of grass, was a man who save for his Horseclans
garb and weaponry could easily have been taken for a
pure Ehleen—tall, larger of build than his companions, with black hair a bit grey at the temples,
guardsman-style moustache as black as the hair and eyes
that could have been black or a very dark brown, his
skin a light olive under the tan and weathering.

But any who took him for Ehleen would have been
very wrong, for he was no such thing, for all that he
spoke that language as fluently and unaccentedly as he
did some score of other languages and twice that number of dialects. His name was Milo Morai and he was a
chief of the Horseclans, one of the triumvirate that
presently ruled the Confederation of Eastern Peoples,
and far, far more, besides.

The carefully selected Ehleen horse guards who made
up some third of his personal contingent on this trip
called him and referred to him as High Lord Milo. So,
too, did some of the Horseclansmen . . . sometimes,
but more usually to them, as to uncounted generations
of their forebears, he was "Chief Milo," "Uncle Milo,"
or on occasion "God Milo."

Although he gave appearance of an age somewhere between thirty and forty years, that appearance was vastly deceiving, and, in truth, not even Milo himself knew his exact age, only that thus far it exceeded seven centuries and that he had appeared just as he now did for all of that vast expanse of years of life.

All of the Horseclansfolk—men, women, children, past and present—venerated this man, for he had always been among them, moved among them, lived among them, fought beside them against savage beasts and savage weather and calamity. He it was who had first succored the Sacred Ancestors—those who became the first Horseclansfolk—guided generation after generation of their descendants in establishing hegemony over all of the Sea of Grasses, far to the west, before he finally had led forty-two Horseclans clans on an epic, twenty-year-long trek to the east and the lands they currently held. In the nearly three-quarters of a century since then, he and they had slowly increased their holdings—for the Horseclansfolk, this was not just necessary but vital, for their natural increase and that of their herds called always for more land, and most good land in the east was already held by one people or another, few of them willing to give it up without a fight.

Therefore, for all that their people were no longer free-roaming nomad-herders and had not been for almost three full generations, still were all in this force proven, blooded warriors, just as had been the force led by Chief Pawl Vawn of Vawn.

The three men squatting in silence were all telepaths and were, despite appearances, deep in conversation. Above eighty percent of Horseclansfolk were, to one degree or another, telepathic, telepathy having been a survival trait on the prairies and high plains which had for so very long been the home and breeding grounds of their race. They called the talent "mindspeak" and used it not only amongst themselves but in communicating with their horses and with the prairiecats—these being jaguar-size, long-cuspided, highly intelligent felines that had been with the Horseclans for almost as long as there had existed folk called Horseclans.

"Uncle Milo," Chief Skaht silently beamed, "I still don't know why you are bringing along all of those Ehleenee; yes, the ones from up in Kehnooryos Ehlahs are part of your guards, but it just seems silly to drag along more of the damned boy-buggerers from Karaleenos. When you need them to fight, they'll probably be off in the bushes somewhere futtering each other, and if you can get them into a real battle, the chances are good they'll run in a pinch, lest they chance ruining their girlish good looks with a warrior's scar or three."

"Oh come now, Hwahlt," was Milo's silent reply, "you know better than that. You've fought in the mountains and during the Zastros business, six years ago, you've fought alongside Ehleenohee, even commanded units of them, on occasion, and you surely know that their warriors—heterosexual, bisexual or homosexual—can be every bit as effective as the warriors of any other people, if properly led, armed, supplied and disciplined.

"As to why I brought along young men of Kahnooryos Ehlahs and Karaleenos, I brought them for precisely the same reason you brought all those footloose young warriors from half a score of clans; man, these are countless acres of prime land in this former kingdom with no lords to hold and rule them, so many were the noblemen killed in the civil wars and then in Zastros' Folly. Ehleen customs of inheritance are strictly patrilineal, as you know, all land going to the eldest son of the house. All of the young men I brought down here are younger sons who will all be more than happy to give military service and then willingly swear oaths of loyalty to the Consolidated *Thoheekseeahnee* and our Confederation of Eastern Peoples in order to receive land on which to raise up a family."

"But what about our Horseclans boys, Uncle Milo?" demanded Sub-chief Djeri Baikuh. "If these damned young Ehleenees get all the land and all?"

There was a broad measure of humor in Milo's beamed answer. "Oh ho, now we get to the bottom of things. Never you fear, Kindred, you have never seen these lands into which we ride on the morrow. They are truly vast, when compared to those lands you have seen; there will be more than enough for all, believe me."

"Are these lands as long and as wide as the Sea of Grasses, Uncle Milo?" queried Chief Hwahlt Skaht.

"Not that large, Hwahlt," Milo replied. "Before the great earthquake and subsidences of so much of the coasts and tidewater lands, the lands that later became the kingdom of Southern Ehleenohee took up some one hundred and seventy or one hundred and eighty thousand square miles, and even today, the Consolidated *Thoheekseeahnee* stretches and spreads over an expanse of one hundred and thirty-odd thousand square miles."

"And just how large is, say, Kehnooryos Ehlahs, Uncle Milo?" the chief asked.

"Between the landward edges of the salt fens and the latest-won portions of the mountains," was Milo's reply, "between the Karaleenos border and the Kuhmbuhluhn border, Kehnooryos Ehlahs covers about two-fifths as much land, Hwahlt."

The chief spit out his grass stem and hissed softly between his teeth, looking very thoughtful, but carefully shielding his thoughts from the scrutiny of his two companions.

But not shielded from the powerful mental probing abilities of him who abruptly joined them.

The agouti-colored cat slipped noiselessly from out the tiny copse between the three men and came to sit between Chief Hwahlt and Milo, his chin resting on the latter's knee and his thick tail overlapping his forepaws.

Even as he yawned gapingly, the westering sun glinting on his long, white cuspids, he was beaming, "Why would my cat-brother, the honored and valiant Chief of the Skahts, think of taking all of his clan away from Ehlai, whence first came the Sacred Ancestors, the progenitors of his folk?"

"To begin with, cat-brother," was Hwahlt's answer, "there is some doubt that this Ehlai is the original Ehlai, amongst the bards of the clans, for some versions of the Prophecy of the Return and How Strange Our Old Lands say that the direction of The Ehlai of our Sacred Ancestors lies in the home of the *setting*, not of the *rising*, of Sun. So there may well be nothing in any way holy about that crowded, overgrazed, mosquito-ridden place up in Kehnooryos Ehlahs at all.

"I mean to take my clan out of it, too, whether we come down here to the Consolidated *Thoheekseeahnee* or take over the lands and titles that King Zenos has offered me and mine, and Chief Ben of Baikuh means to go, too. Nor are we two the only chiefs considering the offers of Karaleen lands; no, there's Vawn, Morguhn, Danyuhlz, Rahsz and more."

Milo was not surprised to hear the chief's thoughts. He of all men knew just how crowded the high island in the midst of the great salt fen was become as the Horseclansfolk and their herds bred year after year. Nor was the ancient man at all displeased at the news, for the clans squatting on Ehlai were becoming more and more inbred, and this fact could be the beginning of racial disaster, yet few of them living cheek by jowl with close Kindred could be persuaded to take Ehleen women or men in marriage. However, were the clans to settle far away from other clans, in Ehleen-populated lands, then perhaps they might begin to scatter their racial seed farther afield and reduce somewhat their present consanguinity.

In fact, did this chief and the others he had mentioned know the full truth of the matter, King Zenos had requested and been gladly given Milo's permission to offer his handsome propositions to the chiefs after the defeat of Zastros' great army, six years back. It had taken longer than he or the young king had expected, but it now would seem that that particular barme had begun to ferment.

To the newly arrived prairiecat, Milo beamed, "Did my cat-brother see or smell aught of danger nearby our campsite?"

The cat had begun to lick at his chest fur with steady strokes of a long, wide, red-pink tongue, nor did he cease his grooming while he beamed his silent reply to Milo. "No two-legs den up anywhere I went in the lands ahead, God Milo. There was one place where once they denned, but no faintest scent of them now lies anywhere within it, only the smells of the beasts which for long have used its shelter. Around the road, yonder toward the rising of Sun is the only place in which there is recent scent of two-legs, and even that is not too recent. This cat . . . wait, God Milo, Shadowspots beams to this cat."

After a moment, still licking, the prairiecat resumed his beaming: "God Milo, Shadowspots has found a sandy place down the river. Two-legs without toot coverings have walked there this day, and small, very narrow boats were pulled up out of the river there. The bones and scales of several fish are scattered there, also the bones of a large water viper."

"Any trace of fire?" asked Milo.

"No, God Milo," the cat beamed back, "only that

which this cat has repeated from the beaming of Shadowspots."

Milo came up to a stand, ordering, "Hwahlt, before anyone goes too far in settling up hereabouts, tell them we won't be camping here after all. Shadowspots has found a place where barefoot men pulled canoes or pirogues ashore on a little riverine beach and had themselves a meal of raw fish and a raw moccasin, leaving behind bones from the snake but not the head. What does that sound like to you?"

The chief's lips became a grim line. "Fen-men! No damned wonder this stretch is unsettled, on either side of the river; those devils must have killed or driven off everyone who tried to live around here . . . if they were anywhere near to the river, that is. Fen-men will never willingly get far from water and their boats, ever, for any reason."

Hurriedly, the carts were reloaded and the march resumed in a southwesterly direction, away from the river and the swamps into which it eventually flowed. The fen-folk were the avowed enemies of every man or woman or child not of their scanty numbers and had always been such for as long as anyone could recall. They were a primitive and a singularly savage people, living deep in the fens and swamps in small extended-family groups, joining forces with others of their unsavory ilk but rarely.

Their most-feared arm was a blowgun which expelled darts smeared with deadly poisons; other than these, most carried a large, multipurpose knife and maybe a second, smaller one; they were said to use spears in hunting boars, alligators and certain other large, dangerous beasts, but they never used such in warfare. Fen-men wore no armor, no footwear of any description and few clothes, for that matter. They went about almost naked and smeared from head to foot with some sort of grease that smelled reptilian

Robert Adams

and was said to repel insects. Adult fen-men shaved or pulled out all of the hair from both scalp and body, but otherwise were of distinctively unclean habits. All folk so unfortunate as to live near them hated and feared the night-stalking killers with their deadly blow-pipes; they were killed on sight, like the deadly species of vermin they were considered to be. But wiser folk tried to avoid fen-men and their haunts altogether, which was just what Milo and the others were doing.

"Better to be safe than sorry," he thought, "but someday I'm just going to have to find a way to eradicate those damned man-shaped things from one end of the fens to the other. I hate to think of counte-nancing, leading, genocide, but the fen-folk have been at war with all the rest of humanity since at least the time of the great earthquakes and I don't think they will ever be otherwise then cold-blooded, creeping, sneaking murderers, coming by night or killing from ambush any man or woman or child they see who is not one of them. Even the Ehleen pirates, who have had shaky agreement with them for a couple of centu-ries now, admit that the fen-men are sly, treacherous and completely devoted to murder as a pleasant pas-time. And people like that cannot be dealt with—I know, I've tried for years with the subrace of them who inhabit the fens of Kehnooryos Ehlahs—save with a bow at ranges that their devilish poisoned darts won't reach."

Chapter I

Even while she emitted an almost-constant contra-basso rumble of contentment, Sunshine was conversing silently with her "brother," Gil Djohnz, who was engaged in washing her in the shallows of the small river that flowed through the verdant croplands of the Duchy of Mehsees. Whenever Gil looked up and to the east, he could see the dirty smoke of the countless cooking-fires rising up from the city of Mehseepolis and the sprawl of the army camp that surrounded it.

A few yards away, three other elephants were being scrubbed by their own "brothers." The nearest of these called herself Tulip. She was a bit taller and a few years older than Sunshine; her "brother" was a half brother of Gil—though Gil, being the son of his father's premier wife, received Bili Djohnz's deference, for Bili's mother had been but a concubine when he was born. Just beyond Tulip lay a much smaller elephant, a young bull, only a little over four years old; this one called himself Dragonfly for some reason no man or beast had ever yet fathomed, and his "brother" was a nineteen-year-old cousin of Gil. On the bank, drying off from her own bath in the fitful wind and the hot sun, stood the largest of all four elephants, a tusked cow who had named herself Newgrass.

Although in traditional Ehleen armies only bulls were used as war-elephants, the smaller and mostly tuskless cows being relegated to heavy draught pur-

poses, all three of these cows had served in numerous
campaigns of the army of the Consolidated *Thoheek-*
seeahnee in armor and in the very thick of battle in the
time before real, war-trained bulls had finally been
sent from the Land of Elephants, the far-western duchies near the shores of the Upper Gulf.

Consequently, the tender grey skins of all three of
the cows now bore honorable war scars—marks left
them by the bite of sharp steel blades, the stabbing of
spear-, dart- and arrow-points, the friction and pinch-
ing of harness and armor. Gil's sensitive soul mourned
once again whenever he saw and felt these scars, recalling as he then did the suffering of his huge but
basically gentle "sister."

For the umpteenth time, Sunshine beamed the question to Gil, "Brother-mine, is it really true, then? We
really will leave for the land wherein Sunshine was
calved, soon? We will really set out next week?"

"Yes, my sister," he beamed back patiently, smiling
to himself at the cow's enthusiasm. "We will set out
for the far-western duchies on next Monday . . . hopefully, but by Tuesday, at the latest, Sun and Wind
willing. A way was found for us to circumvent the
machinations of the Grand *Strahteegos*, who would
have—had he been allowed his way—kept us here in
virtual military slavery until I had a long beard as
white as snow; kept us for no reason of which I can
think, for now there are a full dozen huge, long-tusked
bulls in the elephant-lines, along with men I have
taught to mindspeak them, so the only uses that you
and our sisters have been recently put to on campaign
have been those of oversized draught-oxen—pulling
siege-engines and wagons and the like—and I am of
the mind that your war service earned you better than
that.

"But now they tell me that that old man is finally
dead, slain by one of his own officers when he went

mad and attacked the leader of Council—him with a sword and a dirk and his chief unarmed. So now we are completely free to leave this dishonorable service to which he saw fit to relegate us and make our way to the land of your birth, with no longer any worry that armed horsemen might be sent galloping after to bring us back into odious and shameful bondage."

He ceased to beam then as he concentrated on removing an embedded tick from deep within a fold of her right ear. He still was at it when an unexpected gush of cold river water struck his head and shoulders with enough force to rock him where he squatted, his consequent imbalance causing Sunshine a jab of pain. When he looked around, he quickly spied out the culprit, who already was refilling his trunk. "Dragonfly!" he beamed sternly. "Did you know that you just caused me to hurt your Auntie Sunshine?"

The dripping young bull shook his head and, while looking about for another, unaware target for his trunkful of water, beamed in a petulant manner, "Well, two-leg, if you don't want to get wet, then hurry up, My mother and the rest won't leave here until you're done, and I want to go back to the elephant-lines, *now*!"

Knowing of old the futility of trying to either argue or reason with the stubborn, selfish young bull, Gil beamed to his cousin, "For the sake of Sacred Sun, Bert, come take this little beast in hand before I'm tempted to render him into army beef."

But another reached the culprit before the young man; she bore him to the ground and belabored him with her trunk until he squealed shrilly, beaming pleas for mercy. But no sooner had his mother, Tulip, allowed him to rearise than he sidled swiftly out of her reach and taunted, "You don't really hurt me. You don't ever really hurt me, I just fool you into thinking you're hurting me. But when I'm all grown up and as

big as Brohntos, then I'll hurt you, I'll crush your
bones and stab my tusks into you until you're very
sorry you ever tried to hurt me when I was smaller
than you are. You'll see, Mother! You . . ."

At that point, the beastlet was again hurled flat on
one side and Newgrass, who had had a few calves of
her own, over the years, belabored him until there
could be no question but that his shrieks and squeals
were those of true and intense pain. When Bert Djohnz
came over, the little bull was more than willing to get
up and leave the vicinity of his grim Auntie Newgrass
with his two-leg brother.

Worriedly, Gil beamed to Sunshine, "Dragonfly dis-
turbs me, sister-mine; he is stubborn, willful, selfish
and vindictive. Now, while he's only four feet or so at
the withers and has not more weight than four or five
men, he's not really very dangerous, but as he grows, I
fear he'll become so deadly he'll have to be either run
off or killed, and I love my sister's kind, Sunshine, I
don't want to see any of them hurt."

The recumbent elephant raised her trunk to tenderly caress the man kneeling on her side with its
sensitive, fingerlike tip. "Yes, man-Gil, Sunshine knows
how much you love her and her sisters. She loves you
deeply and so, too, do Tulip and Newgrass . . . and
even that little bull, Dragonfly, he loves Gil Djohnz,
brother-of-elephants.

"The way that Dragonfly behaves and misbehaves
and threatens, none of it is really his fault, brother-
mine; rather it is because he is growing up with only
mature elephants, not naturally, in a herd environ-
ment, with others of his own age with whom he can
prank and play and fight and slowly establish just what
will be his place when at last he is himself mature.
When we reach my place of birth, he will have a herd
and you will see a great change in him, brother."

As he mounted Sunshine after she had dried and

was ready to return to the Elephant-Lines in camp, Gil saw on the distant road a galloper raising a plume of dust as he spurred hard toward the city, a string of remounts racing after him. From this distance, Gil could not be certain, but he thought that that many remounts would only be brought along by a Horseclans galloper.

Even while Gil and his elephants were wending their slow, unhurried way back to camp, Sub-chief Djaimz Baikuh, drooping in his saddle with weariness, approached the city gate, identified himself, and was granted entry and given a guide to conduct him to the one-time ducal palace, now become a labyrinthine complex of old and new buildings and housing the Council of *Thoheeksee* and their staffs, plus all of the bureaucrats and functionaries necessary to the newly established government.

Thoheeks Mahvros convened the meeting of those other *thoheeksee* who had happened to be in or near to the palace-citadel complex. All who hurried to answer the urgent summons for the emergency meeting were obliged to rack swords and leave other cutlery in the new receptacles located just outside the doors of the chamber, then submit to searches for hidden weapons by the guards, but vividly recalling the terrible events of the third-from-last meeting of the Council, the objections were few and weak.

Thoheeks Grahvos commented, "Mahvros, we can't cast valid votes on any matter of real importance—there're only eleven of us here."

Mahvros shook his head. "There's no need I can see to vote on anything, important or unimportant. This meeting was convened only to officially notify you all that the replacements for Captain Chief Pawl Vawn's squadron of Horseclanner archers is a few days east of

Thrahkohnpolis and will be here within a fortnight or less."

He paused and took a deep, deep breath. "With them rides Milos Morai, High Lord of the Confederation of Eastern Peoples, our overlord . . . in case anyone had forgotten. You'd best all start putting your personal affairs and those of your vassals and desmenes in proper order for his perusal or that of whomever he decides to make our prince and *ahrkeethoheeksee*."

"Now just wait a minute!" yelped *Thoheeks* Vikos, agitatedly. "I thought one of the prime agreements when this Council of *Thoheeksee* was first established was that it was being established to prevent the further proliferation of despotic kings to sit on thrones and grind us all down until we could take no more and rose up against them in bloody, costly rebellions. To my mind, a prince is no better than just another name for a tyrannical . . ."

Thoheeks Grahvos slapped one horny palm on the table and roared, "Enough, now, dammit, Vikos! Do I have to shake sense into your hot head again today? In this instance, 'prince' is simply what the High Lord chooses to title his *satrapeeosee*, his highest-ranking deputies, who rule but only in his name and that of the Confederation."

"What of these *ahrkeethoheeksee*, Grahvos?" asked another of the men. "Will they be of us or northerners put over us?"

Grahvos shrugged. "I couldn't say, my lord, though I would imagine that the *ahrkeethoheeksee*, at least, will be chosen from among the present *thoheeksee* and possibly the prince will, too . . . but I would rather that we weren't and I mean to tell the High Lord precisely that, and in just those words."

Young *Thoheeks* Pennendos looked stunned, appalled. "My lord, my lord, you mean you'd see our overlord put some alien over us before one of our own blood and breeding?"

"And damned right, too!" rumbled *Thoheeks* Bahos' deep voice. "And if he didn't advise just that, then I would, too. Maybe you're too young to remember, but I'm not—*thoheeksee* fighting like gutter curs over some stinking piece of offal, hiring on warbands, taking plowmen out of the croplands to push pikes and die in trying to forward a claim to the crown and office no better than some score of others. And one Bahos right along with them, too, infected by the same cursed plague of ambition as they. That pest is apparently endemic to our blood, my boy, and that's why we dare not see one of us made prince of this land."

Mahvros looked down the table to *Thoheeks* Sitheeros, saying, "My lord, for some reason, the High Lord has indicated a desire to meet your elephant-master, the man Rikos Laskos, so you must immediately summon him to Mehseepolis. As for me, I can be glad that at least we finally got the new guest wing of the complex completed last year; otherwise, we'd all have to be moving out of suites and in with each other or down into the army camp for the duration of the High Lord's stay amongst us, here. Now, at last, you all know just why *Thoheeks* Grahvos pushed that project so hard during his last year of tenure as Council Chairman and I during the earlier months of mine own."

Thoheeks Fraiklinos of Fraiklinospolis declared, "Well, I for one would be more than happy to see this nebulous overlord of ours even if it meant sleeping and biding in a pigsty for the next year. Something has got to be done about the raids against mine and the other western duchies, and our own reorganized fleet just does not seem capable of doing more than helping to pick up the pieces long after the damned foreign raiders are gone back to wherever they lair up."

Grahvos sighed. "Yes, our current fleet—if I can call it that!—indeed sorely lacks experienced senior officers, thanks to Zastros' prize *nautikos* and his idiotic idea of taking on the whole fleet of the Ehleen pirates off the Lumbuh River delta. It would seem that not even one veteran naval officer survived that debacle. And of course any who swam ashore there would've been taken and tormented to death by the bestial fen-men.

"Such as we have are young men learning as they go along, and I fear it will take time to season them in command positions, none of which is of much help or solace to you and your folk of the western *thoheek-seeahnee*, my lord; just remember as you curse and revile them, that for all their present ineptitude, they are trying."

"You're damned right they're trying!" grated Fraiklinos. "Very trying indeed, are they!"

"Well," Grahvos said, "I do know that our overlord has a large and fine fleet in his Confederation; it is, in fact, none other than the fleet that destroyed the best part of the fleet of Zastros, the fleet of Prince Alexandros Pahpahs, Lord of the Ehleen Pirate Isles. Perhaps a reformed pirate will be what it takes to put paid to this worrisome host of active pirates, eh?"

Fraiklinos grumped. "At this point, my lord, I'd be more than willing to try a fleet of demons and apes; certain sure, they would be of more real help than our so-called fleet; they could in no way be more useless."

Where once, as late as three hundreds of years—scarcely an eyeblink of geological time—before, had been green, verdant lands, tall forests and winding freshwater streams, the waves of a long, wide bay now lapped at beaches and muddy deltas, their oceanic salinity always tempered by the quantities of water borne down to that new bay by the rivers and streams from north and west and east. Some of those rivers were indeed mighty and they already had begun to build from the silt and sand and rock that the water brought from drier places islets and deltine peninsulas on which grew grasses and shrubs and small trees, their roots catching and holding more soil and rocks to enlarge and solidify their precarious perches.

There were, by then, few living creatures who could recall the vast cataclysms that had spawned this bay. It had been a time of terror, a time of horror, a time for many of death. In the dark, early-morning hours, a great, unsuspected tsunami had come ashore all along the sleeping coastline and advanced destructively far, far inland, a wall of cold, salty, relentless water; even beyond the main force of the tsunami, the courses of rivers were reversed to flood over their banks, killing and destroying even more.

Though bad enough, the tsunamis were far from the worst ills to afflict the lands and all that dwelt thereupon. There came a seemingly endless succession of earthquakes and tremors that changed the ages-old courses of streams and rivers overnight, dumped ponds and even lakes from out their beds, tumbled cities, buried towns and forests under slides or drowned them, swallowed up farms and homes. Volcanoes dormant for uncountable millennia suddenly rumbled into full, frightful, fiery life all along the chains of eastern and southern mountains, darkening days with their windborne dust and ash, belching molten lava and superheated stones to fire hundreds of square miles of montane forests.

Then, suddenly, as much as a hundred miles inland, all along the eastern coast, the land subsided and the sea came pouring, boiling in. On the southern coast, it was even worse, for the entire peninsula long ago called Florida sank until most of it was, at best, a salt fen, only its rare highlands really above the highest tides.

A second great earthquake sank most of that area once called Louisiana, along with vast stretches of land to the west and the east of it, becoming only an estaurine bay of the vastly enlarged Gulf of Mexico. The Caribbean Sea had shown its own rapaciousness, too, avidly gobbling up coastlines, islands, cays and keys. Most of those lands, islands and islets left above water were smaller, lower and still racked by earthquake aftershocks and some volcanism.

But elsewhere, new lands were formed—the Bermuda Islands having been transformed by risings into a virtual archipelago, almost circular, and almost completely surrounding a shallow salt lagoon, in which lay a broad, hilly island of seabed rock, bare as a picked skull.

After the earth had ceased its agonized spasms, the survivors—plant, animal and human—began to adjust to the new order of lands and seas, to breed and repopulate, to build anew. Some years later, subsequent to a civil war in Kehnooryos Ehlahs, the losers enshipped, sailed down one of the rivers and out to sea, finally making landfall at the collection of new and older islands some hundreds of miles off the east coast.

In the beginning, they made their homes on some of the less rocky, more southerly islands, refurbishing ancient ruins, farming where decent soil remained, breeding small numbers of stock beasts on the strictly limited graze, fishing, and in times of desperation, raiding the coasts and riverways of their previous homelands to the west. But after, themselves, suffering the effects of raids, they first built a citadel on the rocky isle in the inner lagoon, then began to ship load after load of fertile soil over to fill in the terraces they were constructing of material mined from the rocks themselves.

Slowly, painfully, abodes were chipped out, multichamber homes mined into the very rock that had underlain seabed ooze from time out of mind until the upheavals had forced it from endless darkness into the glare of the sun and the silvery rays of the moon. By the time that few of the third generation of islanders were left alive, much had been accomplished and the isle was mostly become green and productive.

Even so, however, there simply was no way to feed the ever growing population from its yield, no matter how bountiful, nor did the drudgery of farming and fishing come easily to these men, who were mostly the descendants of noble warriors, not of farmers and laborers. And so, sometime in the fourth generation, they slid into piracy on shipping—both coastal shipping and maritime—and began to mount regular raids on the coasts to the west, not just against their own ancestors' place of origin but against all of the lands and cities their ships and men could easily reach.

At first, the raiders brought captives in only as slaves, for the work of making their home a near-impregnable fortress went on. Ways were found to block all save a single, treacherous channel to the open sea from the lagoon—native seamen could negotiate it easily and with relative speed, while non-natives perforce had to feel a way along with a leadsman always astride the bowsprit, the snail-crawl progress making of a stranger's ship an easy target to the guards on the cliffs on either hand.

Stones were quarried from the newer, bare-rock isles and barged across the lagoon to the older, lower isles, there to be used in the construction of fortifications and underwater obstacles to hinder the landings of boats on the beaches. Other fortifications and lookout towers were built atop the highest pinnacles of rock. In addition, shipload after shipload of rich soil was brought in from the less populated portions of coastlines and was used to fill terraces built into the lagoon–sides of the surrounding isles.

But as the years followed one after the other and the raidings and piracies and sea-fights and storm-losses of ships and whole crews went on, the slaves began to outnumber the free men and women in the isles, and, at length, one farsighted Lord of the Isles persuaded the Council of Shipmasters to proclaim an end to slavery, giving every living, hale, male slave the right to either ship aboard one of the raiders as a free crewman and warrior or remain ashore to perform one of the numerous necessary trades or crafts in support of the fleet. The pirates and raiders also began to let it be known that slaves of mainland masters with enough guts to attach themselves to raiders' shore parties or otherwise get to the Sea Isles would find a welcome there, just so long as they paid their way and lived according to the Laws of the Isles.

Over the years, a true society developed, an ordered society, with customs and laws and usages of its own. The Lord of the Isles, chosen upon the death of his predecessor by the Council of Shipmasters, was usually—but not always!—a descendant of one of the original Ehleen settlers, and while no one of these families was even near to being of the purity of lineage that the mainland Ehleenohee called *kath'ahrohs*, most of them did try to kidnap and marry Ehleen women of good family, now and then in their raidings; moreover, they made sure that a priest of the Ehleen sect was always in residence in the Isles, honored after a fashion and supported handsomely.

At a time about a hundred and fifty years after the settlement of the Isles, a non-Ehleen Lord of the Isles, Lord Djahn Krooguh, who had been a mainland slave before becoming a pirate, made a momentous and a very valuable discovery. This lord happened to be a telepath, and, having mentally communicated with various beasts in his youth, before being enslaved, he sent out a beam to a pod of *eheethosee*—great black-and-white dolphins, called by other peoples grampuses or orcas or killer whales. Shortly, to the real terror of his crew, his small ship was surrounded by the *eheethosee*—their dorsal fins towering up higher than any of the men, some of them almost as long and as broad abeam as the cockleshell ship. Nor did any one of the crewmen believe for one minute that their very new lord could or was conversing in silence with the pod of sea-monsters, not at first.

But in time such communication came to be accepted among the folk of the Sea Isles and a tenuous bond between man and ork—as they came to be called, adopting a barbarian word for them—was established. Lord Djahn sought out telepaths or those with the ability to develop into such amongst his people and tried to place at least one aboard each of the active ships; so too did all his successors, and, eventually, the telepathic ability became one of the criteria for not only becoming Lord of the Isles, but even succeeding to a command of a ship.

Not only did the orks provide security for the Isles, they became most adept at exploring coasts and harbors for raiders, or seeking out prey on the open seas for pirates. On occasion, two or three or more of them had butted the side of a ship in unison, disordering the crew just before a pirate ship closed with the vessel.

Although the orks were far from averse to consuming dead bodies cast into the water—thus easing the problem of disposing of deceased Isle-folk without attracting sharks and other dangerous scavengers to the environs of the Isles—the sleek creatures often remarked that they preferred seals or fish or whales, so not a few of the pirates wondered now and again over the years just what kept the valuable marine allies so drawn to them. None of them ever learned, dying still ignorantly accepting the fact of the orks' inexplicable allegiances.

Two hundred-odd years after the initial settlement, the folk of the Isles were become wealthy, their huge fleet was the largest and most powerful and modern, and enough of the mainland principalities had, over the years, suffered enough losses, broken enough teeth on the massive natural and man-made defenses of the ocean citadel to now leave well enough alone and accept their occasional losses or pay tribute in specie or goods to the Lord of the Sea Isles in order to keep his ravening, ferocious raiders from their coasts and coastal shipping.

The only mainland state that did not suffer either sea-robbers or tribute was Kehnooryos Ehlahs; some third of a century before, all raidings against them had ceased, and few of their ships had been lost since then to the ships of the Isles. Then, just as High King Zastros had been readying his huge host to march northward on his chosen course of conquest, the young Lord of the Sea Isles, Alexandros Pahpahs, had set sail for Kehnooryos Atheenahs, capital of Kehnooryos Ehlahs, and after conferring with the rulers, allied his folk and ships with the mainland confederation that had grown out of the united stand against the High King of the Southern Ehleenohee.

Moreover, possibly in earnest of the alliance, he had brought back to the Sea Isles upon his own return one of the rulers, who was the recent widow of him who had been the fourth of the original two men and two women who had ruled over Kehnooryos Ehlahs for nearly fifty years.

Sea Isle folk who heard the news thought that his ship would bear some withered, wrinkled crone. They were wrong. The young woman who leaped lightly from rail to wharf looked, despite her actual sixty-odd years, to be no more than twenty-two or twenty-three and a true *kath'ahrohs*—with a dense mass of blue-black hair, eyes so dark as to appear black and an olive complexion beneath her tan.

The High Lady Aldora Linsee Treeah-Potohmahs had quickly proven herself a singular lady in a host of ways. Very well coordinated, she had on the voyage to the Isles learned to scamper up and down the rigging of the sailing ship as rapidly and surefootedly as any of the able-bodied seamen. She was a master of many weapons, making up for the bulk and bulging muscles she lacked with a flexibility and speed that had to be seen to be believed; the wearing of heavy armor did not seem to ever tire her and slowed her but mini-mally. She could swim as fast and with as little appar-ent effort as any Sea Islesman, and her telepathic ability was stronger and farther-ranging than that of any man or woman of the Sea Isles folk.

She also proved herself stubborn and willful, stalk-ing unsummoned into a meeting of the Council of Captains to demand that she be aboard one of the ships being sent to coastal waters to interdict High King Zastros' fleet, prevent it from entering the Lumbuh River and giving aid and supplies to the land forces. She shouted them all down in the course of that stormy meeting, even Lord Alexandros and the Senior Cap-tain, Yahnekos, his stepfather. When a Captain Moh-mahros had had enough female impertinence and made to put her out of the chamber by force, she dislocated his shoulder and his elbow and cracked three of his ribs so speedily and with so little apparent effort that many of the others did not immediately realize just why the man had come to lie, white-faced and groan-ing, on the carpet before the wisp of a grim-faced girl.

Eventually, having worn down most of the opposi-tion, she got her way, of course, shipping out aboard

Lord Alexandros' personal bireme, pulling her part of an oar on the benches with the rest of the ship's complement and, in the course of the protracted, destructive, very bloody battle against the Southern Ehleen battle fleet, distinguishing herself as a paladin-par-excellence.

So respected was she become for her warlike traits and skills that she faced no argument when she elected to be one of the volunteers who went upriver in the smallest, most shallow-draft vessels to mount night attacks against the camps of the High King sprawled along the southern banks across from the sections defended by the High Lord Milo and his allies.

After the deaths of Zastros and his queen, after the abrupt cessation of hostilities on the mainland, the Lady Aldora took part in some practical voyages, even tried coastal raiding for a while. Then, however, having driven home her point, gotten her way, she put off her armor and weapons and sea-boots, taking up the attire and ways of a Sea Isles woman, living in the palace with Lord Alexandros—first as his mistress, then, after a while, as his legal wife. She was not his only wife, of course, for he wanted and needed heirs, sons, while she was barren and knew it for fact, fifty years' worth of lusty lovers having all failed to ever quicken her. When first she began to enjoy regular sex with Alexandros, she hoped against hope . . . but she was of too practical and realistic a basic nature to pin the succession of his house and title on such vain hopes, so she insisted that he seek out and wed other women, even presenting some of them to him; one of the girls she had personally kidnapped from Kehnooryos Mahkehdonya and another from a seaside city in Ehspahneeah, far and far to the east across the great Ocean.

Aldora found herself to be naturally attuned to and very comfortable with the free and easy sexual mores

of the Sea Isle womenfolk, mores so like to those of
the Horseclans with whom she had matured. She never
took another legal husband, as did most of the polyan-
drous women of the Isle, but she felt free and was,
indeed, completely free to enjoy many lovers from
among the captains, pirates and raiders while her husband busied himself with the necessary functions of
procreation on his other wives. But when they were at
sea together, Lord Alexandros was hers alone for the
length of the voyage and she took full advantage of
him and his rare ability to fully fulfill her, as lover, as
matelot, as caring friend, as knowledgeable teacher in
the ways of the sea.

She found that she did not miss the mainland or its
people at all, after a while; what she did miss was
horses and the great prairiecats. The only felines on
any of the Isles were domestic or feral housecats, kept
to check the depredations of rats and mice, and there
was not one horse to be found. There was a small herd
of runty, wild ponies on the largest of the low isles,
but all of her attempts to mindspeak them had proven
them possessed of little ability to none at all, with but
dim intelligence. The folk of the Isles used them mostly
for meat and hides, like the feral swine that shared the
isle, these latter being far and away the intellectual
superiors of the ponies, capable of mindspeaking with
humans, but not much inclined to so do, rather assidu-
ously avoiding close proximity to their two-legged
predators.

But with the great orks, Aldora found herself at
home. The mindspeak of the massive marine mam-
mals was almost as powerful as her own rare talents,
and the creatures seemed to take to her as they did
and had to no other human, living or dead. A pod of
varying strengths always was resident in the clear waters of the sandy-bottomed central lagoon, for sharks
seldom entered from the sea beyond the circling isles

and, consequently, the lagoon was a safe place for calving.

In company with her newfound friends, Aldora explored the most distant reaches of the lagoon, fearful of no other living thing while she swam among the sleek black-and-white beasts. Not even the long, scaly *krohkohthehlishsee* that crawled and swam in the salt swamp on the southernmost side of the Isles dared to venture into the lagoon when orks were nearby, for their armor-plated hides were no match for the crushing strength of an ork's jaws, and fast as their flattened sculling tails could propel them, the orks could effortlessly swim rings around them; also, orks could seldom bring themselves to pass up a tasty snack of reptile meat.

When once she suggested to Lord Alexandros the extirpation of the crocodilians—which numbered among them some true giants of fifteen and twenty feet in length and took ponies and pigs on occasion, as well as a human swimmer, now and then, or a sentinel careless or foolhardy enough to leave one of the three fen-watchtowers alone and afoot—he had demurred.

"No, love, like the orks, those dragons are allies in our defense, fearsome and treacherous allies, sometimes, but still allies."

"Allies?" she demanded. "What the hell are you talking about, Lekos? The orks are intelligent, can reason; those damned things are mindless, just toothy eating-machines, and about as picky about their fare as a damned shark."

"Well, for one thing," he replied patiently, "they provide efficient burial service for corpses and quick disposal of such garbage as the swine find unappetizing. But the most important thing is that they make of that fen a deathtrap to any would-be invaders.

"Fourscore or so years back, a party of mainlanders made to dig out and deepen the water courses through those fens in order to get some of their ships through it and into the lagoon. They began at dusk, one night, while others of them kept the attention of our men near the entry-channel, away to the north. A few justly terrified warriors and seamen were found in the tops of a few trees or squatting within one of the two whaleboats left behind, and they swore that over a full thousand men had entered that benighted fen, perhaps a tenth of their numbers had won back to the sea, a few dozens had found safe places and the rest had all died horribly, done to death by the dragons.

"Until that occurrence, our folk had actively hunted the beasts for their fine leather and the flesh of their tails, but the then Lord of the Isles forbade any further incursions against them, and it has been so ever since. They are only killed when they are caught in or near to the harbor, too close to this isle or otherwise threatening one of us. As I say, they are considered to be allies in defense of the Sea Isles, my dear."

Chapter II

It not being a military operation, the party led by sometime Captain-of-elephants Gil Djohnz left on time, with the dawning of the Monday morning. Passing through the various unit camps, they noted them all to be abustle, but this was not in any way remarkable, for drills and training marches, practice alarms and parades were commonplace occurrences in the permanent garrison of the army of the Consolidated *Thoheekseeahnee.*

In the years since the twenty-five-year-old Horseclansman had been forced—at barely twenty—to accept a captaincy in that army, he had grudgingly, and then only for the sake of army discipline, given lip service to the seemingly endless lists of rules and regulations and general orders and special orders and service customs by and under which that army lived and trained, marched and fought, but in his heart of hearts he had never ceased to thank them all—well, at least the most of them—every bit as silly and senseless as he had when he had first arrived here with Sunshine, Tulip and a handful of his kinsmen.

As he rode along on Sunshine, at the head of his column of elephants, horses, humans and carts, out of the camp and its environs and out onto the road to the west, he did feel a little hurt that his old friends *Thoheeks* Sitheeros and Sub-*strahteegos Thoheeks* Tomos Gonsalos had neither of them taken the time to come the night before and bid him a last farewell,

share a mug of wine, at least; he had kept half each of
an eye and an ear cocked for sounds of them throughout the preceding day and night . . . vainly, as it
turned out. True, they three had enjoyed a feast and
well-lubricated revel the weekend before at the quarters Sitheeros maintained in Mehseepolis, but even so
. . . He sighed and shook his head.

Taking a look behind, he beamed, "Slow down,
Sunshine, the pace you're setting will tire the horses
too quickly. It's a very long journey, you know; we'll
not be there tonight, or tomorrow night, or for many
and many a tomorrow night, my dear, so there is no
need to race or rush."

The elephant's return beaming bore with it a tinge
of exasperation. "Sunshine cannot understand why her
brother felt it necessary to bring along those delicate,
easily tiring little creatures anyway. They and their
rabbit-eared cousins that draw those carts, they are
superfluous, really. Do you and your two-leg brothers
not have three powerful and very intelligent creatures
of my sort to bear you along and draw your carts?"

Gil thought fast. "Sister-mine," he beamed, "we
two-legs were of a mind that it would not be dignified
for our brave, brainy sisters, whom we so love and
respect, to enter back into the Land of Elephants
appearing as mere beasts of draught and burden; this
is why the mules and horses accompanied us, that
should fighting become necessary, my sister and her
sisters will not be hitched up or burdened down and
thus will be immediately able to put their awesome
power into full use against such foes as we might
face."

At this, Sunshine beamed a warm, all-encompassing
tide of pure affection into Gil's mind, simultaneously
renewing her vows of love and endless loyalty to him.
She shortened her walking stride, and as she did, so
too did the other, following elephants.

While beaming in return his own love for and loyalty to his massive mount, Gil thought deep within a carefully shielded recess of his mind that he was become over the years most adept at elephantine psychology. Before many days had passed, he was to ruefully recall this smug expression of hubris.

Thoheeks Mahvros read the just-delivered message and turned back to the councillors—nineteen of them, this day—saying, "The party of our High Lord lies camped about the Monastery of Ayeeos Antohnios of the Stones, while the brothers ferry them as fast as human flesh may endeavor across the River Lithothios. Brothers and soldiers together are rigging cables to float the wheeled transport across, the ferry vessels being apparently too small or lightweight for such task."

Thoheeks Bahos cracked the prominent knuckles of his big hands and shook his head. "Dammit, Mahvros, we're going to have to get around to replacing that damned bridge . . . and soon, man! That used to be the main trade road, but of late years, the traders have been compelled to swing way north and west and make use of that damned treacherous ford up by the ruins of Castle Lambdos, and naturally they jack up their prices for the extra effort and risks."

Mahvros nodded. "Yes, all true, but that's just one bridge, and there are others placed in spots of more strategic importance that must still take priority. Moreover, now that our lands are settling down—the outlaws, the brigand bands, the renegades and all similar dangerous scum eradicated—the road crews are running short of state-slaves and we may soon start having to institute regular levies of farmers and townsmen to fill out the labor groups, are we to maintain the repair schedules originally decided upon."

To the chorus of groans and incensed mutterings that this last evoked around the council table, he raised an open hand and said, placatingly, "I know, I know, gentlemen, such would play pure hob with activities of an agricultural nature. But please consider: What good to us, to our people, is an army that cannot move quickly from a place it is not needed to a place where it is needed? We all must begin to think of the best things for the realm, not merely of petty, personal concerns. Each and every one of you is fully aware just how much tribute-grain and other foodstuffs goes to our army, not to even mention other supplies, and in order to justify such sacrifices, we must be able to make full use of the army, which means decent roads, strong bridges, well-paved fords and safe passes in the mountainous areas."

"The damned army and nobody else is going to eat regularly do we go about taking the workers out of the fields to sweat over roads," said *Thoheeks* Pennendos bluntly. "Why not use part of the army to raid the northern barbarians for slaves . . . ?"

Jumping to his feet, leaning across the table, red-faced, *Thoheeks* Sitheeros shouted, "You half-wit ninny! Your lands lie far from the barbarian states, mine are tooth by jowl with them, and our realm has at long last hammered out a reasonably secure peace with them. Now *you* want to start a border war. What's in your head, boy? No brains, clearly. Horse biscuits, perhaps?"

Involuntarily, Pennendos flinched back from the big, powerful man. In a tightly controlled voice, he said, "My friends will call on you shortly, Lord Sitheeros, and . . ."

"And nothing!" snapped *Thoheeks* and Acting *Strahteegos* Grahvos, in a tone of utter exasperation. "Sitheeros, sit down and shut up! Pennendos, you're

still a young man, but if you're going to call out every
man who ever names you a shithead, you will never
make old bones; Sitheeros could make a bloodpudding
of you with one hand only, and if you aren't aware of
that fact, you truly are a shithead. You and your
overly hot head often make me wonder if perhaps
Council did not err in confirming you to your lands
and titles; the confirmation is not irreversible, you
know, so beware." The older man maintained a hard,
cold stare until the younger dropped his gaze.

From Sitheeros' side of the table, Thoheeks Vikos
spoke up. "I'm as committed to the common weal as
any man here, God knows, but really productive farming is a year-round job and a hard and time-consuming
one, at that. Are all of the workers to be taken from
off the land for even a couple of weeks, an entire crop
could be lost."

Mahvros nodded. "We are all as aware of the facts
as are you, Vikos, and we have taken all facts into
consideration in plotting out our contingency courses.
In the event it becomes necessary to draft land-workers
for road crews, we will expect those *thoheeksee* called
upon to send us one able man in every three for forty
days of work. When they return, the *thoheeksee* will
replace them in equal number from those still on the
land, and so on. At no time will more than a third of
the land-workers be absent from the fields. This will be
a sacrifice, true, but far from a ruinous one, you must
admit."

Vikos nodded. "Those remaining will just have to
work harder and longer every day. And I suppose
you'll maintain a constant labor force by dint of stag-
gering the arrival and departure dates of the levies due
from the various *thoheekseeahnee*, eh?"

"Just so," said Mahvros, then, sighing, he pled,
"Now, please, may we get back to consideration of
our overlord and his entourage?

"Lest he be further delayed on that onetime trade road, I suggest that we send out an honor guard commanded by one of us to bring him and his immediate staff on more quickly to Mahseepolis. Do I hear any volunteers to head up that guard of honor, gentlemen?"

Thoheeks Sitheeros nodded, saying, "I could use the exercise, Mahvros, I'll lead them. Hell, I'll even use some of my own lancers, if you wish, and we can just leave the army horsemen in camp."

But old Grahvos shook his head. "No, Sitheeros, thank you, but it were better that the honor guard be of our common army, not of a great magnate's personal following, for, if you'll recall, private armies are just what caused our homeland so much grief within recent memory. We'll have Tomos to pick us out a score of lancers, a sergeant or two and a young officer to actually command; you'll be a noble supernumerary, Sitheeros, officially commanding only your personal bodyguards."

"Only twenty measly lancers?" yelped *Thoheeks* Pennendos. "No, I think we should send out at the least a squadron each of heavy horse *and* lancers, my lord, possibly some war-elephants, too. Twenty lancers smacks to me as but the pitiful effort of some small, weak, utterly impoverished foothill principality of uncultured near-barbarians, and I doubt not but that any Ehleen gentleman would share and echo my sentiments."

Grahvos sighed, while Mahvros snorted and opened his mouth to make reply, but the older man caught his eye and shook his head, then addressed *Thoheeks* Pennendos in a patient tone. "My young lord, this matter is but another example of one of the more important reasons why this Council exists: that the older and wiser heads may give guidance to the younger and less experienced of our number, lead them in the proper path and hope that they will afterward remember the way.

"My lord, one sends forth large and impressive forces either to make war or to impress and intimidate and thus prevent warfare from occurring. Neither is to be contemplated in this instance. The man, the personage, approaching Mehseepolis is our own, dear, very much respected overlord, Milos Morai. Compared to the lands and peoples and wealth and forces he could raise and command, ours is but little better than that poor, weak hill-principality you envisioned in your ill-conceived argument.

"Also, do not forget that we all still owe this man recompense, reparations for the damages wrought by the host of Zastros in its progress through the southerly provinces of Karaleenos; no doubt, while with us, our overlord will be of a mind to set the rates of payment on these old debts, so we do not wish to render a first impression to his mind of a fluid wealth that we do not, in fact, own."

Thoheeks Pennendos shook his head. "I still don't see why we should supinely allow this strange foreigner to easily set his foot down upon our collective neck, rule us as subjects, put an outlander prince over us and milk us of our remaining riches for who knows how long to pay off debts incurred by a dead man."

Mahvros stared down the length of the table, raised an eyebrow and asked, "My lord Pennendos, were you ever dropped on your head as a babe? If so, that might be the reason for your lack of wit, so often demonstrated to us all in this chamber."

Thoheeks Bahos stirred his massive frame and rumbled, "Now, Mahvros, let us cease to sink to the level of personal insult. Our Pennendos, here, is bright enough, he's but young and has not seen so much of life as have we. Remember, he was not on that ill-fated debacle of Zastros' devising, he was then too young.

"My lord Pennendos," the huge man continued, "you must know that the mighty host of the late and unlamented King Zastros did not suffer so much defeat as utter dissolution up there on the Lumbuh River, years back. Then and there, there was, there existed, nothing that might've prevented High Lord Milos from leading his own mighty host—which was nearly as large as Zastros' had been at its strongest—down here to burn, pillage, rape, enslave and thoroughly wreak havoc upon the length and the breadth of the then kingless Kingdom of the Southern Ehleenohee. Had Zastros or full many another of us seen a former foreman so prostrate before us, you know that that is precisely what we would have done.

"But this High Lord Milos Morai of Kehnooryos Ehlahs did not. He acted with an unbelievable degree of humanity, restraint, magnanimity, Christian charity. He asked only that we deliver up to him the king and the queen, leaving us specifically free to bear away with us all that we could carry—weapons, gear, tents, animals, wheeled transport, everything—moreover, he had friendly guides come down from out the western mountains and show us to sources of unpoisoned water all along the way.

"Also, he freely offered us the loan of troops to secure and maintain order in this homeland while we reorganized a government and rendered ourselves once more a peaceful, productive land. In the early talks, he never mentioned the subject of reparations; Grahvos and I it was brought it up and had Mahvros—who did the actual negotiating—promise payment when once more the lands were reset on an earning basis, for right is right, young sir, and an honest man is owned by his just debts until he has repaid them to the last jot and tittle.

"As for the setting of feet upon collective necks, my lord Pennendos, I had much liefer have the foot of a generous and forgiving stranger upon mine than that of a grasping, greedy, cruel, arrogant poseur of a near relative. Though I have as yet to have the honor of meeting him, this High Lord Milos seems to me an overlord that I and you and the rest of us can easily live with and under, and I feel him and his overlordship to be a blessing of God upon us and our so long afflicted land."

Milo Morai sat on a sandstone bench beside the aged, arthritic Father Mithos, *eeohyimehnos* of the Monastery of Saint Anthony of the Stones. The buildings behind them still showed clear evidences of the ruin that had been unremittingly visited upon them during the long years of civil warring, raids and general chaos. But even in its present state, stripped of most of its ancient treasures, portions of roofs here and there still undergoing repairs, the purity of line of laid stones and columns bore out as ever the skill and real love that had originally gone into the erection of the complex.

Father Mithos was one of the only three of the original brothers to survive. He was maimed and hideously scarred by steel, lash, rope and searing heat—tortures wrought upon his flesh by cruel men seeking the hiding places of the last few treasures of the order; vain tortures, as it turned out, for Father Mithos was possessed of great faith, a tempered will and the warrior heritage of his noble forebears.

More accustomed to the vain, proud, supercilious and often downright criminal churchmen of his northerly realm of Kehnooryos Ehlahs, Milo had at first found this erudite, deeply religious, but withal both gentle and humble man truly refreshing. As the days had gone on, with the brawny brothers working the long days through at ferrying the men and horses some bare handful at a time across the treacherous stretch of river in their tiny boats, the High Lord had found himself to be beginning to not only respect Father Mithos but to really like him, as well.

After a sip of the cider, Milo remarked, "Father Mithos, it is a bit surprising to me that the main trade road has not been put into better order and that the bridge, here, has not been rebuilt. I must remember to speak of both projects in Mehseepolis."

Both of the old man's thumbs were now but withered, bumpy, immovable claws, so he needs must use his two palms to raise and then lower his cider-cup, and he did this slowly, painfully, in deference to calcifications in joints sprung on rack and strappado. With a skill born of long, patient practice, he set down the cup and smiled, his scarred lips writhing jerkily aside to show his few remaining teeth.

"Do not trouble yourself of the *thoheeksee*, my son. They mostly are good, righteous, godly men, and they have done more than many ever expected they could or would to set this land to right within the space of bare years rather than decades.

"As regards the trade road, I can understand why it has not been improved more than it has. For one thing, there are few reasons to move the army in this direction, but many to move it to north and south and west, so understandably, those roads are foremost in the minds and plans of the Council and repair crews. Also, the traders have taken to using another track and a ford well up north of here, though I feel certain that were the bridge again sound and whole and usable, they would return to the old road.

"The bridge was the property of this house, you know, my son. We maintained it and, when necessary, repaired it, and we waxed wealthy on the tolls for use of it. But as our wealth grew, so too did our overweening pride. Truly it is averred that pride goeth before a fall, never doubt the words, Milo. We waxed proud and rich and slothful and the Lord God brought us down, far, far down, visited upon us deaths and sufferings and hunger and loss.

"Five years ago, brigands nested behind those walls and in the toll-castle down by the river, there. There were but three of us brothers left alive and we were all in sad condition, tramping the roads and begging, starving in rags. But then *Thoheeks* Grahvos—may God bless and keep him, ever—sent his army against the brigands and drove them all forth, killing some in battle, hanging others and enslaving the remainder. He freed their captives, then sought out Brother Miklos, Brother Thiodohros and me. He had us restored in body and brought here to reoccupy our lands and begin to restore our order and buildings to the use of the Lord God.

"Now, God be praised, there are three-and-twenty of us here, to sing of the glories of God and to do His holy work. Our vines and fruit trees have been replanted and they will, in God's own time, produce the bounty of yore. We have harvested two crops of grain and soon will reap yet another. Early on, we gathered in poor, homeless, near-wild goats and sheep and cattle, two asses, two oxen and an injured horse which last we slowly nursed back to health, only to find that he is a war-trained horse and most ill suited to the needs of a band of peaceful brothers of God. According to God's will, the beasts have multiplied and continue to do so. The pastures have been refenced, the folds and sheds rebuilt, and hayfields sown. God willing, we someday may again own swine to batten upon the mast of our forest. And also, someday, when He has fully forgiven us of our pride and sloth and other impieties, God will show us the way, will allow us leave to rebuild that bridge.

"Already has the Lord shone His face most brightly upon us here, my son, far and away more brightly than our many sins deserved for us. Therefore, do not trouble the *thoheeksee* in Mehseepolis on our account, for we all are fed, clothed, housed and content with the Lord God's blessed bounty."

As the sun began to set behind the monastery forest, the old abbot arose from his seat and, tenderly assisted by a tall, brawny brother who had stood behind him in meek silence for the hours he and Milo had sat and sipped and conversed, made his painful, hobbling way back to the main building. But Milo was not halfway back to camp when, with a pounding of bare feet, the tall brother caught up to him, perspiring lightly but breathing normally despite his run, for which he had rolled up his sleeves almost to the shoulder and tucked the hem of his robe into his waist-rope to display heavily muscled limbs bearing the puckered scars of a man who had worn armor and swung steel for many a year. Walking toward Milo, smiling, the monk strode with a pantherish grace, and Milo thought that the man had probably been a deadly swordsman in his salad days, no doubt still could be had he not traded his armor for a robe of unbleached wool and his sword for his faith.

He dredged the monk's name out of his memory. "Yes, Brother Kahnstantinos? You would have words with me?"

The monk nodded brusquely, there on the trail along which other brothers were passing on their way up from the day's atrocious labors on the river, too dumb with fatigue to do more than mumble to the tall monk and stumble on toward the monastery complex.

"Someplace private, and it please my lord."

In Milo's pavilion, the monk sipped at the wine, savored it on his tongue and complimented Milo on his selection of vintage, as well as on the workmanship of the gilded silver wine-goblet. His speech and bearing were unmistakably those of a gentleman to the manor born.

After thanking him no less elaborately, Milo asked bluntly, "Well, then, my lord monk, what have you for my ears only in privacy?"

The monk contemplated the dark depths of his wine for a long moment, then looked up with sad eyes and said, "That which I should not utter, for in so doing I will be gainsaying a man whom I respect and love above all other living creatures I ever have known in all of a bloody, violent, misspent life; but still I must say it, my lord, though it damn me.

"My lord, things are not nearly so good here as Father Mithos would like to believe. Indeed, he does not even know of the worst of our afflictions . . . I don't think . . . for those of us who do know shield him from them. We know that he will not live much longer, you see, and we wish him to die in peace and in as near to comfort as this rude, poor place can afford him. For if any man born has ever earned the right to a peaceful, painless demise, it is him. They crucified him, you know, my lord.

"After the sacrilegious swine had done their worst to his poor flesh and bones to force from out his lips the hiding places of the holy treasures, they decided that he must not know that secret after all. That was when they fashioned a cross and bound his shattered, broken body upon it and rode off and left him to die among the other corpses of the murdered brethren. He might well have so died, there upon that cross, save that two shepherd brothers who had been absent in search of some sheep of the monastery herd and had wisely lain low until the raiders were beyond the horizon came back in time to cut him down and nurse him back to as close to health as the poor, mutilated old man ever again will know. Following a few more close calls while they still were nursing him, the two brothers sagaciously quitted the wrecked monastery as soon as he could walk for any distance, for here they were become only sitting, helpless victims.

"In my boyhood, this monastery was noted for the fine vintages its vineyards produced. My late father was a taciturn man, yet he rejoiced openly whenever one of his agents was able to buy a pipe of the wine produced here, completely disregarding the literal pounds of silver that that pipe had cost. But that famous vineyard is now no more, my lord, and it will be many a year before the new-planted ones can produce even a small keg of wine.

"The monks of earlier years also were widely known for their brewing of herbal- and fruit-flavored cordials, but that too is now a thing of the past, even had we the wherewithal. Some nameless idiot of a bandit tried his clumsy hand at it and managed to blow up the distillery, the building that had housed it and himself, as well. The copper-scrap, of course, was looted and borne away, and it will be years yet to come before we can afford to replace it, poor as we are here.

"You recall, my lord, that Father Mithos mentioned that someday again he would like to see a few pigs feeding on the oak mast?"

Milo nodded. "Yes, my lord monk."

"The monastery once ran herds of fat swine and their specially cured and smoked pork-products were known far and wide. So, you see, it was not just the bridge or the bequests that made this place a famous and a very rich one. Lay brothers included, there were at times as many as seventy souls laboring at one thing and another hereabouts. Yes, they lived well, but it was all from the fruits of their own hard work, and they also shared unstintingly with those in need.

"Father Mithos is a good and a saintly man. He does not really, as I said, know it all. What he does know, I believe he unconsciously sees through a rosy mist, as it were, imagining the best where objects are unclear to him. He is aged, most infirm at his healthiest and . . . and I fear that the terrible, horrible torments he endured and, with God's help and infinite mercy, survived may have beclouded his mind."

"Quite likely true and fully understandable, if so," said Milo, adding, "To my sorrow, I've learned more over the years about torture than I ever had any desire to know, and, yes, protracted torment does quite often affect the minds of its victims . . . and sometimes of its perpetrators, as well.

"But that aside, I take it you want me to, are imploring me to speak of the straits of you and your brothers, here, to the Council of *Thoheeksee*, in Mehseepolis. That is it, isn't it, my lord monk? All right then, I will do so, you have my word on it, one gentleman to another."

The man with the black, square-cut beard shook his head slowly. "No, my lord, I am no longer a gentleman or anyone's lord, only a simple, humble servant of God. But . . . and it please my lord . . . there is one other thing that I would ask of you." At Milo's nod, he went on, "The stallion that Father Mithos found and took in and healed, he is a fine, beautifully trained destrier, obviously foaled of the very best bloodlines and sound as a suit of proof, now. However, he eats more than any other beast we own and, as he was never broken to aught save being ridden into a fight, is useless to us; I am the only one that he will abide astride him, and that must be bareback as we have no gear for him. Yet Father Mithos will not put him out. Would . . . does my lord think that perhaps he would be willing to trade a draught mule for the horse? He would make for my lord a splendid charger."

The morning mist still lay in a thick, fleecy blanket over the rack-studded river when Milo, riding a gelding palfrey and leading a loaded pack-mule, rejoined Brother Kahnstantinos. The High Lord wore knee-high boots, leather-lined canvas trousers, an arming-doublet and a half-sleeved shirt of light mail. There was a quilted-suede cap on his head, and a wide, cursive saber hung from his baldric.

When he had dismounted and hitched the horse and mule to a brace of saplings, he followed the monk through the second-growth woods to halt before a split-rail fence enclosing a grassy expanse of pasture.

"I fed him and groomed him and turned him out about a quarter hour since," said the tall monk. "He's likeliest beyond that fold of ground out there drinking from the pond."

A shrill whistle from the monk brought a tall, dark-mahogany stallion, with four white stockings and a long, thin blaze of white, up over the fold of ground. At a slow but distance-eating amble, the horse approached them and came to a snorting, stamping halt just the other side of the fence from the monk, who took the fine head into his arms and petted the beast with a gruff tenderness.

Silently, Milo sought the mind of the stallion. "How does my horse-brother call himself, think of himself?" he beamed.

The stallion started so abruptly that his jerking head flung the monk backward onto his rump, that man's own surprise and pain being expressed in terms more heard in cavalry lines than in monasteries.

Moving slowly, warily, the big equine drew back just beyond the reach of either man. "How can you speak to me, two-legs? Your kind cannot really speak to my kind, every horse and mare knows that."

"But I can bespeak you, horse-brother," beamed Milo. "So, too, can most of the two-legs of my herd. For this reason, we need not place cruel, pain-making metal bits into the mouths of our horse-brothers, for they are truly our brothers, our partners, not our mere slaves.

"Now, what do you call yourself, horse-brother?"

Helping the tall monk back onto his feet, even while he silently conversed with the bemused but still-wary stallion, Milo signaled the man to fetch and lead back with him the palfrey and mule. The monk came back just in time to see Milo step from the topmost rail of the fence over and astride the bare back of the stallion. With his thighs tightly gripping the dark-red barrel and his sinewy hand grasping the full mane, the man kneed the warhorse first to his slow amble, next to a faster amble, then a canter, then a full gallop.

Lifetime horseman and veteran cavalryman that he was, Brother Kahnstantinos still was startled when, after galloping the full circuit of the pasture twice, Milo sent him sailing over the four-foot rail fence, out into the woods, then back over it again for yet a third circuit of the pasture at a hard gallop, maintaining his seat effortlessly and doing it all, incredibly, without a bridle and reins.

When he had brought the big horse over the fence a third time, Milo slid from off him and said, "He's all you attested and more, my lord monk. I'll take him into my service. This mule is now yours; he's five years old and healthy and he's as docile as any good mule ever was or will be. He's double-broke—can be used for either draught or for riding or, as you can see here, for packing loads—he now bears two fifty-*keeloh* bags of grain, one twenty-*keeloh* bag of dried beans, one of shelled maize and a small cask of brandy for Father Mithos. I realize that in total this still is a dirt-cheap price for so fine a horse as this one, but there will be more yet to come to you, believe me, my friend."

Walking over to the stallion, the tall monk once more took and embraced and petted his head, murmuring, "May God bless and keep you, old friend. I will miss your companionship sorely. But it were better that you be among warriors than among monks."

Chapter III

Captain-of-squadron *Vahrohnos* Bralos of Yohyül-tönpolis, the officer chosen to lead the twenty-four lances sent east to meet and guide on to Mehseepolis the High Lord and his contingent, soon had proven himself to be a man after *Thoheeks* Sitheeros' heart. He was accompanied by a young lieutenant, one Pülos of Aptahpolis, when he made his call upon the *Thoheeks* of Iron Mountain. When all three gentlemen were seated and served and the slaves had departed the room, when all of the ritual courtesies had been observed, the captain got down to business.

"My lord *Thoheeks*, Sub-*strahteegos Thoheeks* Tomos Gonsalos has seen fit to afford me the impressive honor of leading two dozen of my lances to meet and escort the High Lord Milos Morai of Kehnooryos Ehlahs, of Karaleenos, of the Pirate Isles and of some barbarian principalities the names of which I cannot seem to get my tongue around. It is my understanding that the Lord of Iron Mountain is to accompany my unit with a number of his servants and bodyguards. I must know just how many men and beasts will be in his party that I may make arrangements for providing proper provender for all and may organize my order of march. It also would help me to know the numbers and sizes of wheeled transport my lord presumes to take along."

Sitheeros shrugged. "It was *my* understanding, Captain, that this was to be a fast-moving column on the

eastern leg, at least; therefore, I meant to keep my
baggage to a minimum—no carts or wagons at all,
only a dozen pack-mules and most of them merely to
bear grain for them and the horses. I'm an old cam-
paigner, Captain, I've probably spent more years in a
saddle on the march than your lieutenant has years of
life. Including the two muleskinners, I'll have nine
servants and eight of my armed retainers, Tenzee barbarians. My remuda will run about twenty head of
horses and a few extra mules."

The captain exchanged a glance with his subordinate
and sighed, then said in a less formal tone, "My lord
has just made my day. Over the course of the last
couple of years, my troops have been right often called
upon to give escort to not a few of my lord's peers of
Council, some of whom have proven . . . ahh, difficult
to properly escort, owning precious little knowledge of
or respect for the military aspects of such a mission.
But I now can see that travel with my lord will be not
only a signal honor but a pleasure, as well."

With an added note of warmth in his voice, Sitheeros
admonished, "You two lads drink your wine, it's a
good vintage from one of my own vineyards—a mountain vineyard, mind you, none of this water–weak
and all but tasteless lowland stuff. Drink that down
and I'll have a real treat fetched up here."

To the servant who answered his pull on a bellrope,
he said, "Go tell Tailos that I said to tap the third cask
on the left, the one with the elephant burnt into the
wood above the bunghole, then you bring me a large
decanter and clean goblets. Have a tray of sweetmeats
and fried nuts and crisp breads brought, as well."

"If it please my lord," said the captain, hurriedly,
before the serving-man had left the chamber, "the
lieutenant and I cannot stay for long, I have duties in
the camp . . ."

Sitheeros grinned and nodded. "Which, judging by

my own warring-years with armies, can be done just as
well in your absence by your sergeants, Captain
Vahrohnos Bralos. So keep your place and drink your
wine, my boy.

"Tell me, aren't you the officer who fell into possession of enough loot to buy both a squadron-command
and your presently held land and title, then managed
to get himself almost hanged by order of our late
lamented Grand *Strahteegos Thoheeks* Pahvlos?"

The captain nodded. "I am that man, my lord."

"I would love to hear just how you were able to
acquire such a treasure, my boy, in a land that had
been so thoroughly plundered as had this one over the
years. You need not tell me unless you want to, you
understand. Yes, I'm curious about it, but I'm not
ordering the tale out of you," said Sitheeros.

"But, of course, my lord," the captain replied. "First,
though, does my lord recall aught concerning one
Thoheeks-designate Hahkmukos, some years back?"

Sitheeros wrinkled his brows for a moment, then
snapped his fingers with a sharp crack. "Why, certainly, the sly bastard who was Zastros' quartermaster
on that debacle up in Karaleenos. Yes, I do remember
him. But he never was confirmed to that title, was he?
I seem to recall that he ended being declared outlaw."

"Just so, my lord," said Captain Bralos. "On-the-
spot investigation by *Thoheeks* Grahvos and the other
senior officers disclosed that not only had this Hahkmukos
greatly exaggerated his relationship to the direct
line of descent of the former *thoheeks*, but he had
entirely neglected to mention that he had left the
thoheekseeahn of his birth under a cloud of suspicion
of parricide.

"I then was a lieutenant of the staff guards—third
son of a *komees*, with no patrimony save a decent
sword, some armor and clothing and gear, a couple of
good horses and damn-all else, the bulk of my fluid

capital having gone toward the purchase of a lieutenancy of foot-guards. On the day of the truce and
conference, my section had been assigned by the guards
captain to serve as security for the pavilion of *Thoheeks*
Grahvos. When now-*Thoheeks* Klaios and his gentlemen were brought to the pavilion and had had their
say, *Thoheeks* Grahvos sent me to summon *Thoheeks*-
designate Hahkmukos to face his accuser and give
answer to the grave charges leveled against him.

"But this Hahkmukos, who was within his tent,
pleasuring himself with a slave-boy catamite, refused
the summons, would not even see or speak with me
himself. This report naturally angered the senior officers and I was sent back with a squad and orders to
shed blood if that was the only way I could bring the
thoheeks-designate back to the pavilion with me.

"So we went back with leveled spears and bared steel
and I had to kill the captain of Hahkmukos' mercenary guards at the onset of it all, but with him cough-
ing up his life's blood in the mire, his men just melted
away from the environs of that tent and I entered with
a bloody sword and 'persuaded' Hahkmukos to dismiss his young slave and don enough clothing to return with me to the pavilion.

"Once there, this Hahkmukos was so rash as to
seize a sword and attempt to violate a sacred truce by
fleshing it in the other claimant, now-*Thoheeks* Klaios.
It was at that juncture that the senior officers there
present decided that the choice should be left to the
Lord God, that, while Lord Klaios' panoply was being
fetched to him from the city, I should take Hahkmukos
back to his tent and assist him in arming for a
deathmatch to decide who would be confirmed *thoheeks*.

"In the drizzling, misty rain, we tramped back to
Hahkmukos' encampment, and while he used his pot,
I went looking for a brace of his mercenaries to be his
arming-men and seconds for the fight, but not a one

was there to be found, other than the dead captain,
whose corpse had been stripped of everything of value.
The troop tents had been struck and the picket lines
were empty. Therefore, while I was assisting Hahkmukos
to accouter himself for battle, I sent two of my spearmen
off to borrow a brace of saddled horses.

"My lord, that man's armor was undoubtedly the
finest that it ever has been my privilege to handle—all
Pitzburk, prince-grade and king-grade, nothing less,
and decorated and inletted beyond all dreams. His
sword, dirk and daggers were a matched set—splendid! But as soon as he had hung his axe from the
pommel of one of the horses, both of which beasts
were mine—they being the easiest for the spearmen to
quickly get at—he begged me give him a leg up, citing
the length of time it had been since he essayed mount-
ing in armor.

"However, no sooner was he in the saddle than he
kicked me full in the face and reined about and left
the camp, headed northwest. One of my men threw a
spear at him but it fell a bit short, worse luck.

Then they both thought it best to see to me, to get
my face out of the mud before I smothered, swooning
as I was, just then.

"When I had recovered enough of my senses to
walk with assistance, I reported back to the pavilion,
feeling like a fool and a failure, but *Thoheeks* Grahvos
seemed actually pleased by Hahkmukos' demonstrated
cowardice, though he did send a squad of Horseclanners
out later to track him and, hopefully, apprehend him.
Magnanimously, he awarded me—in recompense, he
said, for my suffering and the loss of one of my horses—
Hahkmukos' fine tent and all that the decamping mercenaries and servants had left of his camp effects."

Sitheeros grinned and nodded. "And just how much
did Grahvos' largesse amount to, Captain?"

Bralos shrugged. "Not all that much at once, my

lord. Two new, sturdy wagons; I kept the best and traded the other one for the mules to draw the one I kept. Sub-chief Captain Vawn took but one look at the flashy, overdecorated saddle and horse-gear that Hahkmukos had left behind and offered me the price of a decent horse for it, and I took him up on it. I considered selling the spare helmet and such bits and pieces of armor as were left, but I ended by adding them to my own sparse panoply; the sword I left with your bodyguards was, in fact, his everyday sword—it's Pitzburk-made, too, but only a duke-grade.

"Although he had begun to run somewhat to fat, Hahkmukos had been about of a size with me, so I just had his chests all repacked and placed in the wagon, intending to have a tailor at the base camp do such alterations as were necessary. Then I had the tent struck and reerected in the guards camp and contributed most of the victuals and wines to the guard officers' mess. And that was that until the army was returned to the base-camp, down below-walls, save that *Thoheeks* Klaios made me the offer of a *vahrohnoseeahn* for a most attractive price . . . could I but raise that much money; I rendered him the thanks I knew due him, but realized that, barring some miracle, I would never even see that much silver or gold at one time did I live a century.

"We had been back for a month or so and then, of a night when I chanced to not have duties, I opened Hahkmukos' chests and began to sort out the clothing, linens, blankets and boots. The largest of those chests was a massive thing, more than a load for four strong men when fully packed, banded and cornered and edged and reinforced with strips and studs of iron and brass, full of inner drawers and compartments. I had already found several small purses of silver in one of the drawers and so was exploring them all in hopes of finding a bit more . . . and I did, my lord, I did.

"The chest was sitting on one end, gaped open, and I had gone into all save one of the drawers. That one opened a fraction of a finger-breadth on only one side, then seemed to jam solidly, and I was unable to either close it back or open it, so I searched about for a blade of a sufficient degree of thinness to get into the opening and try to pry it open. Finally locating a slender dagger, I worked its blade into the opening and began to gingerly twist it. At last, the troublesome drawer came out . . . empty of all save three folded scarves of silk.

"But then I noted something odd, my lord. That drawer was exactly alike to the others save in a single respect: it was only about half as long. Exploration with fingers and dagger-point revealed that the recess from which the drawer had just come was no whit different from the other recesses above it—all of them being lined with high-quality cedarwood—save only that it was not so deep as were they.

"It was then that I recalled, my lord, certain details of the flight of the wretched Hahkmukos, of how when I entered his tent to help him to arm, a drawer had stood open and empty from the *outer* side of one of the smaller chests and of how when once that drawer had been shut, I had never again figured out how to reopen it or even fathomed just where it was located.

"Thinking again on this arcane matter, I went around to the other side, the outer side of the chest, moving the lamp so as to give me better light. There was no visible handle or mechanism, of course, but I squatted there and began to push and pull at each and every stud and band on that lid. At great length, when I was become frustrated to the point of murder and madness, a brass stud sank in smoothly under a fingertip and I heard a faint click from someplace within the lid. Keeping that stud depressed, I pushed again at every one of its mates I could reach, and when an iron one sank inward, a drawer opened slightly out of the lid's outer face.

"I knew from the moment that I lifted the first soft velvet purselet out of the hideaway drawer that it was far too light to hold either silver or gold. When I opened the drawstrings and shook the contents out into my palm, I thought that surely my heart would cease its beating at the beauty of the large purple amethysts that rolled out."

Sitheeros hissed softly between his teeth. "They all were bags of amethysts, then, Captain?"

The officer shook his head. "No, my lord, there was one more of the amethysts, two of sapphires, and one each of blue-white diamonds, yellow diamonds, rubies, emeralds, topazes, aquamarines, garnets, opals, and a larger bag containing an assortment of fine pearls."

Before the captain could say more, the servants arrived with the wine and edibles, and the gentlemen kept silent until the servers were departed.

After the wine had been savored and extensively praised, Sitheeros asked, "So, Captain, there you sat with handfuls of precious gems; so what did you do then?"

The officer smiled. "After thinking it through, I went to Sub-*strahteegos Thoheeks* Tomos Gonsalos—I don't think that he ever sleeps, my lord, so late can he be found at work in his headquarters on almost any night—and spread the bags of gems before him and told him the tale, then asked what I should do.

"He heard me out, examined the contents of the bags, then told me to pour us both a stoup of Karaleenos brandy."

"Lieutenant Bralos," Tomos said, "in addition to being a brave man and a conscientious man, you have just proven yourself to be an exceptionally honest man. Let me tell you, not many men would've brought this king's ransom in gems and asked me the honorable disposition of it, not one bit of it. But you did, miracle of miracles, you did. You are henceforth proven in my eyes, you are just the sort of officer that this army needs, hell, you're the sort of man of which no land ever has enough."

Gonsalos took a lens from a box on his desk and used it to peer closely at one of the blue-white diamonds. "Look at this, young man. This particular stone and not a few of the others are old, very old, old beyond reckoning, for no stonesmith has ever again learned of just how the ancients cut their stones and made so many tiny smooth places upon them."

Seated stiffly upon the edge of a camp stool, Lieutenant Bralos said hesitantly, "My lord, I had thought . . . Hahkmukos was, after all, the chief quartermaster for High King Zastros in Karaleenos; perhaps these stones were looted from out that land . . . ?"

Gonsalos just shook his head. "Oh, no, the land through which Zastros and his doomed army passed had been emptied and cleared out long before the army's first mounted scout waded his horse across the Ahrbahkootchee River. No, these beauties did not come from out my homeland.

"So, what do you mean to do with your new wealth, my boy, keep them or sell them? There is an assortment of lands and titles just now up for sale to men of good breeding and proven character, you know, most of the parcels coming complete with hereditary titles, more or less battered holds and more or less occupied towns or even walled cities."

"But who . . . where can I sell such a treasure and be certain that I'm not being cheated, that I'm getting a fair price, my lord Sub-*strahteegos*?" Bralos asked helplessly, adding, "My lord must see, my late sire was a *komees*, yes, but far from wealthy in aught save lands and children, so my knowledge of gems and gem-sellers is very scant."

"Hmmm," mused Gonsalos. "Let me think of it for a moment, my good Bralos." Seemingly absently, he went back through the contents of the twelve smaller bags, lifting out a stone here and another there. When what looked to be a pool of fire lay winking in the lamp-fire upon his desktop, he replaced the bulk of the stones in their purselets and asked,

"Bralos, you mentioned that you had found silver in one of those drawers. Coin? Of what approximate value?"

"A hundred and sixty *thrahkmehee*, my lord, mostly of King Hyamos, though appearing new-minted still," replied the lieutenant.

Gonsalos grinned. "Nearly a full year's pay for a lieutenant of foot-guards, eh? But still and all, it's a less than inconsequential piffle compared to these gems and their value. Even so, it should be enough to hold you for a few months." His grin widened. "With careful budgeting, of course.

"Now, as you may know, my first cousin is Zenos XII, once king and now prince of Karaleenos. I'm going to send this sample lot of the gems to him. He has always had a fondness for stones of the cut of the ancients and he still owns an impressive collection of them, despite all the turbulence of the past years. I am certain that he will buy some of these samples, and I intend to ask that he obtain the best possible prices for the remainder . . . carefully hinting that there are more where these came from.

"As for the rest of them, I can think of no safer place for them, just now, than within that secret drawer wherein you found them. Do not breathe a single word of any of this to even your lovers or your dearest friends; if talk you have to, talk to your horse and in strictest privacy.

"Now, polish off that brandy and hie you back to your bed. The drums will roll at the usual time and you'll be expected to perform your usual duties."

"So, my lord *Thoheeks* Sitheeros," continued Captain Bralos, "I was sought out at drill some months later, ordered to wash and change to dress uniform, then to present myself to the adjutant at the headquarters of Sub-*strahteegos Thoheeks* Tomos Gonsalos. When I did so, the sub-*strahteegos* had me ushered into his office, opened a small boiled-leather chest and counted out to me ten and a half pounds-weight of gold Zenos."

Sitheeros whistled and shook his head silently. Each unclipped Zenos of Karaleenos contained a full ounce-weight of pure gold, and the rate of exchange at the time of which they were conversing would have represented a sum of between three and four hundred thousand *thrahkmehee* of purchasing power in the then-depressed economy of the war-scarred, impoverished land, wherein gold had commanded vastly enhanced values.

Gonsalos had said, "My cousin, Prince Zenos, would like to see and examine another selection of similar size. Even should he not decide to buy all of these as he bought all of the first lot, he will see that you receive the top prices for them from whomever—if any man living has unlimited access to well-heeled dealers, it's my cousin, and none of them is so witless as to try to cheat him.

"Have you decided in which *thoheekseeahn* you want to buy land and title, young Bralos?"

Upon being told of the offer from *Thoheeks* Klaios, Gonsalos had sat for a few moments, pulling at his chinbeard. Then he had nodded once and said, "You should not buy land you've never seen and at least walked over from a man you know but briefly. I'm

going to have an order drafted temporarily detaching
you from the foot-guards and assigning you to my
headquarters; you'll be taking it back to your captain
from here. Bring all of those gems back with you—I'll
make the selections and lodge the rest in my strongbox.

"On the morrow, you'll be leading out a score of my
horse-guards. Your destination will be the *Thoheekseeahn* of Ahndropolis. If, after you've seen and examined the land, talked over the inherent rights and
obligations of the holder and, most important, decided
whether or not you can live under or even really like
your prospective overlord, you still want to buy what
he has to sell, you can give him the two pounds-weight
of gold you'll have carried down there and promise
him the rest—in gold—when you have been properly
invested. How much did he say he wanted, anyway?"

Lieutenant Bralos had replied, "One hundred and
twenty thousand *thrahkmehee*, my lord Sub-*strahteegos*."

"Hmmm, sounds reasonable, about what your average *vahrohnoseeahn* seems to be going for down here
these days, but even so, see if you can haggle him
down to a hundred thousand, my boy. Remember,
rank also hath its definite responsibilities, and the folk
and erections on that land will be yours, once you're
invested their lord," said Gonsalos, adding, "And you're
probably going to have to carry those folk for as long
as it takes to get the land into production again, not to
mention rebuilding town walls, habitations and, probably, even your hold. Then you'll have to furnish your
hold and town residence, hire on a certain number of
garrison troops and other functionaries to mind the
place in your absence . . . unless you intend to sell
your lieutenancy and retire. Do you so intend, Bralos?"

"No, my lord Sub-*strahteegos*," Lieutenant Bralos
had answered. "I like the army and I had actually
intended to buy a captaincy-of-cavalry, could I afford
it after buying land and title."

Gonsalos had smiled broadly and warmly. "Good, good, that's what I'd hoped you'd say, Bralos. You're a fine young man, a good officer, and you'll be an equally fine squadron captain, I'm sure. When you're ready to purchase that captaincy, let me know."

Thoheeks Klaios and his sparkling, vivacious young wife had treated Lieutenant Bralos less like a favored guest than like a loved member of the family from the very beginning of his stay with them. He could see that although ravaged, overgrown and showing the evidence of neglect, the land was basically good and, with hard work, could be put right and productive again. The walls of the town were in need of extensive repairs and the hold looked as if nothing short of total rebuilding would suffice to make it livable and defensible again; however, the *thoheeks* was quick to tell him of the granite quarry in his *thoheekseeahn* and of a few skilled stonemasons locally available; he also made mention of his agreements with neighboring *thoheeksee* to trade dressed stone for baked roofing-tiles and building-brick.

In the end, Bralos had been able to haggle the price of his lands and title down to one hundred and twelve thousand *thrahkmehee* in gold. *Thoheeks* Klaios not only freely gave Bralos a very favorable tax-structure for ten years into the future, but offered to have his own seneschal oversee the governance of whomever Bralos hired on to rule in his absence.

Bralos had ridden back to the camp below Mehseepolis thinking that matters had worked out very well for his aspirations to date. All now needed was his investiture, the payment of the rest of the gold to his new civil overlord, then purchase of a squadron captaincy, which last he would have scant difficulty selling to another nobleman should he ever find himself in need of the money or should he decide to retire to his lands and start the breeding of sons to inherit them and his new title.

However, thanks primarily to the press of military duties, that investiture was long in coming. By the time that he was invested, Grand *Strahteegos* Pahvlos the Warlike had taken over the army and begun to tailor it to his personal tastes, readying it for the march west to Kahlkopolis. He and his troop fought well at Kahlkopolis, capturing an enemy banner and receiving the personal notice and public thanks for Captain Portos himself.

But then, during the return march, Bralos, part of his troop, a young ensign of foot and some pikemen were seconded to serve as garrison for the city of Ippohspolis, loaned by the Grand *Strahteegos* until the new city lord could hire on troops of his own. As said new lord, knowing a good thing when he saw it, dragged his feet incessantly, Bralos and the rest vegetated for almost a year before someone back at Mehseepolis finally remembered and recalled them.

No sooner, however, were the sometime Ippohspolis garrison back in the camp below Mehseepolis than Bralos and his troopers needs must ride out with their squadron on a foray against a far-southern *opokomees* whose armed band had taken to raiding his neighbors round about and who had forwarded the pickled head of the herald Council had sent down to try to reason with him. Ambushed before they had even reached the border of the *opokomeeseeah*, the squadron had sustained heavy losses and, with Bralos and his troop covering it, had executed a retrograde movement . . . tails between legs.

Before he had suicided of pure shame, the captain of the squadron had effusively praised the bravery and sagacity of Lieutenant Bralos to the Grand *Strahteegos*, Tomos Gonsalos and Council. The humiliated officer had strongly recommended Bralos for squadron command, but by the time the squadron and the remainder of the expeditionary force had returned once more to Mehseepolis with the head of the rebel *opokomees* and a long file of chain-laden bandits to be gelded and put into slavery on the roads, it was to find that the Grand *Strahteegos* had sold command of the squadron to "a more mature man," an officer of the onetime royal army almost as old as Pahvlos himself.

Naturally, Bralos could not request leave to journey down and be invested until the new captain had gotten to know the officers and troopers of the squadron, and by the time things had shaken down and the vacancies in the ranks had been filled, they and half the squadron of the Horseclansmen were sent off into the northwestern foothills after a reorganized band of bandit marauders which had taken to harrying certain of the border *thoheekseeahnee* and even raiding across the border, taking the chance of agitating the now-peaceful barbarians.

Early on in the campaign, the new captain had made complaint at the evening meal of dull pains in both arms and, sulphurously cursing the cold, damp air, had retired to his tent and bed rather early; just before dawn his servant had found him cold and dead in his bed. This had left Captain Chief Pawl of Vawn as senior officer of the expeditionary force.

The Horseclans chief had ridden up to where a gaggle of light cavalry officers stood grouped near to the dead captain's tent while servants prepared the body for the pyre.

From his saddle, he had demanded, "Who's the senior lieutenant of the squadron, gentlemen?"

Acting Squadron Captain Bralos and Captain Chief Pawl had found that they worked well together, a something that could not have been said for the Horseclansman chief's short, stormy relationship with the now-deceased man who had originally been appointed senior officer of the combined force by Grand *Strahteegos* Pahvlos.

There followed a succession of short, vicious, bloody skirmishes with portions of the bandit band, none of the small fights accomplishing anything worthwhile, due to the fact that the bandits, when stung, retreated across the border which the Council troops had been expressly forbidden to do, for whatever reason.

At last, of a wet, blustery night, while Bralos sat in the tent he had inherited along with squadron command, poring over sketch-maps of the hills while an *eeahtros* changed the bandage protecting a fairly fresh sword-cut on the young officer's bridle-arm, the guards had admitted the cloaked Chief Pawl.

After shedding the sodden, dripping cloak and hanging it in such fashion that water from it would not pond on the tent's flooring, the slender, wiry man sat down and poured himself a measure of watered wine from the jar, swallowed appreciatively, then asked, "How's the arm, Bralos? Healing well?"

"It hurts less and itches more, so I suppose it's healing," was Bralos' reply, "but for an expert's comments, you'll have to ask Master Geros, here. Well, Geros, old friend?"

The *eeahtros* smiled fleetingly. "My lord Captain, it is progressing as well as can be expected, since the lord lieutenant insists upon using it as if it were sound, day after day."

Sipping at the cup of wine, the Horseclansman then sat and chatted of inconsequential topics until the *eeahtros* had completed his tasks and departed into the rainy night. Then Vawn drew his stool closer to Bralos and spoke in hushed tones.

"Look you, Bralos, we could carry on like this until next year this time and not do anything of value up here. The few hunters that the *thoheeksee* have loaned us may know wild game, but they know damn-all about military operations. Winter is approaching fast and I do not want to be up here to meet it, nor do I look forward to going back to Mehseepolis with nothing but casualties and used-up supplies to show for our efforts.

"When you go after rats, you first put a brace of terriers at the bolthole before you let the ferret down the burrow. The border, up there, is these rats' bolthole, and we'll never scotch more than two or three at any one time until we get that bolthole covered properly, don't you see."

Bralos shook his head. "But what can we do, Captain? We were warned in no uncertain terms not to cross over into the barbarian lands. If only we could be certain of a time when and a place where barbarian warriors would be along their side of the border . . . but I can see no way for us to do that."

The Horseclansman's thin lips parted as he grinned. "Oh, but there is a way to do just so, Bralos. With the dawn, I'm going to be riding up there with two of my men and a local type who says he not only knows how to reach the village of the chief, but knows that worthy of old. I'm going to be leaving you in overall command, but I want you to do nothing save patrol the perimeter and not fight unless attached. The men and the horses can all use a few days of rest . . . and so too can you and your arm."

"Captain, I beg you not to go," pled Bralos. "If you do, it will be in direct contradiction to the personal orders of the Grand *Strahteegos*."

Grinning even more widely, Vawn drew out an oilskin documents pouch, unwound it and fumbled through papers until he found the one he wanted, then proffered it to the younger officer, saying, "If you read it, Bralos, it states that under no circumstances is any officer of the force to lead his command across the border, even if in hot pursuit of bandits.

"Well, I am not going to be leading my command anywhere, they're going to be hunkering down here in camp along with you and yours. I'm simply riding up there with a couple of my relatives to pay a friendly call on a fellow-barbarian chief and chew the fat with him."

Bralos shook his head. "Captain, you are not a barbarian, not in any way such; those people up there are, and they all hate Ehleenohee. Most likely, if ride you insist, you'll be riding to your death in those hills."

"Oh, but I am a barbarian," Vawn assured him. "I and my kindred are no whit different from the folk of those mountain tribes, Bralos. Yes, they ate most Ehleenee . . . but with good and sufficient reasons: not only did your ancestors drive theirs from the rich lands that you now hold, but your race and theirs have been more or less at war over lands ever since. It is precisely because those tribes and I are both racially and linguistically akin that I think I can talk them around to helping us eradicate a common menace: those damned bandit raiders.

"I will be taking along two prairiecats to scout and act as both hidden guards and messengers. Should both of them come back without me or any of my party, then you may be certain that none of us will ever come back and that whatever else is done about these bandits up here will be fully in your hands; Lieutenant Sub-chief Bili Vawn, my half brother, has orders to completely subordinate himself and his force to you and abide by your decisions."

"Is there nothing that I can do or say to dissuade you from this suicidal folly?" asked Bralos despairingly.

"Did I think it certain suicide, I'd not be doing it," Vawn assured him. "Let's just call it a calculated risk, a quality with which warfare is riddled. But I've dealt with mountain tribes quite often, up north, in Kehnooryos Ehlahs, learned to speak their dialects and respect their cultures. I know and you know full well that some new something must be introduced to end this seemingly endless little war of attrition against the bandits, and I think that with a bit of help from my far-distant cousins, that new strategy can be speedily accomplished."

"But . . . to so risk your very life . . . ?" Bralos began.

Vawn laughed. "Friend Bralos, I and you and every other officer and trooper and clansman of this or any other force risks life each time a horse is forked or an attack is ordered or shining steel is drawn or arrows fly.

"Now, I must bid you a good night and seek my blankets." He stood up and reached for his cloak. "Dawn always comes early, it seems."

Captain Chief Pawl Vawn of Vawn had succeeded in his aims, returned from his mountain mission with presents and a dozen warrior-guides out of the Maginiz Tribe. Then, for over a week, the force had carefully herded the chary bandits, avoiding combat as much as possible, but heading the foe in a chosen direction until, at last, the earlier-chosen time and place was reached. Then Bralos and Vawn threw every effective against the concentrated band: Bralos' Ehleen squadron, Vawn's Horseclansmen, some twoscore armed retainers and hunters on loan from the local *thoheeksee* and the dozen Maginiz fighters.

It was of course a running, mounted fight from its inception, both sides being horsemen, and as usual when the bandits had had enough, they began to stream over the nearby border. But presently, frantic, desperate men began to spur-rake frothing horses back over that selfsame border, many of them hotly pursued by grim, well-armed mountain tribesmen, both ahorse and afoot and all with certain bloodsoaked scores to be settled.

Not many of the largish band survived, and of those who did, the ones who were marched south in chains considered themselves extremely blessed with good fortune, for even the gelding and branding and life of slavery toward which they were being driven was far preferable to the sure fates of those survivors who had been claimed by the tribes of the mountains.

The force and their captives happened to return to the camp below Mehseepolis at a time while the Grand *Strahteegos* and most of the rest of the army were away somewhere in the east persuading a *thoheeks* to be reasonable and seek confirmation of his inherited title from Council rather than trying to proclaim himself King and successor to Zastros. Pahvlos' absence had left Sub-*strahteegos* Tomos Gonsalos in full command of the camp and such forces as remained therein.

Chapter IV

Grand *Strahteegos* Pahvlos the Warlike and the army still were absent on campaign when Lieutenant *Vahrohnos* Bralos of Yohyültönpolis returned from thirty days' leave, during which time he had been invested with his newly purchased civil rank and lands. The investiture had been witnessed by a covey of the squadron officers and by Captain Chief Pawl Vawn of Vawn along with some of his kindred subordinates. The guest-witnesses had stayed on to take part in the great hunt that had preceded the feastings and had all consumed their fair shares of the game and other foods, wines, beer, pear cider and other potables. The nongame foods and drink had been ostensibly provided by *Thoheeks* Klaios but had, in point of fact, been paid for by some ounces of gold loaned the overlord by Bralos.

Once back in camp, the senior lieutenant of the now-captainless squadron had thrown himself with a will into preparing the unit for field service. Replacement troopers had to be fitted in along with replacements for horses and equipment, while still-serviceable items required cleaning at least and often repair and refurbishing after the long, hard use in the wet, misty foothills and mountains. But Bralos knew what needed doing and he did or saw it all done to perfection.

At long last came the day when the army returned, carrying the pickled head of the *thoheeks* who would have had himself recognized king of the Southern

Ehleenohee. A wretched column of those who had borne arms against Council's army and had had the misfortune to not die in battle were herded in the rear, ungently shepherded by lancers, while a delegation of lesser nobility from the *thoheekseeahn* rode in the van with the Grand *Strahteegos* and his heavy horse bodyguards.

Bralos allowed a bit over two weeks for the returned army to refit itself to garrison life, then he requested an audience with Senior Captain *Thoheeks* Portos, overall commander of cavalry.

The big, tall, black-haired officer greeted him warmly. "My very heartiest congratulations on your investiture, Lord Lieutenant *Vahrohnos*." He had smiled, waving Bralos to a chair. "I suppose that you now wish leave to quit the army for your civil responsibilities, and to feel so is reasonable, but please allow me to reason with you, nonetheless. You see, Council is going to need a strong army for some time yet to come, and officers of your water are most difficult to come by . . ."

"Please, my lord *Thoheeks*, your pardon," Bralos courteously injected, "but it is not my desire to leave the army; rather do I desire to purchase higher rank in it. I would be a squadron captain of light or medium cavalry, my lord."

Portos stared hard at him. "Is it then so, young Bralos? You must be aware that such rank does not come cheaply, nor is credit at all acceptable, nothing save hard coin—preferably, gold."

Wordlessly, Bralos had lined ten golden Zenos on the desktop between them. Then the haggling had begun. By its end, some days later, he had purchased the captaincy of his lancer squadron for about two thirds of the sum that his barony had cost him.

Thoheeks Sitheeros, nibbling at a crisp, deep-fried

songbird, crunching the tiny, hollow bones between his big teeth, took a sip of his fine wine, then asked his guest, "But why did our late Grand *Strahteegos* try so hard to have you hung—you should've heard the unholy row in Council when he was voted down on that score—and why did you take your squadron and leave the camp, the army and the environs of the capital until Pahvlos' demise?"

Captain-of-squadron *Vahrohnos* Bralos of Vohyültönpolis just shook his head, washed down a mouthful of spicy, salty crisp bread and said, "My lord *Thoheeks*, that is a sorry tale, but if you would hear it, then I'll tell it."

Bralos' first, informal meeting with Grand *Strahteegos* Pahvlos was upon the occasion of the party welcoming the new captain *vahrohnos* to the brotherhood of the army's higher officers, the traditional festivities having been organized by Senior Captain of Cavalry Portos and Sub-*strahteegos* Tomos Gonsalos, who had but just received word of his own civil promotion to *thoheeks* in his northern homeland of Karaleenos.

After brief congratulations, the old man had chatted for some two hours with others, then sought out Bralos again, seating himself beside him and splashing a little watered wine into his goblet from a convenient ewer.

"It is my understanding, *Vahrohnos*," he had said, "that you began your career with this army as a junior lieutenant of the foot-guards, distinguished yourself in battle at least twice, were commended for that and other services by both Senior Captain Portos and *Thoheeks* Grahvos. After you had purchased a lieutenancy and troop command in the lancers, you were mentioned in Portos' dispatches from the field of the Battle of Kahlkopolis, too. Yes, you own, have earned, the high regard of some exceedingly important men, both in the army and in the civil sphere. Your new overlord, in fact, *Thoheeks* Klaios, seems to regard you almost as a family member rather than as just a noble vassal."

"My lord Grand *Strahteegos* knows far more of me and my life than I would have dreamed," said Bralos, wondering even as he spoke to just what purpose the senior officer had searched out these facts.

Taking his goblet stem between his sinewy fingers and rolling it absently, the Grand *Strahteegos* had smiled and said, "The more that a commander knows of his men and, most especially, of his officers, the better; remember that, Captain Bralos. But that which I have not yet learned of you is this, my good captain: we both know that your younger son's patrimony was barely sufficient to buy your first, junior-lieutenant rank, and you just might've been able to have won enough gambling to have secured the troop-lieutenancy in the lancers. But when we are come to discuss baronies and squadron captaincies, we are speaking of really large sums, far and away more gold than any officer-mess gamblers ever saw in one place at one time. So just how did you come by so much hard gold in a land stripped so bare as ours?"

It was in Bralos' mind, just then, to tell the prying old man that his personal finances were none of his business, but such an answer would not be politic, not to so high-ranking a man, so he used the reply on which he and Sub-*strahteegos Thoheeks* Tomos Gonsalos had long ago agreed. Smiling, he said, "Loot, my lord. The worth of some gems I took during a campaign before you came to command us."

Old Pahvlos threw back his balding head and laughed, then reached and grasped Bralos' forearm, squeezing it warmly, cordially. "Young man, you will go very far in this or in any other army. We two will discuss this matter and that of your career with Council's army at some other time and place, but for now"—he raised his voice and, shoving back his chair, stood up—"my good Captain *Vahrohnos*, I must bid you and this company a fond good night, for old bones require more frequent rest than do younger bones."

Bralos had done very well by his squadron, so that soon he had no slightest trouble filling the ranks, and indeed, was obliged to maintain a waiting list for would-be troopers and first-rate sergeants. At the suggestions of Senior Captain *Thoheeks* Portos and Sub-*strahteegos* Tomos Gonsalos, he raised both the asking-price and the other requirements for ensigns, sub-lieutenants, troop-lieutenants, senior lieutenant and sub-captain, after first buying back the ranks of those few men who did not or could not work with or under him, and even so, hardly the day passed but that he found himself approached by top-notch officers or one time officers or wellborn young men, all clearly eager to lay their credentials and money before him.

Of course, lieutenants and captains of units losing personnel to the Wolf Squadron grumbled and groused that he was pampering his unit, turning them into overfed, underworked, elegantly dressed, indulged show troops, unfit for anything save parades; but even as these few envious officers spoke, they knew well the falsity of their words of accusation, for Wolf Squadron was performing yeoman service in the seemingly endless round of campaigns into which Grand *Strahteegos Thoheeks* Pahvlos the Warlike had plunged the army. Elegant as was the appearance of the officers and other ranks of Wolf Squadron when they were seen on occasions of formality, in the field they all fought with the ferocity of their totem beast, a lean winter wolf.

Provided with the quantities of golden Zenos which kept coming, through Sub-*strahteegos Thoheeks* Tomos Gonsalos, from the north, Bralos found himself able to see to it that all ranks of his command possessed the necessities in quality as well as in quantity, plus not a few luxuries to compensate them for hard, faithful service.

He had taken over his newly purchased squadron at the end of a cold, wet autumn, and after a detailed inspection of the weapons and equipment of the four hundred-odd officers and men, he had set up in his own mind a list of priorities, cleared them with Senior Captain *Thoheeks* Portos, gone to Sub-*strahteegos Thoheeks* Tomos Gonsalos for a weight of gold, then betaken himself to the collection of buildings at the base of the hills on which sat the fast-growing city of Mehseepolis and sought out certain suppliers of military paraphernalia.

He had had to settle initially for plain, but thick and warm, blanket-cloaks for the most of his squadron, but with the promise in writing that immediately the requisite numbers of dense wolf-pelts were become available, they would be added to trim the hoods without additional charge; however, he had seen all of the cloaks bleached out, then dyed a uniform soft grey, with the same color being applied to the twenty-three-score horse-blankets he bought at the same time from the same family of dealers. This same family were able to also lead him to both a leatherworker and a specialty smith who contracted to undertake a joint project to produce knee-high boots with wrought-iron splints and elbow-high gauntlets sewn with iron or steel rings for all the squadron.

The smith—a heavyset man with wavy brown hair and curly beard, an exceptionally hairy body and the largest, thickest moustache that Bralos could ever recall having seen set under a big and raptorial nose—had served his guests cups of a powerful cider and questioned them at length in relatively good Ehleenokos spoken with an unusual accent. Finally, shoving aside the sheaf of sketches he had made and the notes he had taken in a script that was not Ehleen or Merikan, either, though bearing more resemblance to the former than to the latter, he took a swallow of the cider, then spoke.

"My lord Captain *Vahrohnos*, what if your trooper be sword-gashed between elbow and shoulder, what then?"

Bralos sighed. "Then, Master Haigh, with luck, he'll be crippled, only. I can see where you're going, but be you apprised that it is traditional that lancers' armor be only helmet and light breastplate. And those who command this army insist upon almost-slavish adherence to tradition, alas."

The smith frowned and pursed his lips for a moment, then flitted the trace of a smile. "What would my noble lord think of a grade of fine, strong, but very light double mail that might be easily sewn into an arming shirt or a gambeson to protect troopers' upper arms and armpits, eh? Since it would not be visible, thus would this mad tradition be served."

Bralos skeptically cast a glance into the rather small shop—only the smith, a brother and three lads—replied, "Man, it sounds good, but it would take your shop years to produce enough of the stuff for my command. We're talking here of two per man and between four and five hundred men."

The smith's lip-corners twitched. "Oh, no, my lord, I do not make this fine mail; it is produced by some . . . relatives, in the north."

Bralos barked a short, humorless laugh. "Master Haigh, not even I can afford Pitzburk prices plus wagoning costs to protect my men, much as I would so like to do."

The smith shouted something through the doorway that led into the shop and forge, something in a harsh-sounding language, and in a moment, one of the lads came in with a bundle wrapped in oiled suede, placing it at a word from the smith atop the table, then departing to shortly return wheeling a carved wooden dummy of a man's torso and a brace of heavy-bladed shortswords in wood-and-leather scabbards.

Still seated, the master smith unwrapped the oiled suede to show an underwrapping of coarse, unbleached woolen fabric as thick as blanketing and also oil-impregnated. Under the wool was the mail.

Bralos thought that the gleaming metal mesh might have been wrought of fine silver, so lustrous was it; leaning close, he could see that each and every small ring was riveted—a quality product and no mistaking it, each ring joined to other rings in eight places and all finely finished and polished.

Lifting one of the three hauberks, for such this lot were, the smith's big, scarred hands rolled and compressed it into a ball that looked impossibly small, then proffered it to his principal guest.

Bralos found it extremely light, yet when he unrolled it and laid part of it out on the tabletop, he could not get half a finger-width of the point of his boot-dagger through it, shove as he did.

Standing, the smith took the hauberk from him and draped it over the scarred, dented wooden dummy. When it was draped to his critical satisfaction, the big man turned back to the table, selected one of the brace of shortswords and drew it from out its scabbard, then he reversed and offered the weapon for Bralos' inspection.

Handling it carefully, for the winking edges showed it to be honed to a very keen degree of sharpness all along both edges of the roughly two feet of broad blade, Bralos knew immediately that he had never seen or handled its exact like before. In some ways, it bore a similarity to the standard Ehleen army infantry shortsword, but it was wider, thicker and differently balanced from that weapon. The central rib would no doubt impart decided strength to it, while the four

fullers down most of the length on both flats reduced
significantly the overall weight.

With the sword once more in his hand, the master
smith shoved the dummy a little farther from the table
and his guests, took a stance and, whirling the weapon
up above and behind his head, shouted some phrase in
the guttural foreign tongue and delivered several cuts
and looping slashes at the mail-draped wooden form.
No one could doubt that he was striking with all his
not inconsiderable strength, for twice a shower of
sparklets flew upward from the buffets, the fabric of
the hardwood dummy creaked and groaned protestingly
and, at the last blow, one of the axles of the dummy-
cart bent and a freed wooden wheel went skittering
across the floor.

There having been no arms to help hold it in place
on the dummy, the mail had of course been moved out
of its original drape, but aside from this, Bralos was
able to detect no slightest breaking or bending or even
scarring of the rings anywhere on the fine steel shirt,
for all that the edges of the sword showed the effects
of hard contacts with steel. Even so, he rearranged the
drape of the hauberk and went at it for a few strokes
with the other sword. At last, he used his left hand to
hold the dummy still and drew back his arm, clearly
intending to thrust at the chest.

"No," said the master smith, adding, "And it please
my lord, no; that sword will break the mail and pene-
trate, though one of your own swords probably would
not do so. That sword was designed to pierce mail and
scale armor at the hard thrust, you see."

Bralos stepped back from the abused dummy and
nodded, smiling. "I thought so when I saw that almost-
edgeless, diamond-shaped point and that ribbed blade.
It's a good design for a sword, though a bit short for
my own tastes. You'd play hell trying to use so short a
blade on horseback."

"My peo . . . that is, the people who developed that sword live in mountains and mountainous foothills, my lord, and own precious few riding horses. They bestride mountain ponies to the site of battle, then fight on foot."

Bralos nodded again. "Which is probably why and how this fine, very strong, but exceedingly light mail came to be, eh? Who are your people, Master Haigh?"

The smith shrugged. "But another race of what my lord's folk call mountain barbarians, though our lands are in no way near to these Consolidated *Thoheek- seeahnee*. Would other tribes leave us to bide in peace, we would do naught save farm our valleys and graze our flocks on the heights, but such has never for long come to pass, and so have we been compelled to learn to practice the ways of war."

Bralos shook his head. "Using those swords and this fantastic mail as indicators, I would say that your people have assured themselves of the wherewithal to practice war quite well. If you can fit it to me, I'd like to buy one of those hauberks from you, one that will hang to about mid-thigh.

"So far as the half-sleeves for my men are con- cerned, how long would it take your tribe to produce five hundred pairs and get them here to Mehseepolis? Oh, and what will the pairs cost?"

Once they had worked out a price that was mutually agreeable, the smith said, "My lord, much of the iron that my people use is smelted locally from ores or rendered from rusted ancient-times artifacts. If my lord desires quicker delivery and would be willing to advance a bit more gold to buy pig iron . . . ?"

Senior Captain *Thoheeks* Portos summoned Bralos to the heavy horse camp on a sunny but bone-chillingly cold January day, snow lying deeply on the ground. Within his plastered, wooden-walled office, a brace of braziers warmed the room to such degree that, with a cupful of brandy, a man could be almost comfortable.

"We . . . you have a problem, Bralos," said the cavalry commander, with his usual bluntness.

Bralos could think of no problems of any consequence within the squadron, so he raised his eyebrows quizzically and awaited elucidation in silence.

"It has gotten back . . . rather, been borne back by certain envious officers," said Portos, "that you are coddling your squadron—overindulging them with rough, warm clothing, decent food and wine or beer, protective boots and gauntlets and ash lance-shafts, where the other squadron must make do with issue oaken shafts. Therefore, the Grand *Strahteegos* has decided that if you can afford to so pamper the common troopers of your squadron, you can equally well afford to increase your squadron strength to four troops.

"Look you, Bralos, I did try . . . for all the good that it did me or you." Portos' dark face was a very study in frustration and anger. "I pointed out that it were eminently unfair to ask you to raise and arm and outfit another troop while allowing Captain *Opokomees* Ehrrikos to maintain only the three. But then that slimy Ehrrikos, waving a hand that bore gold and gems on its every finger, protested his near-penury, cited your flaunted affluence . . . and that was that, the old man signed the order.

"So, now, my boy, you must recruit, and recruit most speedily, at the least ninety troopers, ten sergeants, three cooks, probably one or two more farriers, a senior sergeant, another horse-leech and at least two more *eeahtrohsee*. Mounts, weapons and armor and horse-furnishings will, of course, be provided by the army. There is the fact, for what compensation that it will be, that you now will have ranks to put on the market—one troop-lieutenancy, two of sub-lieu-

tenant and four of ensign. How long do you think it
will take you? I'll get you all the time I can."

By the end of that week, Bralos had over a hundred
troopers, a senior sergeant and twelve section-sergeants,
all of the needed specialist troops, a troop-lieutenant,
a sub-lieutenant and three of the ensigns—all five of
the officers, all but two of the sergeants and a goodly
portion of the troopers come out of the other squadron of lancers, the Panther Squadron, commanded by
none other than Captain *Opokomees* Ehrrikos of
Thakhahrispolis.

Portos rode up to the headquarters building of Wolf
Squadron rocking in his saddle with laughter, tossed
his reins to the waiting trooper and slid to the ground,
still laughing. Seated in Bralos' snug office, with a
goblet of brandied wine in his big hands, the senior
captain controlled himself long enough to give his host
the tale.

Foaming with rage, Captain *Opokomees* Ehrrikos
had stormed into the heavy horse headquarters and
demanded immediate words with the overall commander
of cavalry. Upon admission to Portos' office, he had
brusquely refused the offer of a tipple and had begun
to rant and rave of the loss of almost a full troop of his
best troopers and sergeants—including two sergeants
from out of his own headquarters detachment and, to
add insult to injury, his personal batman—no less than
three sub-lieutenants, two ensigns and the senior lieutenant who had been in charge of his headquarters for
years.

"Desertion?" queried Portos blandly, suspecting un-
told the true answer, even as he spoke. "We'll apprehend these miscreants in no time, never you fear,
Opokomees, the scouts will tell us which way they
went, and then I'll send some of Captain Chief Pawl's
Horseclanners to . . ."

"No, no, no, no no!" the visiting officer half-shrieked,

shaking both gloved fists and stamping one booted foot upon the floor in his agitation. "The pigs didn't desert, my lord *Thoheeks*, not legally; no, Petros and the rest of those drooling idiots I called my officers came to me and demanded back the prices of their ranks . . . and, of course, I had to give them the money. The others, those scoundrelly sergeants and the idiot troopers and my cretin of a servant, they all just took everything that did not belong to me and went over in a body to join that goddam Wolf Squadron. They're hunkering there, now."

"Well, lord *Opokomees*," inquired Portos, "what do you want me to do about it all, pray tell? If the troops did not desert, then they still are members of my command who simply have chosen to serve me and the army in a different squadron. Admittedly, the other ranks should, strictly speaking, have gone through channels to effect a transfer to another unit of horse, but now that it is done, I can see no reason to censure them."

"I don't want them censured!" Captain Ehrrikos half-shouted. "I want the lowborn scum back! I'll see the bare white spines of every one of those damned sergeants . . . and that backbiting batman, too!"

"It is all as I have heretofore stated, Captain *Opokomees*," said Portos with chilly formality. "This . . . ahhh . . . rearrangement of officers and troops will not discommode me or my brigade of horse, and so I can think of nothing that would impel me to involve myself in it. Have you considered riding over and pleading with Captain *Vahrohnos* Bralos to return them to Panther Squadron?"

Ehrrikos turned livid and grated from between tightly clenched teeth. "I did . . . earlier today. The bastard of a shoat and a goat, he *laughed* at me, laughed at *me*, to my very face. He said that did I put less gold on myself and more upon the backs of and in the bellies

of my troopers, I might still have more of them within
the precincts of my own camp and fewer of them
within his. Then the misbegotten son of a diseased ape
informed me that as he was very busy with interview-
ing newly come personnel, he would have to cut our
visit short. The *gall* of the upstart, only a damned
vahrohnos, and not even that for long!"

Portos tried hard to keep the smile from off his face,
the laughter out of his voice. "Well, then, Captain,
have you considered seeking an audience with the
Grand *Strahteegos*? You seemed to have his ear and
his favor earlier this week, as I recall. Perhaps he
would see that you got at least your other ranks back.
Neither he nor I could tell your noble officers what to
do, not after you allowed them to sell back their ranks
in Panther Squadron."

The officer's lividity deepened, darkened, and he
ground his teeth. "Lord *Thoheeks*, it was our Grand
Strahteegos Thoheeks Pahvlos who sent me here, to
you as cavalry brigade commander to resolve this stinking mess. He said that he would leave resolution of the
current matter up to you, trusting as he does your
judgment, and he . . ." Ehrrikos paused and ground
his teeth once more.

"Yes?" prompted Portos. "The Grand *Strahteegos*
had other words, Captain?"

"He . . . he said . . . it was of a rather personal
nature, my lord," said Ehrrikos, a little lamely.

"Even so, I will hear it, Captain. Now," Portos
demanded, ordered.

Even in his anger, Ehrrikos could not mistake the
authority in the voice of the senior captain, and he
could not but obey. "He said, my lord, that if I was
desirous of keeping my rank and the command of
Panther Squadron, the two troops I had remaining and
the third that I must immediately begin to recruit, I had
best sell my finger-rings, my arm-rings and my golden

chain and use the money from them to outfit my troops
for winter campaigning and begin to feed them more
and better rations. He . . . he promised that was Panther Squadron not the equal at least of Wolf Squadron
by spring, that . . . that the entire army would be witness to my impalement."

Lolling in the chair in Bralos' office, the big, brawny
Portos could no longer restrain himself, gusting once
more into laughter that continued until tears were cours-
ing down his scarred cheeks into his beard and he must
perforce hold with both hands his aching sides.

"And would he?" asked Bralos. "Captain *Thoheeks*,
could the Grand *Strahteegos* have an *opokomees* publicly impaled for such cause?"

Sobering a bit, the brigade commander replied,
"Whether he would or not is really anyone's guess; old
Pahvlos is not easy to fathom. But if he felt he had
cause, sufficient cause, he most assuredly could. His
successes—past and present—have made him virtually
a law unto himself, insofar as Council is concerned.

"But in this case of *Opokomees* Ehrrikos' callous
mistreatment of his squadron, I doubt that Pahvlos
would go that far. Most likely, if Ehrrikos sees fit to
ignore Pahvlos' 'advice,' he will just have him well
striped, stripped of his military rank and enough of his
personal treasures to cover refurbishing the squadron
and meeting the prices of rank of the remaining officers, then send him home in disgrace. No doubt,
Ehrrikos' overlord will be sufficiently displeased to
punish him, too. But impalement, no, I doubt it, Bralos,
not crucifixion or maiming, even."

"My lord," Bralos said, "I would ask a question of
you."

Smiling, Portos nodded. "Ask away, then, my good
Bralos."

"The provisions I have made for the men of my
squadron—decent clothing, equipment and food—

should these things not be provided to all men of the army *by* the army, rather than leaving such necessities' provision up to individual commanders who, in most cases, either cannot or will not? Sub-*strahteegos Thoheeks* Tomos Gonsalos has told me that in both the Royal Army of Karaleenos and in the Army of the Confederation, things are just so—all soldiers' needs being issued by the army."

Portos took his barely touched goblet from off the desktop and took a sip, then sighed. "The biggest and, to Pahvlos and many another noble officer, most important reason is that the present method, with all its undeniable faults, is the traditional method in armies of the Southern *Ehleenohee*. The most pressing reason that this was not adopted by Grahvos and the rest when Tomos first advised its adoption, years back, before Pahvlos came, was and is the simple fact that the Council could not and cannot afford it . . . yet.

"Hell, Bralos, I dislike it as much as any other officer or man. I would much rather be putting such funds as I come by into my new duchy, rather than using them to clothe and equip and feed my troops, but they are completely dependent on me and I realize that fact, recognizing my responsibility to them and to the army.

"But until, if, when, Council sees fit to step into the management of the army, has the necessary income and effects a reorganization of sorts, you and I are just stuck with making the best that we can of an old, bad, but long-established situation."

"All right, then, if the squadron is to be my responsibility, I want it to be my sole responsibility, my lord, all of it. I want leave to buy the present horses from Council, the furnishings for them and my men's weapons," said Bralos.

"Sweet Christ on Your Cross!" exclaimed Portos. "Man, do you have any conception of the kind of money you're speaking of laying out here? Just how rich *are* you, anyway?"

Bralos nodded. "Yes, I know the figure almost to the coppers, my lord, Sub-*strahteegos* Tomos and I added it all up with the help of a quartermaster officer and a remount officer, both sworn to secrecy. It will put somewhat of a dent in my present finances, but I still can afford it."

"Why do you want to do such a thing?" demanded Portos, incredulity in his voice, a stunned look on his face. "It . . . the thing just makes no sense to me."

"Should I leave the army, for whatever reason," answered Bralos, "I want to go with the knowledge that the men who served me so well for so long and under such trying conditions will each own at least the value of a good troop-horse and their weapons and armor. Another thing is this: many of my men are—rather were—farmers, herders and suchlike. My barony—hell, the entire duchy, for that matter—is underpopulated, now. Whenever things wind down and the army need not be so large, I want to take all of my squadron who wish to go with me back to my lands, to till and sow and herd upon them. For those men not so inclined, both my overlord and I will need small armed bands of retainers."

Portos stared hard into Bralos' eyes, then dropped his gaze. "A bit earlier, I was speaking to Ehrrikos on the responsibilities of rank. Bralos, you shame me, you shame all of us officers, in your concern for the present welfare and even the future welfare of your troopers. How I wish all of my cavalry officers were alike to you.

"Your request will, naturally, have to go to the highest authority, to the Grand *Strahteegos* himself. But I will personally bear it to him and pray that he approve it; if he does not, then I'll put it to Council. That's the best I can do."

"My lord is more than generous, may God bless him," Bralos said with sincere feeling.

"Yes, I recall that ruckus in Council," said *Thoheeks* Sitheeros, while using his powerful hands to crack nuts. "A duel resulted from some of the name-calling engendered in that day's civilized debate. Grahvos finally summoned Tomos up to the palace and closeted with him for a while, then rammed the measure through by way of a half-Council vote. That can be done, you know; most business can be decided by the votes of seventeen councillors only, not the full thirty-three.

"So, then, that was how you got on the bad side of our late Grand *Strahteegos*, hey?"

"I'm now certain that that was the beginning of the Grand *Strahteegos'* antipathy toward me, my lord. He insisted after that that my squadron be listed as mercenary cavalry; I suppose that he thought that such a designation would limit my ability to recruit replacements and sell officer ranks, but of course it did not," replied Bralos.

The spring thaw saw the beginning of nearly two years of almost constant campaigning for the army of Council, beginning with a long march into the far-northwestern corner of the Consolidated *Thoheek-seeahnee* and a protracted war against an alliance of a number of tribes of mountain barbarians. The army stayed in those mountain for more than six months, almost until snowtime, seldom engaging in large open battles, but one hit-and-miss ambuscade or running fight or assault upon walled or stockaded hold and village after another. The cavalry, particularly the light cavalry, took heavy losses in this campaign.

Once arrived back at the camp under Mehseepolis' walls, Bralos set about buying horses and equipment to replace losses, carted out wainloads of damaged items for repair and had broadcast a call for men to fill out his ranks . . . and they came, despite the measures taken by his peers in military rank to prevent them so doing. They came because—despite the brutally hard service to which Wolf Squadron had been subjected— very few troopers had been lost due to malnourishment or frostbite, most casualties being the result of enemy action or common accident or mischance.

Although the snows came, this unpleasant fact did not prevent the army being marched forth on another campaign for the year, this one to the south and lasting the most of the winter.

Barely had the next spring been ushered in when Wolf Squadron and half of the Horseclan Squadron were dispatched again to another stretch of border to deal with yet another pack of bandit-raiders whose ongoing depredations were become the bane of two more *thoheeksee*. So once more Bralos rode north with Captain Chief Pawl Vawn of Vawn.

This action did not take as much time, for Chief Pawl was senior officer from the start, and immediately it was seen by him and Bralos that the border was being used just as the other bandits had used it, he rode into the mountains with local hunters and chewed the fat with his fellow barbarian chiefs, and shortly he and Bralos were headed back to Mehseepolis with a long coffle of slaves-to-be and but few losses from among their own ranks.

It had been during the campaign of the previous winter—that one conducted along the ill-defined border of the sinister Witch Kingdom, which lay somewhere deep within the dank, dark, overgrown wilderness of ghoul-haunted fens and monster-teeming swamps, where huge and often deadly serpents slithered, where carpets of lush vegetation concealed beds of quicksand and bottomless pools of brackish water—that Grand

Strahteegos Pahvlos had acquired a lover. This boy of about fourteen or fifteen, Ilios by name and the recognized bastard of a *thoheeks*, reared in his father's household and extended most of the same education and advantages as had his legitimate half brothers, was as pretty as a young girl, and Pahvlos' possession was envied by those officers and soldiers of similar tastes; the rest referred to him in private as "Ilios *Pooeesos*." It had been determined much later by general consensus that the coming of this Ilios had marked the very beginnings of old Pahvlos' abrupt change of character, when he first began to drive the army unmercifully in the field and exact upon the flesh of his soldiers such exaggerated outrages of discipline that, had he not died when he had, he might have sundered the army apart. As it was, he came quite close to tearing apart the Council of *Thoheeksee*.

Chapter V

Upon arrival of the victorious cavalry column at the crossroads just beyond the army's camp, Captain Bralos, having rather urgent business in the commerce district of Mehseepolis, ordered his senior lieutenant to take the squadron into camp, while he and his personal guards accompanied the lancers and Horseclansmen guarding and guiding the hundred-odd chained prisoners bound for the state slave pens, these situated behind a palisaded enclosure just beyond the city's west gate, the ever-present stenches of it, the main abattoir and the tanneries nearby borne away from the city on the prevailing winds.

A low hill with a wide, flattish top a few hundred yards west of the tanneries had become the new location of executions, the former one, when Mehseepolis had been merely a ducal city, having been used as the site of the slave pens. Bralos and the column of horsemen and stumbling war captives slowly passed the place of terror, of torment and death. There apparently had been no recent crucifixions, for all the line of uprights sat without crosspieces, bare save for black crows perching atop three of them, with wistful hope. Beyond them, Bralos could discern the bulk of the permanent gallows, large enough to hang as many as a dozen miscreants at once. A powerful shudder suddenly coursed through the length of him, and he tore his gaze away to look up at the blue skies . . .

only to see the buzzards patiently gliding, circling the abattoir and slave pens.

Inside the outer palisade, a quartet of burly, cruel-looking men shoved and cuffed and cudgeled the bone-weary captives into several files, counted them and reported to a languid, bored-appearing man who had earlier introduced himself to Bralos as one Kahsos of Ahkapnospolis (his lack of title indicated him to be a younger son whose patrimony had been a small city or walled town, but in polite conversation, he would still be addressed as "lord," of course).

Leading the way to the smallest of the buildings, the gentleman ushered his noble military guest in, saw him seated, then poured two battered brass cups half full of a sour, unwatered wine, before seating himself and starting to dictate a receipt to a scribe whose ankles were fettered and joined by a chain.

When he was done and the slave scribe was busy with the sanding and the affixing of the seal to the document, the gentleman said, "My lord *Vahrohnos*, you could not have brought these slaves to us at a better time. When the last batch were gelded, an appalling number of the bastards had the effrontery to die on us, many more of them than is at all normal after geldings, so old *Thoheeks* Bahos, who heads up the Roads and Walls Committee in Council, is fuming, fit to be tied, swears he's going to send out a real surgeon or *eeahtros* and insist he and his helpers do all future geldings."

"Who had you had doing them before, Lord Kahsos?" asked Bralos. 'Some of your guards?"

The reply made him sorry he had asked. "No, my lord *Vahrohnos*, a man name of Pehlzos, used to be a swine-breeder, works now over at the abattoir. He's going to be madder than hops at the loss of his three coppers for each pair of balls if the man lived, one copper was he to die.

"Very funny story, my lord *Vahrohnos*, about the time we threw a slave and Pehlzos come to find out when he went in his bag, the damn bastard didn't have but the one ball, and while Pehlzos was squatting down there with that single ball in his hand, arguing about how we was still going to owe him the going rate and all, that slave bastard, he jerked one hand loose of the straps, took up one of old Pehlzos' knifes and put it through his own heart, right there. I ended up giving Pehlzos a half-copper for that one, and he was bellyaching about it and over it for weeks; still brings it up now and then."

A few yards outside the city gates, Bralos signaled his guards to rein up, kneed his horse over to the side of the road, leaned from his saddle and retched until nothing more would come up. To solicitous words from the guards, he remarked, "That country gentleman's wine, or whatever the stuff really was, was fouler than swampwater or ditchwater running off a new-mucked field. Far better that it be back at home in that ditch than sloshing about in my poor belly."

"Well, then," remarked his guards-sergeant, Tahntos, slyly, "will my lord be wanting to stop by a wineshop to get the taste of that brew from out his mouth?"

"No, my good Tahntos." Pausing long enough to see the disappointment register on Tahntos' face and that of the others before continuing, he said, "But all of you have my leave to visit Master Keemohsahbis' place while I call upon Master Haigh's smithy, across the way . . . just so long as you all stay sober enough to easily stay on a horse and ride with me back to camp, that is."

Seated again in the crowded little chamber off the smithy, Bralos gratefully savored the tart bite of Master Haigh's strong winter cider for a few moments before broaching his reason for coming this day.

"Master Haigh, that fine mailshirt I bought from

you, away back when first we two met, saved my life on this last campaign, making it to my mind worth every last *thrahkmeh* of that steepish price."

The master smith did not appear at all surprised at the news, only inquiring, "Would my lord care to tell what happened?"

Bralos shrugged. "Not much to tell. We were chasing after bandits in the northern foothills, up on the border. That particular day, the unit I was leading was following a very winding and extremely narrow trail through heavily wooded terrain. I had just ridden past an old tree when one of the bandits leaped down from a place of concealment on a thick limb and hacked at my back with a heavy saber.

"Now it was a shrewd blow, delivered with full strength, and had I been without that mailshirt, I'd've been down dead or dying with a severed spine and some hacked-through ribs and that bandit would've been up in my saddle and spurring away, leading the rest of my unit into the maw of an ambush at the gallop. As it was, the edge did no more than cut through the straps of my breastplate and ruin a shirt, though the force of the blow drove the air clean out of my lungs and sent me up into the withers of my mount.

"Not having expected to have to strike a second blow, my attacker paused for a split-second, then, when he drew back to hack again, the back of his blade struck a tree limb, and by that time I'd regained at least my balance if not my breath, gotten my own saber uncased and come close to taking off his sword-arm between wrist and elbow.

"It is a well-known fact that lancers are armored only on the fronts of their bodies, you see; indeed, two of my men were slain in just that same way during this campaign just past, and I mean to do my best to put a stop to it . . . at least within my squadron,

Master Haigh. But I'll need your services in order to do it."

The smith shook his head. "My lord, I cannot go any lower on my price for those double mailshirts . . . well, not enough lower to matter, at least. Much as I respect and admire your solicitude for the welfare of your warriors, wealthy as I know you to be, still must I say that I entertain doubts that you could or should pay the two or three hundred thousand *thrahkmehee* that so many shirts would cost, and besides, it would take me over a year to get so many down here to you. A great deal of time and painstaking labor needs must go into each and every one of them are they to be perfect and of dependable quality. In addition, did my lord not tell me upon the occasion when first we met that the somewhat silly traditions of his army forbade additional armor for lancers?"

Bralos grinned. "Quite true, as regards that last, my good Master Haigh, but there have been some significant changes for me and mine since that day, too. The old, callous traditions still apply to most of the rest of the army, but the Grand *Strahteegos*, in a fit of pique, declared me and my squadron to be mercenaries, not any longer true Ehleen soldiers, which means that the strict interpretations of army traditions need no longer be applied to Wolf Squadron, you see.

"Insofar as your first statements are concerned, you're quite correct; to buy shirts like mine for the entire squadron would be much beyond my means at the present time. But on the march back down here to Mehseepolis, I've reasoned out another idea. What would you quote me tentatively on five hundred *single*-thickness mailshirts, to be assembled of larger rings?"

"It would be far quicker and cheaper, my lord," replied the smith, "to just order up as many backplates. I could probably fulfill part of that order myself, here in this shop, and for the rest, I could job them out to some other good smithies I know of . . .?"

But the officer shook his head. "No, I dare not be so blatant . . . not yet. No, I was thinking of having one of the locals, hereabout, enclose these shirts I envision between two layers of thin leather or linen-canvas. They'd be or at least look like jerkins, in the squadron colors, and thus not be an affront to the Grand *Strahteegos* each time he saw one of us."

"I understand." The smith nodded, grinning. "But look you, my lord, there is a better, cheaper way to give just as much or even more protection to the backs of your horsemen. I'll show you, but please excuse me while I fetch some things out of the shop."

The man returned with a basketful of what looked at first glance to be bits and pieces of scrap iron and steel, but when he had laid a handful upon the table, Bralos saw them to be thin squares of steel, not yet polished and still discolored from the tempering, each of them pierced with a small hole at two corners on one edge. After laying the squares out in staggered lines, the smith looked back up at his guest.

"These, my lord, are a part of special order we're doing up for a customer who wants a jazeran, a scaleshirt, which while bulky and heavy is the best protection from both edge and point short of a breast-and-back of Pitzburk plate. And they're cheaper than either plate or mail, too. For him, these plates will be riveted in overlapping rows onto a double-thick jack of saddle-skirting leather. But there are other ways to use such plates, too, my lord.

"The innermost layer of your canvas jerkin could have a thin layer of cotton batting stitched on, then squares or lozenges of good steel atop that, each sewn or riveted as you'd wish, and another thinness of batting, then another of canvas sewn in a quilted pattern. Add brass or iron guides for the straps of the breastplate, eyelets to the armholes to affix the mail-lined half-sleeves you've already bought, and you'd have an arming-jerkin with a well-hidden difference."

Bralos studied the arrangement on the tabletop, frowning in deep thought, considering this new, fresh suggestion. Then he looked up and demanded, "But what of the collars to protect the throat, Master Haigh?"

The smith waved his hand. "Simple, my lord, very simple. Long, curved plates that will overlap a bit in the front. Sew enough thick braid onto the collar that it would be stiff anyway and conceal the thong used to join the overlapping plate ends."

Still frowning, Bralos asked, "But what of the weight, the bulk?"

The smith sighed. "The bones must come with the mutton, my lord. But, look you, this will be replacing the ordinary arming-shirt. The weight of the steel in back will, if anything, help the man's body to balance the weight of the breastplate and spauldrons, and even with the weights of everything—steel, rivets, canvas, thread and batting—added together, I'd be so bold as to say that it will weigh a bit less than a double mailshirt."

Bralos chewed at his thumb for a moment, then inquired, "Can you have one of these padded shirts made up so that I can examine it? Also, that way we'll know for certain about how much of everything will be needed."

"What are the colors of your Wolf Squadron, my lord?" asked the smith by way of a reply. "Crimson and silver . . .?"

After he had arranged with Master Keemohsahbis to have two pipes of a middling wine he knew to be favored by his troopers carted out to his camp, along with a half-pipe of a far better example of the vintner's art and some small casks of brandy to go to the squadron officers' mess, Bralos collected his slightly tiddly guards and rode back to camp.

There he strolled about to see that everything needful was being done, called for a fresh horse to be saddled, visited his own quarters long enough to doff his armor and change to clean clothing, then rode over to Sub-*strahteegos* Tomos Gonsalos' headquarters. Had anyone with the authority stopped him and asked him why, he was quite prepared to lie, to say that he was searching for Senior Captain *Thoheeks* Portos to render his report on the campaign in the foothills and deliver up the receipts for the banditslaves and the chains in which they had been delivered to the noisome slave pens.

But when he saw the crowd and hubbub around the plain building housing Gonsalos' offices, he almost reined about and rode back to truly report to the overall commander of cavalry. He did ride on, however, as far as he was allowed to ride. The Council Guardsmen who halted him and courteously requested that he dismount then just as courteously demanded to know his reason for approaching the area of the sub-*strahteegos*' headquarters.

Bralos swallowed the testy, impatient answer that had been upon the tip of his tongue; for all their show of courtesy and good manners, Council Guardsmen had a well-earned reputation of blooding their steel first and determining if such had been necessary well after the fact, and aside from his gauntlets, he now wore nothing that would resist the honed edges of their weapons any better than his flesh.

"Lieutenant," he lied glibly, "I have but just led my squadron in from a campaign in one of the northern *thoheekseeahnee*. I found that word had been left for me to report to the Lord Sub-*strahteegos Thoheeks* Tomos immediately upon my return. I am responding to that order; I cannot do less, Lieutenant."

"Of course not, of course not, my lord Captain *Vahrohnos*," the guards officer agreed readily, "but let it please my lord to understand, far more important men than the Sub-*strahteegos* himself just now are visiting him, so perhaps later today or tomorrow might be a better time to report."

Bralos shook his head. "Lieutenant, the message said 'immediately upon my return,' and it has been my experience that the officer always chooses his words carefully and means just what he says. I will report today, now, and that's that."

The guards officer nodded once. "Very well, my lord Captain *Vahrohnos*, but my lord must then surrender his sidearms to me and he must allow himself to be searched. My lord has his functions, I have mine. One of my men will take care of your horse and weapons."

The adjutant would have stopped Bralos, shooed him away back to his camp, had not Tomos caught sight of him through the partially opened door of the larger room where he and several other men sat around the largest table. Excusing himself, he strode out to greet Bralos warmly.

"You're back far earlier than anyone expected you to be, Bralos. What happened, did Chief Pawl despair of ever catching that pack of marauders? If so, old Pahvlos will've been proved right; nevertheless, you can bet a month's pay he won't be at all pleased."

Bralos shrugged. "Not at all, my lord. Oh, yes, we had trouble for the first week or so, but then Captain Chief Pawl devised strategy that gave us an inexpensive victory and above a hundred fresh slaves for the state."

"*Slaves*?" came a contrabasso rumble of a voice from within the large room. "Did someone out there mention slaves? I'm here to tell any man that my road crews need every one they can get, are the repair and replacement schedules to be kept up to date."

This was followed by the grating sound of a chair being pushed back, then a few heavy steps, and the door was shoved farther open by the thick, hairy arm of a big, muscular man of middle years. "Tomos," he rumbled, "who is this officer and what's this of slaves?"

Gonsalos stepped back and said in formal tones, "My lord *Thoheeks*, please allow me to present to you Captain-of-squadron *Vahrohnos* Bralos of Yohyültönpolis. He and his squadron have this very day returned from a short but very successful campaign against bandits in one of the border *thoheekseeahnee*, and he was telling me of the numbers of prisoners they had taken and brought back for state-slaves.

"Captain, this nobleman is a *Thoheeks* Bahos, a member of Council."

Not sure just what else to do, Bralos straightened and rendered the massive man a correct military salute.

The saluted man just grinned. "So you're the young man who so twisted the tail of our revered Grand *Strahteegos*, hey? Do you know that a few days after the first Council debate on whether or not you should be allowed to pay Council hard, honest gold for the right to be completely responsible for your squadron, I wound up back in armor, fighting a formal duel with that hotheaded young whippersnapper *Thoheeks* Vikos? Did you know that, young sir? Of course you didn't. And you didn't know that I showed him his folly in trying to fight me, old man or not, either. True, he's now faster than me, but I'm still lots stronger, so I just let him wear himself out, slow down a bit, then I finished the thing quickly, nearly sundered his helm, I did, they say. Hahahahah!"

It was then that Bralos was shocked to hear himself ask, "My lord *Thoheeks* Bahos, may Captain *Vahrohnos* Bralos inquire of the *thoheeks*?"

Still grinning broadly at memory of his victory over his younger peer, the big man nodded, saying, "Of course you may, young sir, and you need not be so militarily formal, either, for any man that our good Tomos pleases to call friend is also a friend of mine."

Bralos took a deep breath and spoke again. "My lord, Captain Chief Pawl of Vawn and I, we captured a hundred and twelve bandits and got back to Mehseepolis with a hundred and seven of them still living and in as good shape as could be expected after a march of that length by men accustomed to riding mostly."

"What of the weapons and the gear and mounts of these bandits?" interjected the *thoheeks*. "Was it brought back, too?"

Blankfaced, Bralos replied, "My lord, we lacked enough pack-mules to bring back much of anything, since we had been up there for so short a time and used so few supplies, though a few officers and men did pick out certain better-quality items."

Bahos nodded. "Well, it's of no real importance; likely it's better that the stuff was left up there, anyway. Most of it was probably lifted from there and now the noblemen will have it back. But what of the bandits' mounts?"

"Most of them were mountain ponies, my lord *Thoheeks*," Bralos answered. "The few full-size horses were in generally poor shape, some dozen or so that looked good we did bring back, two thirds of the beasts going to my squadron, one third selected by Pawl of Vawn for the use of his Horseclansmen."

"Good, good," nodded the massive nobleman, "horses cost money. But you wished to ask a question of me, I believe . . . ?"

Bralos took another deep breath and launched into it, saying, "My lord *Thoheeks*, what is the point of squandering supplies and horses and trained men to bring back captive warriors who never give Council even one day's work because they die of the black rot in the slave pen after being gelded by an elderly pig farmer who works at the abattoir?"

The big man's smile evaporated in a trice, and his face became as dark as a lowering thundercloud. But when he spoke, his voice was a tightly controlled, soft rumble. "Who told you these things, young man?"

"Why, the keeper of the slave pen, my lord, one Kahsos, told me of his hiring of the old man to do the gelding, while one of his men told one of my body-guards about the high rate of loss from the black rot after the man, Pehlzos, had done his bloody work," said Bralos.

Turning on his heel, the big man opened both doors wide agape and stepped back, saying, "My good young sir, please humor me by coming in, seating yourself, having a stoup to drink and telling my companions of these sorry things."

As *Thoheeks* Bahos himself seated the somewhat bemused Bralos and filled a cup for him from one of the ewers, then introduced him to those men seated around the table, he finally understood why so many fully armed and alert Council Guardsmen were sur-rounding the building. No less than five of the most powerful members of the Council of the Thirty-three sat about that table, including his own commander, Senior Captain *Thoheeks* Portos.

Portos said, "Well, you and Pawl Vawn must have worked some sort of miracle to be back this fast. So well done a job should rightly earn Wolf Squadron a bit of rest . . . but it probably won't. I don't know, it's just as I was telling all these gentlemen prior to your arrival, Bralos, something has gotten into Pahvlos; he seems intent anymore to run the whole army ragged to little real purpose."

"Portos, Portos, we'll get back to all that," said Bahos, "but for now I'd like you all to hear some information that this fine young officer has stumbled across. My good Bralos, tell again just what you told me out in the foyer."

Senior Captain *Thoheeks* Portos purposely chose the longest and most circuitous route from the headquarters of Sub-*strahteegos* Tomos Gonsalos back to the headquarters of the cavalry brigade, he and Bralos riding knee to knee ahead of and out of easy earshot of his bodyguards, conversing in low, hushed tones.

"You made yourself some very good friends on Council, this day, my good Bralos," said Portos. "Those four, back there, along with a brace of their faction and leanings who were unable to make it for this day's clandestine meeting out here, are capable—by ways of the multiple duchies and voting proxies systems—to pass or defeat most varieties of business that come before Council without so much as letting any other members of Council know that voting is taking place. And that, my boy, is power—raw, unquestionable and so never questioned power. Poor grace as you're in with Pahvlos, you may need such friends, too, one day soon or late."

"What of Lord Kahsos, Portos, what will be done to him?" asked Bralos.

Portos shrugged, shaking his head, so that the plumes of his dress helmet swished and the loose cheekplates rattled. "With a bit of luck, he'll be censured, striped publicly and exiled back to his civil holdings to be further punished by his overlord, probably. But lacking that bit of luck . . . ? *Thoheeks* Bahos, jovial as he can be, is still a very hard man who can be most vindictive when he feels himself to have been wronged or hoodwinked—and you know he feels just so in this particular instance—and he also nurtures a deep, wide streak of bloodthirstiness in his character, which means that the larcenous Kahsos may well find himself adorn-

ing one of those crosses outside the walls, that or
minus his balls and working on a road gang, out in the
thoheekseeahnee somewhere."

Looking and sounding as troubled as he had felt all
day, ever since he had turned the war captives over to
the unsavory Lord Kahsos, Bralos asked, "Portos,
why are . . . why must state-slaves be castrated?"

The tall, darker man shrugged again. "They just
always have been. It's tradition that they be deballed,
is all.

"Now, wait a minute, dammit!" he ordered, seeing
the look of distaste on the other officer's face. "Yes, I
fully agree, our Grand *Strahteegos* has indeed run the
word and term 'traditional' into the ground, very
deep indeed into the ground, used it to mask or to try
to justify all sorts of flagrant nepotism and personal
likes or dislikes of one kind or another, but in this
instance, we are not in the least concerned with his
misuse of 'tradition,' mind you.

"I was long ago told that the practice dated from the
very start of our race in these lands. In those ancient
times, there were very few of us, all male warriors,
and a hellacious lot of the barbarians, both male and
female. As our distant ancestors came ashore and
fought and settled the lands they had conquered,
they captured barbarians as slaves; however, these
slaves sometimes escaped to breed up still more of
their savage kind against the Ehleenohee, so at length
it was decreed by the leaders that any male slave kept
solely for labor must be deballed, that should he escape captivity, he would not be able to sire more
barbarians. For long and long, this rule applied to all
male slaves, both publicly and privately owned, but
as the barbarians drew back out of the tidewater and
piedmont lands and the supply of more new slaves
became a rather chancy thing, private owners began to
discover the advantages of allowing their slaves to

breed more slaves. But the state-slaves continued to be only eunuchs or female. It is still that way, that's all I can say on the subject, Bralos. Whether you personally like it or not, that's the way things have always been, now are and most likely will continue to be in times to come.

"What you and I and the rest of the officers and common soldiers of Council's army have to worry about just now is the strange changes that have been and are coming over the man who owns the power of life or death over us all, Grand *Strahteegos Thoheeks* Pahvlos the Warlike. And with him in mind, I had best mention now that you are going to have to pay your squadron out of your own purse again, this month . . . and no doubt but that Pawl of Vawn will be needing to borrow from you again to pay his Horseclansmen, too. Captain-of-pikes Guhsz Hehluh, canny, maybe prescient old bastard that he is, insisted on six months' pay in advance, last spring."

"What in the holy name of . . . ? Portos, have you any faintest idea just what he is up to? It's not that I mind seeing my officers and troopers paid out of my personal funds, nor is it all that much of a strain on my assets—yet—but it is not at all the wisest course for a commanding officer to follow: to hold back the due monthly stipends of hardworking, hard-marching, hard-fighting soldiers who have won for him and Council every battle he has put them to for years, now," declared Bralos.

Portos sighed. "I know, I know and you know and one would think that with all his years of experience with armies *he* would know, as well. At the meeting of senior officers last week, he declared his intention to take the army, all of it, on a long march that might result in some fighting before it was over. Up to the old royal capital and back here, refit and resupply, then back on the march over to Sahvahnahspolis . . ."

"And for sure heavy casualties from the accursed swampers," Bralos half-snarled. "Not to think even of the way the horses and the rest of us will suffer from the heat, the insects, snakes, foul water, *krohkohthehliohsee* and God alone knows what other hellish afflictions. Why the hell try to pick trouble with the swampers, anyway? And just what has his mad schedule of marchings got to do with his withholding of his army's pay and allowances? Doesn't he know that a good many of the officers and even a few of the common soldiers have wives and children around and about this camp who need money on which to live, since they cannot draw army rations, usually?"

"As I said . . ." began Portos, then paused. "Oh, that's right, you were not there at the commencement of our discussion this evening, Bralos. Well, at last week's senior officers' conference, Pahvlos harangued us all at length, and with more heat than was necessary, in regard to the fact that one of the principal things wrong with this army, one of the significant ways in which it differed, to its true detriment, from the old, royal army, was that it contained far too many womanizing men. He declared that he was of the conviction that the company of women and the breeding of children, so far as common soldiers or officers who were not landholders was concerned, should be activities not to be engaged in while still on active service, but rather after retirement. He ordered us to encourage any married or near-married men in those two catagories to put aside the women and disown the children. He then suggested that we put our troops to scouring the settlements around the camp perimeters of any females of any ages, class or calling."

"Portos, has he gone stark mad, then?" asked Bralos, with obvious concern. "Should he try to enforce something so heinous on Council's army, he'll precipitate a true mutiny, they'll tear him to pieces, him and any

officer or man who tries to come between them and
him. For, after all, many of the officers and some of
the common soldiers, as well, are in no way or means
career warriors, they serve as they do—and that's
damned well, as you and I both know and as the
Grand *Strahteegos* should know—because of a sincere
desire to help Council bring peace to our borders and
order within them. That's why I'm still forking a horse
up here at Mehseepolis instead of going about setting
my *vahrohnoseeahn* to rights down south. And I serve
you fair warning, friend and Senior Captain *Thoheeks*
Portos, before I see my men pushed to the point of
mutiny against legal authority, I'll take them all and
ride south to my own lands and the Grand *Strahteegos*
Thoheeks Pahvlos can take his bumboy and his crack-
pate ideas about running an army and march straight
into the lowest, foulest, hottest pit of hell."

Chapter VI

The cat-footed, silent servants presented basins of warm, sweet-scented water on which rose petals floated to each of *Thoheeks* Sitheeros' guests as well as to their master himself, followed by soft, fluffy cotton towels. Others came in to take away the trays which held the foodstuffs, but when they made to bear away the dregs of the wine, the *thoheeks* spoke.

"Bring another decanter of that vintage. There's still the end of a tale I'd hear."

He turned, smiling, back to Captain-of-squadron Bralos and said, "Have you the time to indulge me, my boy?"

Bralos replied, "But . . . but I would've thought that, as a member of Council, you surely would've heard it all, long since, my lord."

The *thoheeks* nodded. "Most assuredly, in several versions, too, but I'd hear yours as well, if I may."

Bralos shrugged. "I am, of course, at my lord *Thoheeks*' command."

Thoheeks Sitheeros settled back in his chair, smiling. "Very well, now, how much rest was granted you after your whirlwind campaign in the foothills?"

Bralos laughed once, a harsh bark. "Three whole days, my lord, then orders came down through cavalry brigade headquarters that I and the other squadron captains should have our units ready for the road within two weeks. In the interim, all common soldiers were to be restricted to the environs of the camp, save only when on organized details without it. Lancers and light infantry were to regularly patrol the perimeter and enforce this promulgation to the extreme of bare steel, if necessary. Expressly forbidden to enter the camp precincts were women of any description or hawkers of wine, beer or cider, although this last was to not include any merchants or vintners supplying officers, of course."

Upon announcement of this last enormity of senselessness, two of Bralos' troop-lieutenants sought words with the captain upon behalf of married sergeants whose wives lived in the peripheries of the camp, and after hearing them out, Bralos called for a horse and rode over to Senior Captain *Thoheeks* Portos' headquarters.

But seeing the brigade commander took much more waiting than was at all usual, and when at last he was ushered in and had stated his case, the harried-looking senior captain just shook his head, brusquely, and barked, "Dammit, Bralos, we have to do it because the Grand *Strahteegos* says we have to do it. If the old man truly considers you and yours to be mercenaries, however, you just might be able to get by with ignoring most of these insanities; Guhsz Hehluh intends to do just that and so, too, do all of the Horseclansmen, the artificiers and the *eeahtrohsee*, I understand."

"And you, my lord Senior Captain *Thoheeks*?" asked Bralos. "Your heavy cavalry are as much on loan to this state and this army as are the units commanded by Captains Guhsz Hehluh and Pawl of Vawn, truth to be told. Have you the intention of submitting your officers and troopers to such injustices?"

Portos squirmed his body uneasily. "Let's . . . let us just say that I intend to look out for the welfare of my subordinates wherever and whenever and in every conceivable way possible, Captain *Vahrohnos* Bralos, as

always in times past has been my wont. Such is always
a good practice for any officer of rank—from the very
highest to the lowest—to follow, I might add. However, an astute officer, one who makes survival a
habit, will recognize superior force and bow to it . . .
if it all comes down to that. As in battle, if faced with
impossible odds and with maneuver impossible or pointless, you have but two options, in reality: withdrawal
or suicide.

"And now, my good Bralos, I have no more time
for you, unless you have other, meaningful business to
broach. Preparing both my own squadron and the
brigade for the march would be more than enough to
occupy all my waking hours, without this other exercise in stupidity, atop all else."

Bralos formally saluted, turned about and departed.
He understood, he understood fully. It was but another playing of the ancient military game: guard your
arse and duck your head. He would just have to take
to sending out the two married sergeants, the three
other sergeants who maintained more or less formal
"arrangements" with women and the lieutenant who
had married the daughter of a merchant of the lower
town as a "detail" each evening and having Keemohsahbis, the vintner, bring in his carts enough potables
for the entire squadron; such was, he decided, the
only sane course to follow in this lunatic war that the
Grand *Strahteegos* seemingly had declared upon his
own command. And this was just what he told Captain-
of-squadron Chief Pawl Vawn of Vawn when that
worthy came riding over that night.

Sloshing the brandied wine about in his cup, the
spare, wiry chief remarked, "You know, Bralos, I
liked—I really liked—that old man on first meeting
and for a long time since, but after all I've seen and
heard since you and me and our men got back from

this latest campaign up north, I'm beginning to wonder if the old bastard hasn't traded in all of his brains for a peck of moldy owlshit or something.

"None of this latest shit, not one particle of it, makes any sense at all, you know. He's halved the pay of them as are still getting paid, says it's going to be saved against their retirements. He says, too, that all loot taken in the future has to go to the army—him, in other words—and that he'll see any man as tries to hold out anything looted well striped the first time and hung the next time, no matter what his rank. He has offered an amnesty to any officer or common soldier who took loot and kept it for himself in the past if he now will turn what is left of the worth of that loot over to the Grand *Strahteegos*."

Bralos felt a cold chill run the length of his spine, felt the hairs of his nape all aprickle. "Where did you get this information, Pawl?" he demanded.

The Horseclans chief shrugged. "Part of the shit that was laid down while we was gone, is all, Bralos. Sub-chief Myk, who led the rest of my squadron while we were gone up north, told me about it, and I hunted out the copy of the order from the pile; you've got a copy too, I'd guess, somewhere in your headquarters. You worried about that Yvuhz dagger you took off them bandits, man? Hell, damn few knows about it, anyway, so just pry out the stones, cover the gold hilt with soft leather and brass wire and forget about it, that's what I'd do."

"Fuck that dagger!" snarled Bralos. "Were that all of it, I'd give our overly acquisitive Grand *Strahteegos* that deadly little bauble in a trice and never again think about it."

"Then what?" asked Chief Pawl, looking puzzled.

Bralos sighed. "Strictly speaking—and I'm dead certain that we had best expect everything to be interpreted in the strictest of terms by our commander in future—the windfall that has established my own fortune could be considered loot."

"No such thing," declared Pawl vehemently. "I wasn't there, then, but I heard about it all from not a few as were. You were given the effects of that slimeball Hahkmukos as suffering-price and loss-price. When informed of how much more you'd found squirreled away in that campaign chest, I've been told, old *Thoheeks* Grahvos had him a good belly-laugh and said that it was a good thing to have such lucky officers in any army."

"Even so," said Bralos soberly, "I think that I had best consider that the Grand *Strahteegos*, who has seemed to resent my affluence ever since I managed to buy a squadron, and maybe even before that, has definite designs upon my gold and my lands. I think I had best seek audience with Sub-*strahteegos* Tomos. Maybe with *Thoheeks* Grahvos, too, for that matter. Have you the time to ride along with me, Pawl?"

After conferring with Bralos and hearing out all his worries and baleful presentiments, Sub-*strahteegos Thoheeks* Tomos Gonsalos sent a galloper with a sealed message tube into Mehseepolis, to the palace of Council. Bralos followed shortly with Chief Pawl, their two sets of personal guards and a heavy weight of golden Zenos.

Thoheeks Grahvos and *Thoheeks* Mahvros received the two cavalry officers warmly in Grahvos' high-ceilinged, airy office, offering a fine wine to wash the dust from their throats and even sending orders that their guards be entertained in the quarters of the Council Guardsmen. Patiently, the two always-busy noblemen listened with clear concentration and patent interest to all that Bralos and Chief Pawl had to tell them. Then *Thoheeks* Grahvos spoke.

"Gentlemen, did I not know better, know just how

much he has done for our Consolidated *Thoheek-seeahnee* since first he came to us, I might think that *Thoheeks* Pahvlos has taken it into his head to truly destroy this army of ours, drive the best elements from its ranks, certainly, and possibly instigate full mutiny.

"First, that very disturbing report, the other day, from *Thoheeks* Portos, and now this—it's all enough to give me more gray hairs at the very thought of what may very well be bubbling away in the minds of the men he's abusing and denying the few simple pleasures that they have certainly earned by way of superlative service to Council's army, many times over.

"As regards your good fortune, Captain *Vahrohnos* Bralos, you must know that no man rejoiced more than did I. However, while I and most other members of Council would consider your acquisitions from that Hahkmukos creature more in the nature of a reward for services, it is indeed quite possible that this new *Thoheeks* Pahvlos might also be of the opinion that the jewels you found within the cabinet are indeed loot, if only because the previous owner must have looted them from somewhere, at some time. Our good Tomos advises us that you have a plan to broach to representatives of Council today. What is it?"

Presently, *Thoheeks* Grahvos rang for a scribe and dictated two official documents. Then, while the man penned duplicates of each, Bralos set a small chest of cour bouilli on the table and from it counted out some twenty pounds of gold.

When the documents all had been sanded, signed, sealed and witnessed and the scribe was departed, *Thoheeks* Grahvos smiled broadly and said, "All right, my boy, it's all done. So far as *Thoheeks* Pahvlos or any of his faction are concerned, you have admitted taking loot, taken advantage of the broadcast amnesty and conveyed to representatives of Council a golden-hilted dagger plus a certain measure of gold. But between us, you have that document recognizing your generous *loan* to Council, it payable to you or to your heirs at the end of ten years along with an interest of twenty-five percent the year, and should you die without formal heirs or legitimate issue, it will be paid to your present overlord or his heirs."

"Please, my lord *Thoheeks*," protested Bralos, "twenty-five percent the year is far too much. Really there should be none. Cannot my lord allow this to be a true gift to the Consolidated *Thoheekseeahnee*?"

The big, brawny nobleman just stood and stared at the younger for a moment, then he addressed *Thoheeks* Mahvros, saying, "The next time that Pennendos or Vikos or another of that stripe launch again into their incessant slanders of our nobility in this realm, recall you this day and this most generous minor nobleman. Thank God that we have good men like him still among us to come to our aid in time of need.

"No, my good Bralos, your generosity is much appreciated, but no. Your loan will be repaid with the indicated interest as indicated in this document."

"All right, Captain *Vahrohnos*," barked the white-haired Grand *Strahteegos* at Bralos, standing rigidly before him, "I know that you prized a jeweled, gold-hilted and gold-cased Yvuhz dagger on that mission to the north, so hand it over and I won't have you striped . . . this time. Also, I want in my hands by nightfall of this day all of the gold or silver remaining of the loot you took in times past. When we come back from this campaign, we will see to the selling of your unconfirmed *vahrohnoseeahn*, in the south, your squadron captaincy and all else you saw fit to squander army monies upon."

"My lord . . ." began Senior Captain *Thoheeks* Portos, who had been ordered to bring Bralos here.

But he was coldly, brusquely cut off in midsentence. "Shut your mouth, Portos! Yap only when I tell you to. My present business is with this posturing puppy."

During the brief interruption, Bralos' gaze flitted to the girlish Ilios, who lay stretched languidly on a couch behind the old man, the long-lashed eyelids slowly blinking, the too-pretty face blank. He wondered whether the pegboy was using hemp or poppy-paste.

"Would my lord Grand *Strahteegos Thoheeks* deign to peruse an official document of the Council of the Consolidated *Thoheekseeahnee*?" asked Bralos, formally and very diffidently.

"Give it to me," snarled the old man, adding, "And it had better have some bearing on your crimes against this army of mine. I've had all that I can stomach of larcenous newly rich scum like you lording it over your betters and buying lands and ranks you but ill deserve."

Upon reading the document, his face darkened with rage. From between slitted eyelids he looked up at Bralos with pure, distilled hatred. "You shoat, you thing of filth and slime, how dared you to commit so infamous an enormity as this? I should have you slowly whipped to death or impaled, do you know that? I hope that I never again see so foul an instance of insubordination as you have herein committed, you fatherless hound-pup! Are you aware, Portos, of what your favorite here has done? Are you? Well, answer me, damn you!"

"No, my lord Grand *Strahteegos*, I am not. I have not yet seen the document," replied the brigade commander.

"Know you, then, Senior Captain, that this infamous malefactor turned the Yvuhz dagger and some pounds of gold over to *Thoheeks* Grahvos and *Thoheeks* Mahvros, and they then not only granted him a full pardon for his misdeeds in not turning all his loot over in the beginning, but recognized his landholdings and purchased title in an official Council document, of which this is a legal, witnessed copy. On the basis of this . . . this"—he waved the document about—"this piece of filth, this thing who calls himself Bralos now is confirmed and recognized by Council as the *Vahrohnos* of Yohyültönpolis, and no matter that he acquired lands and title with gold that was as good as stolen from this army of mine. And not only that, but that aged fool of a Grahvos so phrased this thing that this puppy now is also recognized by council as a captain-of-squadron of mercenary light cavalry/lancers."

"But, my lord Grand *Strahteegos Thoheeks*," remonstrated Portos, "ever since the Captain *Vahrohnos* bought the entirety of responsibility for his squadron, you have been referring to him as a mercenary."

The old man glared at Portos for a long moment, then grated in a frigid tone, "Senior Captain, do not ever again display such a degree of temerity as to feed me back my own words, not if you'd keep that ugly head on those shoulders and the flesh on the bones of your back. You and everyone else with two bits of brain to rub together knew just what I meant when I called him a mercenary scoundrel, and it was not a description of his rank or his status in my army, either. If you don't—really don't—know just what I meant, then you are an utter dunce and should not be commanding a section, much less a brigade, in any kind of an army!"

Looking back at the still-rigid Bralos, he growled, "All right, my lord Captain *Vahrohnos*, you and your sly chicanery have stolen a march on me . . . this time. But be you warned, I am long in forgetting and I never forgive. I mean to see you dead for this, soon or late, I mean to see you die under circumstances that will reflect no slightest shred of honor on either you or the misbegotten house that was responsible for putting a thing like you out into the world, of afflicting decent folk with the fox-shrewd stench of you. Take your slimy document and get you out of my sight! *Dismiss!*"

Outside, Bralos mounted but sat his horse until Portos came out, his olive face black with suppressed rage, his big hands clenching and unclenching, his movement stiff, tightly controlled. But he spoke no word to Bralos until they were both well clear of the army headquarters area.

"Bralos, had it just been reported to me, I doubt that I would've, could've, believed it. But I *heard* it, heard it all. I can only surmise that the man is going— hell, has gone—stark, staring mad. Man, you just don't talk to the senior officers of your army that way unless in strictest privacy. He had some choice slights for me, too, after he'd dismissed you, and hearing him I could not but think of how good it would be to see him laid out on a pyre, for all that we have no officer capable of replacing him. He couldn't be as vicious toward me as he could and was toward you, of course, because I'm his peer in civil rank and I could call him out, force him to fight me breast to breast in a formal duel. But what he could get away with saying, he said.

"I tell you, friend Bralos, immediately I get back to my place, I'm going to have to write out an account of all that just happened. I couldn't put such a job to a clerk or it would be over the whole army in an eyeblink of time . . . and that we definitely do not want; there's trouble enough brewing already, thanks to that old man. Then I'm going to dispatch it to *Thoheeks* Grahvos, at the palace; you can add a statement to it, if you wish to so do."

But Bralos shook his head. "No, the more you stir shit, the more and worse it stinks. Besides, you can say aii that needs the saying, Portos."

What with one seemingly unavoidable delay after another, the army was a week late in leaving for the

old capital, taking the circuitous northern route now
used by traders over roads recently refurbished by
gangs of state-slaves. Bralos and his remaining men
watched the army march out of the sprawling camp
and set foot to the eastern road, led by light cavalry—
not a few of these their comrades, Bralos' troopers
and officers—and with their supplies and baggage,
their remudas and beef herds behind them.

It had been at the very next called meeting of senior
officers after the explosive interview with the Grand
Strahteegos that this newest catapult boulder had been
dropped upon Bralos. After covering the order of the
march column as regarded infantry, supply and baggage, specialist units and remounts, each category preceded by the name of the officer to command it and be
at all times responsible for it, the Grand *Strahteegos*
finally got around to the cavalry.

"Senior Captain *Thoheeks* Portos as brigade commander will, of course, exercise overall command of
the horse, directly under me. He will also be in command of his own squadron of heavy horse. Captain
Chief Pawl Vawn of Vawn will be in command of his
Horseclans medium-heavy horse. Captain-of-war-ele-
phants *Komees* Nathos of Pinellopolis will be in overall
command of his six bulls and the three cow draught
elephants, assisted by Captain-of-work-elephants Gil
Djohnz.

"Lastly, as regards light cavalry, Captain-of-squadron
Opokomees Ehrrikos will, for this campaign, command his own three troops and an additional three
troops which will be seconded to him from out of the
Wolf Squadron, with the senior lieutenants of both
squadrons to assist him."

Bralos could not move or speak for a moment. He
looked every bit as stunned as he felt, and, noticing
this, not a few of his peers and superiors began to
mutter amongst themselves.

Raising his voice, old Pahvlos went on to say, "Captain-of-squadron *Vahrohnos* Bralos of wherever, having shown himself treacherous and most disloyal to me and my army, will remain here with one troop to maintain order in the camp, where those I can trust can keep an eye on him."

Bralos came to his feet at that last, his fury bubbling up in him, his hand clamping hard on the hilt of his saber.

"*Draw it!*" hissed the Grand *Strahteegos*, cruel glee shining out of his eyes. "Go ahead and draw that steel of yours, you young turd out of a diseased sow. Draw it before all these witnesses; that will be all I need to put a hempen necklace around your scabby throat, sneak-thief, poseur, illegitimate puppy."

Bralos was on the verge of doing just that, suicidal action or no, but a powerful hand clamped cruelly hard about his upper arm, and in a whisper, *Thoheeks* Portos' voice said, "Let be, son Bralos, let be, I say. Don't play directly into his hands. He's clearly, obviously trying in every way he knows to provoke you, making no slightest secret of that fact. He couldn't strip you of your gold, so now he would have your blood, your honor and your life, so don't just hand him that satisfaction. You outthought him before; do it again. That will hurt him far more than a honed edge would."

When Bralos let go his well-worn hilt and sat down, there was a chorus of released breaths all about the crowded room.

Putting the best face he could upon his keen disappointment, the Grand *Strahteegos* crowed, "You see, gentlemen, you all saw it, didn't you? The craven criminal will not even speak to refute my words; he's patently not only guilty of his crimes, then, but an honorless coward, to boot."

Bralos rose more slowly this time, came to rigid attention and said, slowly, clearly, very formally, "Captain-of-squadron *Vahrohnos* Bralos of Yohyül-tönpolis prays that he be allowed to appear before a full panel of his peers, that they may hear all evidence for and against his guilt of the charges made by the Grand *Strahteegos Thoheeks* Pahvlos and decide, therefrom, his culpability or innocence. If found guilty by them, he will leave the army. If found innocent, he will demand that his accusers meet him breast to breast, fully armed, in a formal duel overseen by Ehleen gentlemen."

The old man's face darkened in ire. "Shut your lying mouth and sit down, you thieving cur! No brave, honest, honorable gentleman needs hear anymore of your nauseating misdeeds from anyone. *I* say you're guilty—guilty as very sin—and that's all that's necessary, hear me?"

"No it is not, my lord Grand *Strahteegos Thoheeks*," spoke up Sub-*strahteegos* Tomos Gonsalos, adding, "According to the traditions of this and every other Ehleen army—past or present—of which I have heard or had dealings, a noble officer accused of cowardice or of any felonious conduct by another officer has the right to demand that a panel of officers to include all who heard the allegations spoken or read them written be met as soon as expedient to hear or view all evidence and thereby judge his guilt or his innocence. It would pain me to have to report to the High Lord Milo Morai that so tradition-minded an officer as you refused to abide, in this one instance, by the traditional method and see justice done, thereby."

Glaring hatred at the sub-*strahteegos*, old Pahvlos made to speak twice but produced only wordless growls of insenate rage, then finally stalked out and left his staff to conclude the briefing as best they could. These men's efforts were not helped by the loud sounds of crashings and bangings emanating up the hallway from the direction of the Grand *Strahteegos*' private quarters. That the old man had at last found his voice was clear to all; the shouted curses, obscenities and shocking blasphemies were proof of it.

When the meeting had been adjourned and the officers had silently filed out of the building, they all—seemingly of but a single mind and regardless of the crush of preparations still awaiting them in their own units—made directly for the officers' mess, chivvied out the cooks and servants, then commenced their own meeting.

"I liked that old man, I did," commented Captain-of-pikes Guhsz Hehluh. "I respected him, too, but after today, hell, I don't know if I want a man like that over me and my Keebai boys anymore. He carried on like a spoiled brat throwing a temper tantrum, there at the end of everything. What the hell would happen to the fucking army was the old bugger to do that in battle sometime?"

"Something's changed him, altered his character drastically, and certainly for the worse," said Captain-of-foot Bizahros, commander of the infantry brigade. "When first he came to lead us here, it was as if I still were serving under him in the old royal army, and I rejoiced, as did right many other officers and men of the old army. But now . . . it's almost as if another person were inhabiting his mind. He always averred in the past that the commoner soldiers must be treated well by all officers, from the highest to the lowliest, must be always shown that officers have the best interests of their men at heart at all times. But now . . ."

"Yes," nodded Senior Captain *Thoheeks* Portos, grim-faced, "but in the present state of affairs, we'll be very fortunate do we not have to put down a mutiny or two during this campaign . . . and if not then, then

surely when we get back and our units once more go
under these ridiculous, divisive camp strictures of no
women, no alcohol save the thoroughly watered issue
and no movement outside the perimeter save on organized details."

"It seems to me, and God grant that I'm wrong, in
this instance," opined Captain of Light Infantry
Ahzprinos, "that our esteemed Grand *Strahteegos* is
dead set upon splitting up our army—destroying any
rapport between the officers and the common soldiers
of their units, fomenting dissension of all sorts between the units and the officers, first playing foot
against horse, then playing mercenary against regular
units and so on.

"Take the beginning of this business today, for instance. He knew damned good and well that Captain
Opokomees Ehrrikos and Captain *Vahrohnos* Bralos
have had differences and are not on the best of terms
even yet, and it seemed he could not rest but had to
pick at that scab."

"What was or is between Bralos and me is our
personal affair," said Captain Ehrrikos bluntly, "and I
did not at all like him using or trying to use it as a foil
to make more bad blood between me and a military
peer. Bralos, I didn't and don't want the responsibility
of a double-size squadron thrust willy-nilly upon me,
but as you must know, I had, have and will have
damn-all choice in the matter, not so long as I continue to serve under this increasingly strange, new-
model Grand *Strahteegos* Pahvlos.

"But Bralos, comrade, you have my word of honor
before all of these gentleman-comrades that your troops
and officers will in no way be made to suffer while
under my command. They'll be asked to perform nothing that my own troops are not asked. I will deal with
them at all possible times through their senior lieutenant or troop-lieutenants and they will be stinted on

neither remounts nor supplies. Our Grand *Strahteegos*
is both my military and my civil superior and I am
sworn to obey his orders, where such orders do not
impinge upon my personal honor, but I'll be damned
if I'll serve him as a rod with which he can punish an
officer to whom he has taken a dislike or that officer's
subordinates, either."

Sub-*strahteegos Thoheeks* Tomos Gonsalos said,
"That is a good and a most noble gesture, Captain
Ehrrikos. You other gentlemen should take it to heart,
recall it when next that old man makes to set two of
you to fighting, tearing at each other like alley curs.
Remember that the continued cohesion and existence
of this army is vital to the continued power of Council
and to the very survival of these Consolidated *Thoheekseeahnee*. If you don't want to see a return to conditions of anarchy and chaos in these lands, then you
must all cooperate to defeat whatever schemes this
once-great man's mind is apparently concocting. For
all I know, he wants to be king, but if he does, it
would seem to me he'd be trying to bind the army to
him, not erode its discipline, fracture its cohesion and
drive its best officers and common soldiers away from
it."

The army was gone for six weeks. Immediately it
had marched back into the camp, while still the trains
were making their dusty way to their depot, with a
cracking of stock-whips and the shouts and foul curses
of drivers and drovers, Captain-of-squadron *Opokomees*
Ehrrikos of Panther Squadron and Senior Lieutenant
Hymos of Rahnpolis reined up and dismounted before
the building housing the camp headquarters of Wolf
Squadron. After slapping as much dust as they could
from their sweat-stained clothing, they entered to con-
front Bralos.

The first look at the officers' faces told Bralos that

something was amiss, and he suffered another cold chill of presentiment. Even so, he saw both the tired, sweating men served cool, watered wine and waited silently for the bad news for as long as he could bear it before finally demanding, "All right, how many men were lost from my squadron, Ehrrikos?"

"One killed, neck snapped when his horse fell at the gallop; the horse had to be put down, too. Three injured; one stabbed in the thigh with a spear, one knifed in some senseless, pointless brawl of a night—the *eeahtrohsee* give him a forty-sixty chance of living—one with his clavicle broken by a fractious remount horse."

"Then why the long faces, gentlemen?" demanded Bralos, still more than certain that something was terribly wrong.

The senior lieutenant opened his mouth to speak, then, but kept silent when Captain Ehrrikos spoke first. "Almost to the old royal capital, there was a small bit of action on the road, you see."

"Bandits?" said Bralos with incredulity. "They must've been mad to nibble at a column so large and strong."

"No, not bandits, but certainly mad, nonetheless, Bralos. There was a gang of state-slaves at work at a crossroads, not working on the main road, but on the one crossing it there. A troop of your boys was riding back down the column to relieve another troop—one of mine—that had been riding rearguard for some hours. When some damned farmboy wight of an infantryman dropped a spear, one of the slaves grabbed it up, used it to slay two slave guards, and then two more slaves were armed. The other guards happened to be on the other side of the road with the marching column between them and the action, so your Lieutenant-of-troop Gahndos of Rohthakeenonpolis bade his men encircle the murderous slaves and disarm or kill them. He's a good officer, that one, Bralos, but of course his early training *was* under me.

"The troopers had to finally kill all three of the slaves—that's where your trooper got the spear wound in his thigh, he came in under your man's lance only to get another in his whip-whealed, scabby back before he could withdraw the point of the spear. At the very end of the action, the Grand *Strahteegos* and his guards came pounding back from the head of the main column.

"Now in that ruckus, one other of your common soldiers, a sergeant, had been thrust in the armpit by one of the slaves he was trying to hit with the flat of his saber; in the withdrawal, the hooked blade of the slave-guard spear caught in and tore loose a good part of the upper sleeve of the sergeant's arming-shirt."

"Uh-oh!" said Bralos, shaking his head. "Pahvlos saw the mail lining?"

"No, not at first. In fact, he was reining about to go back when his damned Ilios *Pooeesos* saw and pointed it out to him," replied Captain Ehrrikos sourly. "But he just stared, then rode on back up to his place in the column, and the march resumed from there.

"That evening, however, when we were barely done with the horses and the cooks were minding the rations, the old man rode in with his guards and a troop of heavy horse, fully armed and with Senior Captain Portos along for good measure, though he had left his pegboy in his pavilion, sitting on his peg, I suppose.

"He ordered me to fall out all of your troops—officers, sergeants and troopers. I did, what else could I do, Bralos? He ordered that they be assembled in ranks unarmed but carrying their arming-shirts, and this was obeyed. Then he and several of his guards dismounted and stalked up and down the ranks, using knives to cut the sleeves from off every arming-shirt save only those of the officers, throwing the sleeves out on the ground before the formation.

"That all done, he preached your three troops a long homily that concerned mostly his belief that an excess of useless armor slowed down troopers and needlessly overweighted their mounts. Nor could he stay a few stabs at you, it seems, telling them that they would not be punished unless they should try to reaffix the sleeves without first removing the forbidden mail inserts from them. He chided them for continuing to serve under a base, thieving, forsworn, arrogant, impudent, insubordinate . . . have I forgotten any, Hymos, my boy?"

"Only some of the more colorful references to Captain Bralos' ancestry and personal habits, my lord Captain," replied the senior lieutenant wryly.

"Well, Bralos, you get the general drift of the old man's slanders," concluded Ehrrikos.

"How did my men take all this, Hymos?" asked the commander of Wolf Squadron. "Do they seem to think the worse of me?"

The youngest officer smiled grimly. "Sir, they considered, first and foremost, the source and thought of all the hardships that he has tried to inflict upon them and all the other soldiers, and they recalled the officer who has so generously cared for them, indulged them, even paid them out of his own purse when his accuser would not. No officer or sergeant needs to tell the troopers of your squadron who is their champion, their benefactor and their truest friend, my lord Captain *Vahrohnos* Bralos, nor can the fevered rantings of even so high-ranking an officer of this army as the Grand *Strahteegos Thoheeks* Pahvlos the Warlike convince the squadron that white is suddenly become black and black, white.

"And Captain *Opokomees* Ehrrikos holds high regard for you, as well, my lord. The Grand *Strahteegos* ordered the mail be buried, but the captain instead saw it hidden and scattered around the officers' baggage wagons, instead."

But when Bralos would have thanked his military peer, Ehrrikos shrugged and said, "Hell, comrade, I'd've done the same for any other whom I happened to feel was being wronged and robbed through no real fault of his own. That kind of mail is damnably expensive stuff, I know; I once priced a shirt of it and walked around in a state of shock for two weeks afterwards."

"But the risk you took for me . . ." Bralos protested, his words cut off by Ehrrikos.

"Damn the risk, my friend, it's you who is at risk, terrible risk, every day and every night while Pahvlos is in this camp. For whatever reason, he truly hates you, he means to have your guts for garters, and no doubt about it. Were I you, I'd keep my blankets rolled and my baggage packed constantly. Be ready to take your squadron and ride at a moment's notice, comrade, for you know that if you flee alone, that monster we now serve will, at his best, send Wolf Squadron on your trail with written orders to bring back your head. At worst, he'll force them to bring you back alive to be slowly tortured to death, or maimed, then impaled or crucified."

"No, I talked all of everything over with Sub-*strahteegos Thoheeks* Tomos Gonsalos while the army was gone," said Bralos soberly. "I have decided that the very next personal insult or public accusation of wrongdoing of any nature or attempt to get at me through the officers or common troopers of Wolf Squadron will be the time when I sell back my rank, demand the long-overdue pay of my troopers, sergeants and officers, mount us all up and set out for my *vahrohnoh-seeahn*, in the south. As Tomos says, Pahvlos is a very old man and is leading a very strenuous life and cannot therefore be expected to live much longer, even does he not so far overreach himself that the Council finds it must put paid to his long-overdue account lest he finally really wreck this army of theirs for good and all.

"In normal times, I like soldiering, but I cannot do it longer under such a man, so I will leave it until he no longer commands."

"I pray that you not wait just a little too long, my friend," said Ehrrikos earnestly . . . and prophetically, though he knew it not.

Chapter VII

Sergeant Tahntos was seated astraddle a contrivance of wood, the sharp edges of two dovetailed boards cutting like a dull knifeblade into his naked crotch. His arms were trussed brutally tight behind his back, elbows to wrists, the hands become a uniform bluish grey from lack of circulation, the muscles of his upper torso looking fit to burst through the skin with the strain. A brace of heavy shields was suspended from each ankle. His eyes were closed, though the lids fluttered from time to time, and save for trickles of blood from each corner of his mouth, his face was pale as fresh curds, his jaws tight-clenched in his agony.

Three spearmen of the Grand *Strahteegos'* foot-guards squatted nearby, watching and occasionally taunting the suffering sergeant in a cruel, childish way.

"Hey, big man, has them boards cracked yore balls, yet? Heheheh," shouted one of them.

"It was one feller, out of Asshole Ahzprinos' bunch of stump-jumpers, he was," another put in, "he scrooched him around wrong and the damn boards cut his pecker plumb in two, he bled like a fuckin' stuck pig, too, died in five minits. Don't thet beat all? Hey, Sergeant, you hear me?"

"Aw, hell, he ain't no fun atall," remarked the third disgustedly. "He ain't screamed or begged or nuthin', ain't made hardly a sound a body could hear lest they was right up there with him. Maybe we oughta ask for to hang another couple of shields on his laigs, I bet

140

you his money *that* would start him in to screechin', boys. What you think, you want to do it?"

The nude, tortured man jerked reflexively as a deerfly bit his cheek, and the movement almost made him lose his precarious balance. Righting himself brought a low groan of pure agony from behind his chewed and bloody lips.

"Here he starts, boys, here he starts," said one of the foot-guards with excitement and evident relish. "Firstest thing you know he gone be a-howlin' like a dog and a-cryin' like a baby at the same time."

"No, he is not." The cold, hard voice came from behind them, and they all whirled about to see a fully armed lancer officer sitting a fine horse, his helmet and breastplate winking in the sunlight, a bared saber at rest against his spauldron. Behind him were ranged a dozen or more officers and sergeants of lancers, all armed, all with cold menace shining from their eyes, but none of their stares so icy, so intimidating as that of the officer who led them.

Dropping the reins on the pommel-knob of his war-saddle, the officer waved a signal to those behind him, saying, "Get Sergeant Tahntos from off that hellish contraption before it unmans him or he dies of pain. If these sadistic swine make to halt or hinder you in the least, you have my leave to put them up there in his place."

After removing the shields from the sufferer's ankles, strong, gentle hands joined to lift his tormented body from off the sharp-edged boards, then the flashing blade of a dagger severed the cords binding his wrists and elbows. While four men carried their comrade back to the horses to lay him facedown across the withers of yet another's horse, two troopers batted and cuffed the three foot-guards about until they had surrendered all of the clothing and the money and personal effects of Sergeant Tahntos.

Finding a store of cords and other things beneath the contrivance, certain of the troopers and sergeants took time to bind the arms of the foot-guards, hoist them all up on the sharp boards, weight their ankles, and leave them, already shrieking piteously.

"No slightest doubt but that they'll be coming after me quite shortly, Hymos," said Bralos.

"They'll play merry hell getting you, my lord Captain," averred Senior Lieutenant Hymos firmly. "Not one officer or man in Wolf Squadron but won't fight to the very death for you. Comes to that, we can hack our way out of camp and . . ."

"And you'd all be slaughtered, darted out of the saddle by the light infantry or shot full of arrows by the foot-archers, and I could not live with the knowledge that I'd been responsible for that kind of a massacre," said Bralos just as firmly. "No, what you will do is first send officer-gallopers to the sub-*strahteegos*, to Portos and to Captain Ehrrikos of Panther Squadron . . . oh, and to Captain Chief Pawl Vawn, too. Most of the senior officers are my friends, and, too, I have friends on Council. The only way that that old bastard could kill me unopposed would be to do it in private, and that's not what he wants at all; for some reason, he wants a public execution complete with all the ritual humiliations and tortures and maimings and a well-witnessed death. No, in custody or not, I'll be safe for the nonce.

"But after you've dispatched those gallopers, I want you and all the rest of the squadron to start getting ready for a march of about two weeks. If we ever come back here at all, it won't be for some time, like as not, so pack up everything. The cooks and the *eeahtrohsee* have been paid for thirty more days, so bring them and the other specialists along, also. Tell the smith to pack everything that he can squeeze into that traveling forge I bought him, and the cooks are to strip the kitchens and snag any edibles they can beg, borrow or steal from wherever.

"You'd better send over a detail now to cut our horses out of the permanent herd and another detail to the depot to harness teams and hitch them to our wagons, then drive them back here to be loaded. Set my servants to packing my own effects, and if the sub-*strahteegos* sends over a small, heavy chest, put it in my largest trunk."

He might have said more, but a pounding of approaching hoofbeats heralded the arrival of Captain-of-squadron *Opokomees* Ehrrikos, his face streaming salt sweat and twisted by a frown of worry. Flinging himself from the saddle of the heaving horse, he ran up the steps and burst into the room, gasping, "Bralos, the old man is even now on his way to arrest you for inciting to mutiny. One of my boys was on an errand to army headquarters and saw and heard them forming up a strong party of both horse- and foot-guards, plus a company of foot-archers. Chief Pawl was there and was ordered to add a troop of his Horseclansmen to the party, but he politely told them to do their own dirty work, that he was not down here nor his men either to help overweening dotards conduct vendettas against their own officers. My boy says that at that, some of the old man's own horse-guard officers had to physically keep him from drawing steel and going after Chief Pawl. It's a crying shame they did it, too; Pawl would've minced his lights nicely.

"Well, good God, man, what are you dawdling for, get your arse in a saddle, I'll delay them for as long as I can . . ."

"Hymos," said Bralos calmly, "send out those gallopers, now, to the sub-*strahteegos* and Senior Captain *Thoheeks* Portos; you need not now send to the other two, since they obviously have been otherwise apprised. Set all of the other wheels in motion, if you please. I'll stay here and chat with my comrade until it is necessary for me to go elsewhere."

Sub-*strahteegos Thoheeks* Tomos Gonsalos stalked into the army headquarters building, his face fire-red and streaming sweat, his brick-colored beard and moustaches bristling. Just behind him came Captain-of-squadron Chief Pawl Vawn of Vawn and several of his sub-chiefs, Senior Captain-of-brigade *Thoheeks* Portos, Captain-of-pikes Guhsz Hehluh and Captain-of-foot Ahzprinos. No guardsman still in his right mind would have essayed to try to stop or even to slow such an aggregation of grim-faced senior officers. And none did.

Before their dogged onslaught, members of the headquarters staff scattered like a covey of quail. Before they all could flit away, Portos reached out a big, hard hand and snagged a junior lieutenant by his flabby biceps, terrified him with a look that smacked of a quick, bloody death, then put him to the question.

"Where is Captain-of-squadron *Vahrohnos* Bralos?"

"In . . . in . . . out in the rear court, See . . . See . . . Senior C-Captain," the unfortunate quavered, his voice cracking several times.

"And where is the Grand *Strahteegos*?" demanded Portos.

"He . . . he is . . . he is there, t-too. To oversee the . . . the first f-flogging, and it p-please your grace." The man sniffled, and when Portos hurled him into a heap in a corner, he wet his crotch and began to shudder and sob, then, suddenly, retch up his last meal. Sub-chief Myk Vawn, as he passed the wretched officer, wrinkled up his nose, suspecting that the next-to-last meal had found another means of egress from the staff officer.

Before the party had reached the back of the build-

ing, they heard the drums begin to roll, and before
they all were outside, they heard the regular, whistling
cracks of the whip commence. But these last continued only until Portos grabbed the weighted tip of the
lash on the backswing and jerked the surprised wielder
from off his feet.

The Grand *Strahteegos Thoheeks* Pahvlos jumped
up from his chair, upsetting it, the small table and the
bowl of fresh grapes he had been sharing with the boy,
Ilios, who himself voiced a shrill shriek, though not
leaving the cushioned chair.

"What is this, Mutiny Day, gentlemen?" burst out
Pahvlos. "You, Captain Portos, give that man back his
whip and let's get on with the punishment. This will be
but the first of many, of course, but I mean to have
that pig singing nicely before this day be done. Next
week, when everything has been arranged, I mean to
see the bastard's spine and shoulder blades and ribs,
before I see his traitorous neck stretched."

Disgustedly, Tomos Gonsalos snatched the whip from
Portos and flung it high atop the roof of the building.
"You old fool," he said to Pahvlos. 'Don't you know
your kind of senseless super-discipline and sadism is
well on the way to tearing Council's army apart at the
seams? Do you even care? Or it that really your aim,
to dissolve the army first, then the Consolidated *Thoheekseeahnee*? Would you be king, is that it? Or . . ."
He frowned for a moment, trying to recall just
how the High Lord had phrased it in his most recent,
most secret letter, then he had it. "Or do you serve
other, more sinister interests, my lord? Are they perhaps far-southern interests?"

The Grand *Strahteegos* continued to stare his indig-
nation and rage at the group, but from out the corner
of his eye, Tomos Gonsalos saw the cryptic verbal
barb find lodging in the bumboy, Ilios, who started as
if touched with a red-hot iron.

But now Portos stalked forward and faced his furious commander, stating flatly, "You had no right to do any more than arrest Captain *Vahrohnos* Bralos and hold him in custody until he was brought to face the officers' panel, and you know it full well, my lord *Thoheeks*. You are, by this heinous act, yourself guilty of criminal activity . . . and you know that, too, my lord *Thoheeks*."

"This man," declared the Grand *Strahteegos*, "freed a common sergeant who had tried to cross the perimeter contrary to my promulgated orders, had fought with and grievously injured some of the obedient men who stopped him, and was therefore undergoing punishment on the wooden horse. This man not only freed the malefactor, but he had three of my fine foot-guards beaten severely by his troops, then bound them and placed them, most unjustly, on the punishment horse, leaving them there to scream and writhe in agony until someone decided that no one man alone could make so much noise and came finally to their rescue."

"I knew you'd bring that up," said Pawl Vawn, "and I investigated the matter early on. The sergeant's wife was near death of the fever, and word was sent to him that she was calling for him. What else was a loving husband to do, stupid rules or no stupid rules?"

"My rules are in no way stupid," declared the old man. "At least, in no way that a civilized, cultured Ehleen gentleman could understand. Of course, you barbarians are a crude, rude, uncultured and often quite obnoxious race at your best. I possibly should not expect men of your limited intellectual capacities to ever comprehend, but I will, nonetheless, try one last time to explain to you.

"Three primary things are the utter ruination of your old-fashioned common soldier. These are unwonted luxuries such as hot baths, too much armor and too little work; an overabundance of drink; and women. I sincerely hope that that insubordinate sergeant's wife is dead, for he will be the better man and soldier without her.

"Women rob a man of his vitality, and often by sucking the life clear out of him. They . . ."

"And what, pray tell," muttered one of the Horseclans sub-chiefs from somewhere within the crowd, "does that overpretty *pooeesos* of yours suck out of you, lordy boy?"

The old man turned crimson and clapped hand to his swordhilt. He stepped forward and demanded, "What creature of slime said that? Dare you to show your face to me, you ill-bred pig?"

"Enough and more than enough!" snapped Tomos Gonsalos. "We are come to free Captains Bralos and Ehrrikos. They will be held for a hearing, my lord *Thoheeks*, but until and if the officers' panel says them guilty of some crime, they are not going to be further punished. Pawl, would you and yours kindly see to Bralos and Ehrrikos? Thank you."

"Guards, stop them!" the old man half-shouted at the quintet of his foot-guards, who had wisely kept still and silent through it all.

Old Guhsz Hehluh slouched forward, hitching his swordbelt around for quicker, easier access to the weapon, and Captain Ahzprinos was not far to his rear. "Tell me, boys," asked the captain of mercenary pikemen, in tones of friendly conversation, "is all this here really worth you dying for?"

The Horseclansmen freed Captain Ehrrikos—seized for "aiding and abetting the attempted escape of the notorious malefactor and mutineer who calls himself Bralos of Yohyültönpolis" and promised three dozens of lashes after Bralos had had his share—while others loosened the deep-biting ropes from Bralos' wrists and ankles, then eased him to the ground and flung his torn shirt over his bloody back and shoulders.

Walking to his friend's side, Ehrrikos squatted and asked—a bit stupidly, as he later admitted to all and sundry—"Does it hurt much, Bralos?"

Through tight-clenched and bloody teeth, the flogged man gritted, "Only when I laugh, Ehrrikos."

While the officers were being chosen for the trial panel—they would act as both jury and judges, could find guilt or innocence, set punishments or rewards for anyone connected with the trial, not just the accused officers, and had the power during their tenure to call anyone they wanted to hear, military or civilian, noble or commoner, man or woman, and could demand to peruse any documents save only state secrets—Bralos was cared for in his tightly guarded quarters by his servants, his officers and the senior among his *eeahtrohsee*. His own bodyguards—save only for the convalescing Sergeant Tahntos, who was being nursed in the settlement beyond the perimeter by his newly dead wife's sister—took watch-on-watch so that there never were fewer than two of them outside his door. His officers haunted the outer rooms, both by day and by night, and a constant cordon of troopers and sergeants surrounded the headquarters building, brusquely disarming any officer or man not of their own who made to enter, assured that the officers just inside would back them up with authority should anyone try to pull rank on them.

Of a day, Sub-*strahteegos Thoheeks* Tomos Gonsalos and Senior Captain-of-brigade *Thoheeks* Portos of Pithahpolis, willingly, smilingly handed over their cutlery to the zealous troopers, then passed in to find Bralos seated in a backless chair, his weals all shiny with unguents, conferring with his senior lieutenant, Hymos.

Drawing up stray chairs, the two visiting officers asked for wine, and Hymos himself went to fetch it, for the two bodyguards still were close to their squadron commander and the two visitors were, after all, unarmed and presumably friendly, besides.

"How is the empanelment going?" asked Bralos.

Portos snorted. "Slowly, thanks to that obtuse old man, thank you. He wants it packed with his toadies, naturally, and we are just as dead set that it will be packed in no such way, but a fair, honest aggregation of honorable gentleman-officers. It helps us mightily that you hold the ranks—civil and military—that you do, for the most of the old man's proven toadies are untitled and low-ranking young men, and we can all thank also the narrow-arsed Ilios for much of that, for he didn't like Pahvlos' old staff, said that they all were aged and ugly and, for all their experience and expertise, not at all the kind of men that should be always around. Of course, the infatuated Pahvlos indulged the whims of the little *pooeesos*, and now he shortly will be hoist up by his own catapult.

"You see, the panel may consist of any number of officers above the minimum of eight for hearing of a case against any captain-of-squadron or -battalion; however, the panel must be entirely composed of officers of your rank or higher. In order to be even considered, a man of lower than your military rank must be your superior in his civil rank."

"So the Grand *Strahteegos*," put in Tomos Gonsalos, "has found himself to be lodged between a rock and a hard place, to his distress. Almost every officer of your rank or higher has recently come to fear or hate and despise the Grand *Strahteegos*, and we have stoutly fought off his every attempt to insinuate officers not technically qualified for inclusion. We have received, today, earlier, a tentative roll of the panel. Of the ten, seven are men well known to you: me, to head it; Portos, here; Biszahros and Ahzprinos; Nathos, the elephant-man; Pintos, the senior quartermaster since

Pahvlos booted him from off his staff because his looks didn't please sweet Ilios; and yet another former staff officer, Lahreeos."

"And the other three?" queried Bralos. "What of them, Tomos?"

Tomos grimaced as if he had just tasted something a bit rotten. "Until three days ago, Captain-of-staff Gaios of Thehsmeeyee was a mere lieutenant, not even a senior lieutenant, he'd not been in the army long enough to have earned a senior lieutenancy; he's one of Pahvlos' and no mistaking it . . . but we may be able to find a way of disqualifying the bugger yet. We can't be sure of the other two—they could be his, they could be ours, they could be strictly neutral, too, men who'll make a decision based solely upon testimonies and evidence heard and seen."

"Why not Guhsz Hehluh, or Pawl Vawn?" asked Bralos. "There's the captain of the artificiers, too, for that matter; Nikos is a good man."

Tomos sighed. "Because the first two are not Ehleenohee, and because Pahvlos declares that all three are mercenaries, not his regular troops, and are therefore completely unqualified to sit on the panel and try a regular officer."

"Now, wait a damned minute," protested Bralos heatedly. "The last I heard from that old bastard was that I was a mercenary who had had regular foot-guards assaulted by other mercenaries. If you need a witness, just go ask Ehrrikos, he was there."

Tomos flashed a glance at Portos, and then both nodded. Tomos said to Bralos, "Be that as it may, for the nonce, the Grand *Strahteegos* has declared and avowed before us both that at no time did he truly consider you and Wolf Squadron to be anything save regular Ehleen light cavalry. He states that it was you and you only he tagged with the name 'mercenary scoundrel' and that if that appellation was not properly understood by you and others, he now regrets it."

"Is it then so?" said Bralos. "Then, pray tell me why the old bugger has not paid this squadron's wages in going on six months? I and Wolf Squadron seem to be and have been mercenary troops when it pleases this lying, conniving Grand *Strahteegos*, but regular Ehleen troops when it does not so please him."

"Well," put in Portos, "there's precious little we can do about that matter at this juncture. But who knows what the futures of any of us may hold? Rest well and long and recover quickly as you can, son Bralos, for by this time next week, we just may have agreed upon an officers' panel to settle everything . . . I hope and pray."

Tomos shrugged. "Hopes and prayers are all well and good, my friends, but judging only upon what has happened, and not happened, recently, I must be pessimistic and conclude that the firm choice of a full panel may take longer than merely one more week."

However, before any panel of officers could be formally invested, the most displeased Grand *Strahteegos* played one of his hole cards, ordering almost all of Council's army on the road to Sahvahnahspolis, far and far to the east of the Consolidated *Thoheekseeahnee*. It was a march that no single officer or man in his command was at all anxious to undertake, calling as it did for some two or three days and nights of marching through and camping in swamps and salt fens which happened to be the territory of huge, scaly, predaceous monsters, deadly snakes, strange and hideous fevers, bottomless concealed pits of quicksand and, by far the worst of all the terrors awaiting them, the barbarian swamp-dwellers or fen-men.

Not a few of the officers and soldiers were terrified at thoughts of even entering that dim, damp, death-crawling realm of the sinister fen-men, who were seldom seen and who killed from a distance with blowgun darts steeped in poisons—estimates of the actual distance, accuracy and lethality of the poisons varied greatly, dependent mostly upon just how close was the individual speaker to fear-induced hysteria at the time of the telling.

But it was cold, hard, incontestable fact that entire companies and battalions of well-armed and -led troops had marched into those fens that bordered most of the eastern and southern coasts and never returned, their bodies not even being found, nor any traces of their weapons and equipment. Such incidents as this had most recently occurred during the infamous "March of Royal Conquest" of the late, unlamented and last king of the Kingdom of the Southern Ehleenohee, which land was now metamorphosed into the Consolidated *Thoheekseeahnee* of Southern Ehleenohee. Leading his vast host of hundreds of thousands, High King Zastros I had marched into the southernmost lands of the Kingdom of Karaleenos on an ill-starred, poorly planned military operation that had ended in disaster and the deaths of him and his queen on the banks of the Lumbuh River.*

On the march north, however, when harassed on his right flank by fen-men, he had sent units into the swamps after the raiders. Smaller units had been lost entirely; of larger ones, ten to fifteen percent of the original units had returned, stumbling from out the swamps all bearded and filthy and starved, afflicted with strange fevers, skin diseases never before seen by the *eeahtrohsee*, bloody dysentery and degrees of madness that bred sleeping and waking nightmares. When he once had debriefed a few of the officer-survivors of the largest unit to come out of the swamps more or less alive, High King Zastros had never again sent

---

*See *Swords of the Horseclans* (HORSECLANS #2) by Robert Adams, Signet Books, 1981.

troops into the deadly swamps and had, indeed, seen that the march-route of his columns was narrowed so as to be well to the westward of the peripheries of the salt fens and the barbarians who dwelt therein, for all that it slowed the progress of his horde considerably.

That the Grand *Strahteegos Thoheeks* Pahvlos was now clearly intent on forcing his entire army into another patch of these brooding places of death was, in the eyes of his already more or less disaffected men, but more evidence that their once-revered commander had changed, drastically and for the worse, and now meant them all no slightest good. Even so, they had taken their oaths, sacred oaths, and so they all, per-force, felt that they must obey . . . all, that is, save for the individuals who found or made the time and the opportunity to take hopefully-permanent leave of their insane commander, the army and all.

The traditional Ehleen punishment for apprehended deserters was simply death—by hanging or decapita-tion, usually. But despite his well-earned reputation as an army traditionalist, there was nothing traditional about the manners in which the Grand *Strahteegos* dealt with deserters or with any other common sol-diers who chanced to break one of his new plethora of rules and edicts—which seemed to ever expand in quantity, even as the earlier ones became ever stricter.

In the little cleared space behind army headquar-ters, wherein he and Ilios, his catamite, lived in a suite of ground-floor rooms, he had had erected two whipping-frames of heavy lumber, a rack and a massive table fitted with straps and manacles. There, shaded by an awning, he and Ilios would sit and drink cooled wine and nibble at fruits and bits of cheese or crisp biscuits while men were slowly whipped to death or perma-nently crippled on the rack or blinded with sharp stakes or otherwise mutilated while chained and strapped to the bloodstained table. And the men used so atrociously for his enjoyment were not deserters, but mere troopers who had tried to visit women beyond the perimeters of the sprawling camp, had been caught bringing women into the camp, had been apprehended with unwatered wine or any other potable than wine, had been caught with pipes, tobacco or hemp in their possession or had transgressed in any way against the hordes of near-senseless rules and regulations that his brain continued to invent and his staff continued to churn out for distribution to his command.

For deserters and those guilty of crimes of a truly capital nature, the old commander had had the official army execution site adjacent to the drill field enlarged to include four permanent poles for crosses, two double gallows, and a raised platform fitted for either a whipping-frame or an impalement stake; another platform held the frame of a rack and a table that was the mate of the one behind his headquarters building. Beneath each of the platforms were low sheds wherein were kept the smaller but necessary implements—braziers, whips, pincers, branding-irons, manacles, straps, ropes, prepared oaken impalement stakes, an assortment of sharp knives of various sizes and shapes, hand-bellows for making coals burn hotter, iron bars for breaking bones, mauls for pulping hands or feet, differing sizes of pliers for drawing or breaking off teeth or for tearing out tongues.

Now the common soldiers drilled beneath the shadows of wheeling buzzards and of flocks of black carrion crows winging swiftly to the grisly feast which awaited them, dangling from gallows-beams or roped to crosses, pretenderized by floggings and savage tortures.

At two meetings of senior officers of the army with their Grand *Strahteegos*, old Pahvlos had blamed the increasingly high incidences of sell-back of rank among officers and desertions of common soldiers on a general breakdown in discipline engendered by excessive coddling of the troops. A prime and flagrant example of this distressing trend was, he noted, that of the thief and mutineer Captain *Vahrohnos* Bralos, onetime commander of the lancers of the Wolf Squadron. He had then harangued his captive audience for almost an hour, each time, on the deadly dangers to discipline and order of treating the common soldier like more than the dumb, unfeeling, seldom thinking brute that he actually was. Such dangerous and larcenous officers as *Vahrohnos* Bralos, he noted, who frittered away ill-gotten monies on such things as expensive clothing, extra—and completely unauthorized by traditional practices—items of armor, food as good as some junior officer messes, better wines than the army could afford and even tobacco, were underminers of morale among the unindulged soldiers and the very bane of an overall commander's existence.

The senior officers heard him out—what else could they do?—but the few who took his diatribes to heart had been of his personal clique before he had begun. Most of the officers recognized just what he was trying to accomplish and knew full well just why he was trying to accomplish it. Unimpressed by him, they all knew exactly why their soldiers were deserting or trying to desert or purposefully injuring themselves; they were doing so for the same reasons that so many junior officers were either trying to sell back their ranks or just resigning and riding off to their homes the poorer. The combination of old Pahvlos' dogged determination to convert the entire army to total abstinence from women, unwatered wine, and the use of either hemp or tobacco if he had to flog, maim, mutilate or kill half of them to do it would have been enough, but with a useless, senseless march into the swamps and salt fens looming in the near futures of them all, it did not take an intellectual giant to perceive that Council's army, now commanded by an obvious madman, was become a distinctly unhealthy place in which to remain longer. Indeed, not a few of the senior officers were thinking seriously of early and quick retirement to their lands or cities, had the old man but known.

Far-flung expeditionary forces had been summoned to return to the base camp under the walls of Mehseepolis, and as these smaller units trickled in to be confronted with the hosts of new rules and list of now-forbidden activities—each one, to the minds of the average man, more nonsensical and stupid than the one preceding it—and the halved pay and the frenetic activity in preparation for an extremely dangerous expedition that, were truth known, no one but him responsible for its inception really anticipated with any emotions save fear and horror, whole bodies of not only common soldiers but sergeants and specialists began to desert. They went over the perimeter by dark of night, or they did not come back from errands or details outside the heavily guarded military enclave. Members of units sent out in pursuit of deserters took to not returning, and it was found that punishing the officers in charge of these units did nothing but to increase the rate at which junior officers departed the army.

At length, the mess had begun to stink so foully that Council was moved to calling as full an assembly as possible and hearing a move to force the retirement of its Grand *Strahteegos*. But old Pahvlos owned vehement supporters on the Council and, as a *thoheeks* in civil life, was himself a member. He had, of course, hotly defended his methods of discipline and punishment, refusing to retire, regardless of his age, which was approaching eighty years, and his supporters on Council had spoken so forcefully in his defense that Council Guardsmen had had to be summoned three times to break up brawls between noblemen. Several duels and at least one attempted assassination had been the eventual and only result of the session, and the disgusted chairman, *Thoheeks* Grahvos, had ended by dismissing everyone with nothing in the way of business settled.

With the captains of both lancer squadrons under arrest, confined to their respective quarters and awaiting hearings by a not yet formed board of officers, the Grand *Strahteegos* dispatched orders to Senior Captain and Commander of the Cavalry Brigade *Thoheeks* Portos to appoint the senior lieutenant of each squadron acting-captain-of-squadron and have them take over command during the campaign, wherein the lancers would as usual ride point, flanks and rearguard, back up the scouts whenever necessary and, themselves, scout out from the perimeters of nightly camps. This order resulted in both senior lieutenants immediately selling back their ranks and in one departing the camp soon thereafter. Nor would any of the troop-lieutenants deign to take over their function even when offered them at no cost.

That had been when the Grand *Strahteegos* had decided to merge the seven troops of lancers into a new "great squadron" and place it under the command of one of his favorite staff officers, Captain Gaios of Thehsmeeyee. This signal honor the tall, willowy officer sought to decline, first pointing out that he was more than fulfilled in his present function, then mentioning at some length his unworthiness for such an honor and his patent inexperience in command of combat troops. These points being all poopooed by old Pahvlos, the staff officer had first offered to sell back his rank, then begged the army commander to allow him to forfeit his investment and revert to lower rank. He was brusquely refused and ordered to pack his gear, mount his horse and ride over to the heavy cavalry enclave, present himself to the commander of the brigade of cavalry and tell him that he was to henceforth be captain of the great squadron of lancers.

Seemingly dutifully, Captain Gaios mounted his horse and rode off, leaving his servants to pack his effects, but he did not ride into the cavalry enclave; rather was he last seen headed west on the main trade road, having left a hastily scrawled letter of resignation on his writing desk.

The Grand *Strahteegos* still was fulminating against the cowardly and backbiting Captain Gaios when Captain-of-brigade *Thoheeks* Portos—outwardly grave, but secretly gleeful—dropped the next bit of bad news.

"My lord *Strahteegos*, Captain Chief Pawl Vawn of Vawn says that no one of his Horseclansmen or prairiecats will be on the Sahvahnahspolis operation; rather are they all preparing to return to Kehnooryos Ehlahs, saying that they have been absent long enough from their wives and families. Before they go, Captain Chief Pawl demands that he be paid the seven months' pay now due them. He adds that he must have the full amount agreed upon in his original contract with Council, not the half-pay that now is being given other units."

The old man's face darkened perceptibly and veins began to bulge ominously in his forehead, but before he could commence an outburst, Captain *Thoheeks* Portos, with skillful cunning, dropped the other shoe.

"Moreover, my lord *Strahteegos*, Captain Guhsz Hehluh refuses to go anywhere for any purpose until the month's pay owed his pikemen is paid along with six more months in advance, their beer ration is restored to replace the watered wine, they are given back the right to come and go as they wish, on and off the campgrounds, on their off-duty hours and are no longer hindered or harassed in their bringing back, possessing and enjoying hwiskee, brandy, winter wine, honey wine, double beer, ales, hemp and tobacco. Captain Hehluh states that if your paymaster does not pay him all that he wants in full and to the last half-copper, then he will march his full unit into Mehseepolis under arms and demand the money of Council."

"He wouldn't dare!" hissed Pahvlos. "Like all barbarians, he is only moving his lips and tongue to hear himself talk."

"My lord should not be so certain that Captain Hehluh will not do just what he threatens," cautioned Portos solemnly. "Remember, he and his men were proven veterans of formal warfare long before they came down to serve the Consolidated *Thoheekseeahnee*. They terribly resent the unaccustomed strictures put upon their lives by my lord's modes of army discipline, and the reduction of their pay by half and the delays in giving them even that have infuriated them."

"Well," snarled Pahvlos, "if the unwashed swine of barbarian, alien sows don't care to serve me in a strictly organized army, let them just march back to their sties and thus remove their hateful stink from under the noses of decent, cultured Ehleenohee!"

"They probably will do just that, in the end, does my lord not indulge them," said Portos. "But they want all monies now due them, and my lord can be assured that they can be expected to take whatever steps they feel necessary to receive it, no matter how drastic or embarrassing to my lord."

Chapter VIII

While the Grand *Strahteegos* spent his time planning for the march to Sahvahnahspolis, fuming at the previously unsuspected depths of treachery and outright cowardice of soldiers and trusted officers alike, dawdling of afternoons and early evenings in that slice of very hell behind his headquarters watching and listening to sights and sounds of horror and protracted death with the boy, Ilios, Council's once-fine, once-large, once-effective army went about disintegrating.

As a last step before actually doing as he had threatened, old Guhsz Hehluh, the grizzled captain of the Keebai pikemen, sent down to aid the new government of the lands that had been a kingdom by Milo Morai, High Lord of Kehnooryos Ehlahs, rode into Mehseepolis with a few of his officers and drew rein before the Council palace.

When, after many delays, he actually found himself closeted with *Thoheeks* Grahvos, he spoke very bluntly, as was his wont. "It's damn good brandy, my lord Duke, but I ain't here to drink your brandy. I come because I got a contract was signed by you and a couple other dukes away back when. I think me and my Keebai boys has given you good service."

Grahvos nodded. "That you and they most assuredly have, old friend. You were and are the very backbone of our army."

"Well," said Hehluh, "we won't be for much longer, not unless that old fart of a Grand *Strahteegos* Council

160

wished off on us slacks off his crazy ideas some and starts paying us in full and regular. Our next six months' pay is already more'n thirty days overdue now, and added to this loony plan of his to march the whole fucking army into the frigging salt fens to no other purpose than to pick a fight with the damn frigging fen-men—and you know damn good and well how many of them men he takes in is likely to come out, you know, you was with Zastros' army—plus his cock-eyed new-model rules that soldiers can't go out of the camp nights to dip their wick, shouldn't have wives or females of any kinds, can't drink nothing 'cept of that pukey watered wine, can't smoke hemp or even to-bacco and gets flogged for even owning a fucking pipe, I ain't at all sure just how long my sergeants and officers and me can keep the boys in the line this feather-brain bastard has done drawn."

Grahvos just sat, motionless and silent, for long moments after the middle-aged professional soldier had finished. When at last he spoke, it was to say contritely and with utter sincerity, "Guhsz, my dear old friend, I have been for long aware that Pahvlos has been changing in strange ways for the last couple of years, and I and some others of us have made efforts to first persuade him, then compel him to give up his military rank and retire. But Council consists of men, and all men are fallible, so Council is divided into cliques, some of them in favor of retiring Pahvlos, some of them very violently opposed, regardless of his mishandling of the army, its officers and its men. Those of us who recognize what he is doing to our army, all else having been foiled by his fanatic partisans on Council—and I tell you this next in strict-est confidence and then only because I know you of old, know you for the sort of man you are and, there-fore, trust you implicitly—even tried to have him as-sassinated, no less than three times, but he is always heavily guarded and, obviously, very lucky, so our hirelings all have failed us.

"Unfortunately, he was appointed Grand *Strahteegos* of Council's army for life or until he saw fit to retire. No provision was made to remove him for cause, because, based on his previous reputation, no one of us could just then suspect that ever there would be any cause to forcibly remove him; as I said, all men are fallible, alas. Therefore, until Pahvlos dies, from whatever agent—illness, mishap, battle wound or murder—or until certain cretins on Council learn what brains are for and begin to make use of them, we are stuck with the old man and all his many faults.

"Now I doubt that I can do much to protect the bulk of the army from their nominal commander, but I can damned well take you and your valuable men from under his insanities. When you leave here, you will have been paid every copper owed you according to your contract with Council and you will be bearing a document stipulating that your pikemen are, until further notice, a part of the Mehseepolis city garrison, under direct command of the city castellan. There are some acres just outside Tomos Gonsalos' enclave, near to the road between there and the lower city, as I recall; I own this land and will give it to Council's use, this day. Move your camp there as soon as possible, and between now and autumn, state-slaves and materials will be diverted there to build you and your force snug, permanent quarters, stables, wash-houses, privies, cook-houses, storehouses and whatnot.

"That should take care of you and your lot. Now, what is the case with Chief Pawl—more of the same?"

"Worse, in several ways," replied Hehluh. "He and his have not been paid anything for over seven months now. He has been borrowing from poor Captain Baron Bralos, generous man that he is, in order to give his Horseclansmen just enough for to keep body and soul together. But he's done had enough and he's remembered he's got a home and family, up north, and that's just where he and his kin are all set to head for."

Grahvos frowned worriedly. "Soon?"

"Not tomorrer, but while the weather's still warm and good," was Hehluh's reply. "I tried to talk him around to coming here to see you today, but he allowed as how he'd been down here more'n long enough anyhow, and it was time he and his folks all went back home and let the High Lord send some more Horse-clansmen down here to take his place. I couldn't fault him for thinking that way; in his place, I guess as how I would too, Duke Grahvos. Not every man jack of them is riding north, of course, but then you know about that a'ready, since you're the one talked them into staying down here and taking up vacant lands and raising stock on them."

Grahvos felt disappointed, however, for he had strongly hoped that, in the end, he could convince even more of the northern horsemen to remain in the Consolidated *Thoheekseeahnee*, and given a bit more time, he believed that he might have accomplished it. Yet another black mark to be charged to Grand *Strahteegos Thoheeks* Pahvlos.

The next blow to fall for old Pahvlos was the plague that struck the elephants, not just one or two, as was usual, but all of them, both the war-trained bulls and the three draught cows; only the young, immature and untrained bull seemed to have not contracted the pest. Neither of the captains-of-elephants and none of the *feelahksee* seemed to have any inkling of just what was wrong with the huge beasts, much less know how to doctor them. The symptoms were recurrent at odd intervals rather than constant, but serious and terrifying, all the same. At one minute, an elephant bull or cow would be its normal, well-behaved, obedient self, and then, in a mere eyeblink of time, it would become wild, uncontrollable and almost murderous, often needing to be chained to solid objects until the symptoms had abated, which might take minutes or hours or a whole day.

The Grand *Strahteegos* felt compelled to count out the elephants in his plans for the march to Sahvahnahpolis. But just then he had more than that to trouble and infuriate him.

With the loss of the medium-cavalry Horseclansmen and their great cats, which latter had proven so useful at scouting and patrolling, he knew that he simply had to have the lancers and gifted veteran senior officers to lead and command them. The only two of these now available and close to hand were under arrest, stripped of their commands and awaiting trial.

He talked the matter over with Ilios, now his most trusted confidant, then—gritting his teeth in suppressed rage—he dropped all charges against Captain-of-squadron *Vahrohnos* Bralos and Captain-of-squadron *Opokomees* Ehrrikos . . . only to watch helplessly as the wretched Bralos packed his wagons, mounted up his squadron and led them out of the camp, headed southwest.

A week later, after Pahvlos had watched an artificier's hands maimed for the heinous offense of having sneaked both a woman of easy virtue *and* a quantity of cheap barley hwiskee into the camp, the entire company of artificiers had packed up their wagons and marched away, too, on the northern trade road.

The old man knew, then, that his eyes never would see the ancient city of Sahvahnahspolis. For, lacking artificiers to lay out camps and build temporary bridges and mend damaged roads, with only a scant handful of scouts and three lousy troops of lancers under an officer he no longer trusted, with no elephants at all, he knew that it might well be worth his very life to try to push what was left of the army into those swamps and their very real terrors. This reverse deeply disappointed him, made him begin to wonder if all of the many changes that he and Ilios had promulgated might have been too much, too soon, perhaps.

As always, these days, in time of trouble or anger or distress of any nature, he went to Ilios—sultry, dark-eyed Ilios, always seductive, willing and pleasing, the most satisfying lover, male or female, he ever had enjoyed. But after he had poured it all out, Ilios had not seemed at all displeased or disappointed; rather had the nearly beardless boy nodded his small head of blue-black curls.

"Don't consider these things a loss, love, rather have you done a winnowing of your army—yours, not theirs, the army of Pahvlos, not the army of those silly, deluded creatures who make up the Council— you have driven out the alien barbarians who would have aided the Council in submission of all these lands to rule and domination by that devil-spawn thing Milo Morai. You have beaten the chaff from off the pure grain so that your army, though now smaller, is become all yours and still is big enough, more than strong enough, to allow you to take over this land whenever you feel ready to so do.

"So be not so glum, my own. I'll tell you, let us order honey wine and cheese and biscuits, then go out and watch that personal guardsman of yours who tried to desert punished. He is to be executed anyway, so indulge me . . . please? I always have wondered how long it would take a man to die after boiling pitch had been poured down his throat.

"After that, we can come back here and make love, love. It's always so very much more exciting after we've watched punishments . . . at least, it is for me."

Old Pahvlos indulged his Ilios, of course; he could not but indulge the dear, sweet boy.

*   *   *

Mostly through Sub-*strahteegos Thoheeks* Tomos Gonsalos and Captain-of-brigade *Thoheeks* Portos, *Thoheeks* Grahvos was able to keep his clique of the Council of the Consolidated *Thoheekseeahnee* up to date on the sad state into which their painfully acquired army had sunk and was continuing to sink under the baleful aegis of their once-revered Grand *Strahteegos*.

"Let us all hope . . . and pray, too," said Portos during the course of another clandestine and tightly guarded meeting at Tomos' headquarters, of a night, "that there is no large-scale disturbance at any time soon, out in the *thoheekseeahnee* or, worse, on the borders, for to all intents and purposes our army might as well be chained in place here, unable to move any meaningful numbers of troops anywhere for any purpose."

"Is it so bad, then, Portos?" *Thoheeks* Bahos had rumbled in a worried tone.

The tall horseman nodded. "That bad and far worse than that, my friend. Cavalry Brigade is become a distinct misnomer, a very sick and very grim joke. My own heavy horse is down by over a third of its former full-strength numbers, and in addition to them, there are only three understrength troops of lancers and the elephants. Captain-of-squadron *Opokomees* Ehrrikos flatly refuses to lead his light horse out of garrison for any reason until he is in receipt of a full, formal and public apology for the many wrongs done him by the Grand *Strahteegos*, and he and we, here, and the rest of the army all know that hell will have frozen over solidly before old Pahvlos so humbles himself."

"What of the other squadron of lancers, the Wolf Squadron, *Vahrohnos* Bralos' men?" asked *Thoheeks* Pahlios, who had but recently returned to Mehseepolis from his distant lands.

Portos shrugged. "He and they are gone, gone south to his holdings, I presume. He was treated far worse by Pahvlos than was *Opokomees* Ehrrikos and for far longer a time; immediately the old man was constrained to drop all his pending charges against those two officers and thus release them from arrest, Bralos packed up and mounted up and left with his men, their families and anything movable that any of them owned. His *vahrohneeseeahn* lies many leagues away, close to two weeks of marching time, I'd say."

Thoheeks Bahos knew better than that, but he kept silent and just listened, even in this gathering of noblemen who all were, they averred, of like mindsets. Young Bralos and his effectives were actually camped in a seldom-visited area of Bahos' *thoheekseeahn*, much closer to the capital than anyone else thought, and they there constituted Bahos' ace in the hole. Should the drastically changed old man who once had been loved and deeply respected by them all try anything like forcing Council out of Mehseepolis with his shrunken army, Portos and his heavy horse would know what to do and the elephants and remaining lancers most likely would back them. They, combined with Tomos' training brigade and Captain Guhsz Hehluh's mercenaries, the Council Guardsmen, the city garrison and Bahos' ace should be more than enough to put down any coup dreamed up by Pahvlos, thought the big, silent nobleman to himself.

"What of the foot and the specialists, my lord Portos?" *Thoheeks* Pahlios inquired further. "And Lord Pawl of Vawn and his beautiful, fearsome-toothed panthers?"

But it was Tomos Gonsalos who answered this time. "Captain Guhsz Hehluh's mercenary Keebai pikemen are camped just south of the perimeter of my enclave, officially because Grahvos ordered them to be transferred to duties with the city garrison, unofficially because it was either something of that sort or see them march north, out of the Consolidated *Thoheekseeahnee* entirely, probably looting along their way in revenge for getting only half-pay for six months by old Pahvlos' harebrained order. That was just the way that Chief Pawl and almost all of his squadron left, and for the same basic reasons: half-pay or none at all and always very late at that, being stringently forbidden such soldierly solaces as strong drink, hemp, tobacco and the company of females within the camp, while at the same time being most strongly forbidden to leave the camp to seek out such pleasure under enforced penalties of flogging, hideous torture, maiming, mutilation, even death."

"But . . . but why, my lord Sub-*strahteegos Thoheeks*?" demanded the newly rearrived *thoheeks* in stunned astonishment. "I've spent more of my own life than I would've preferred in armor in armies and I've never before even heard of such stupidities; why, every commander worth his salt knows that withholding of a common soldier's simple pleasures for reasons other than announced punishment is the surest way to breed discontent and desertions. Why was the Grand *Strahteegos* punishing our mercenaries and underpaying them? Is Council so low on fluid funds, then?"

Portos took over the sorry recountal at that point. "Lord Pahlios, it is not and was not, then, only the mercenaries who were being so cruelly and stupidly abused by Pahvlos. No, his strictures apply and applied to the entire army, officers excluded, of course. He claimed that in the old royal armies, it had been determined that congress with females decreased the vitality of common soldiers, and I suppose that he hoped that if he kept them all pent up for long enough, they would end up taking *pooeesosee* as he did some two years ago, just before all of this insanity commenced."

"*Rubbish!*" snapped *Thoheeks* Pahlios scornfully. "A man is a man, common or noble; I've futtered more females in my lifetime than I can begin to count, but never a single man or boy, and I've fought and won some damned hard battles, too."

"That Pahvlos, even at his rather advanced years, has taken a young man to camp-wife is not at all surprising or outside his nature, you know," remarked *Thoheeks* Bahos, speaking to them all. "If you'll recall, I was in the royal army for a stretch myself. Even then, Pahvlos kept his wife and children at his hold, far away, and a handsome young ensign or three in the army enclave, hard by the capital. Everyone knew him as a carrot-grabber, back then, not that he was the only one of exalted rank in the royal army, of course; I think that that practice, especially amongst noble officers, was much more common in the days before the rebellions and civil wars than it has been since."

"And I, for one, am just as glad for it, too," said *Thoheeks* Grahvos gravely. "For in my own royal army days, I saw more outright murders and senseless duels rise out of the bitchinesses and jealousies that seem to proliferate out of man-on-man sexual liaisons like flies from out a cesspit than I could recount if I lived twice my present age. Indeed, I was most pleased when I noted so little of it in Council's own army."

"As for the rest of it," Portos went on, still speaking to *Thoheeks* Pahlios, "smoke of any sort seems to upset the nose of the delicate Ilios—that's Pahvlos' love-boy, my lord. It makes him sneeze, makes his eyes to water, so everyone is dead sure that that's why the ban on smoking either hemp or tobacco in the army. And, incidentally, our Grand *Strahteegos* has taken it solidly into his head that the army, what's now left of it, at least, is not Council's, but rather *his*, and he so refers to it. As regards the proscription of any alcohol save only the well-watered mess-wine, I and those with whom I've discussed it are all utterly in the dark, for widespread misuse of alcohol was never any sort of real, recurrent problem in our units. And this last does not sound to have come from the delicate Ilios, for he does drink; in fact, he and Pahvlos regularly sit in the shade behind the headquarters building, sip wine and eat fruit and dainties while they watch common soldiers flogged and tortured and, occasionally, killed."

"They *what*?" burst out *Thoheeks* Pahlios, horror and incredulity reflected on his face and in his brown eyes.

"Just so, my lord," drawled Tomos Gonsalos in his Karaleenos accent, "and then, or so I am told, they both retire to his quarters and make love."

"It's nothing less than monstrous!" Pahlios remonstrated. "How is it that such an animal still commands our army, Grahvos? Though it does sound a bit to me as if this catamite has twisted him about a finger and adversely influenced him, robbed him of most of his wits insofar as running an army is concerned. Has there been any thought of having this boy, Ilios, quietly . . . ahh, eliminated?"

Thoheeks Mahvros, new chairman of Council and for long Grahvos' protégé, sighed. "Of course we've tried, Pahlios, we've hired certain men to kill both of them on occasions, no less than three attempts on the old man, but he's got more guards than you could shake a stick at, not to mention a seemingly charmed life. His food is prepared in his private kitchen by cooks who have been given to know that they will assuredly be praying for death long before it is granted to them if anything that even might be poison sickens or kills him."

"But back to your question about the regular foot and the corps of specialists, my lord *Thoheeks* Pahlios," said Tomos Gonsalos. "He did his usual number on the artificiers—denying them women, strong tipples, hemp, tobacco, restricting them all to the confines of the camp as if he commanded some slave-army, paying them only half of the contracted monthly stipend— but, oddly enough, they stayed on and merely grumbled until he had both the hands of one of their sergeants mangled and crippled for some trifling offense against his new rules. It was then that the entire unit of artificiers, officers and men alike, packed up and marched out of camp. And my lord must know that without a corps of artificiers, the remnants of our army might as well be sunk four feet deep in the sand for all of the moving any large number of them can do, for only some of the roads and bridges are passable for heavy transport, even yet." Responding to the beginnings of a contrabasso growl, he added, "This last, through no slightest fault of *Thoheeks* Bahos and his committee, but simply through a dearth of state-slaves, suitable materials on hand where and when needed and difficulty of transporting said materials elsewhere quickly."

"And as regards your earlier question about the finances of our government, Pahlios," put in *Thoheeks* Grahvos, "we are sounder now than we ever have been before, and sufficient monies were transferred to Pahvlos to meet all of the army's expenses, in full, and regularly. He simply chose to not pay his troops more than half the money they had coming."

"So where's the rest of it, Grahvos, or does anybody know? Where does old Pahvlos say it is?" asked Pahlios. "And does anybody believe his assertions?"

"Never you fear, it is all safe and fully accounted for," he was assured by *Thoheeks* Mahvros. "For all his other and heinous faults, the Grand *Strahteegos* is no thief or embezzler of army funds. The army paymaster, who recently retired, tells me that he had a full accounting done before he turned everything over to his successor and every last half-copper could be seen or traced to fully justified usage."

"All well and good, then," said *Thoheeks* Pahlios, "but still I must pose the question: What are we going to do about Pahvlos? When and how and how soon are we going to put him out to pasture or put him down?—which last is more along the lines of what he deserves for all the harm he has done us and so many others."

No one had an answer to his questions, however, not then and not there, but less than two weeks later, the Grand *Strahteegos Thoheeks* Pahvlos the Warlike lay dead upon the floor of the Council Chamber, the hilt of a slender dagger standing up from his back, he having been killed by *Thoheeks* Portos, but only after he had run up to the weapons racks, grabbed out his sword and a dirk, threatened to sword *Thoheeks* Grahvos and others, dirked *Thoheeks* Mahvros in the shoulder and called on his adherents to come and join him in what would have amounted to civil war. And such a war would have almost certainly rent the new-made nation apart, destroyed all that so many had labored so long and hard to erect.

Two hours after the necessary murder, newly appointed Sub-*strahteegos Thoheeks* Portos rode into the enclave of the army headquarters at the head of his sometime brigade of cavalry, fully armed for war. Leaving his officers and troopers to round up all of the late Grand *Strahteegos'* people and explain to them the new, hard facts of what was now to be, Portos dismounted and stalked through the main building, back to the private quarters of his late victim in search of his next chosen victim.

The brace of personal guardsmen in the corridor outside the door had been chosen more for their good looks and youth and grace than for any attainments of combativeness or fighting skills, so they were but a momentary hindrance to the tall, thick-muscled veteran warrior. He left one of them stark dead and the other crawling slowly up the empty corridor, sobbing weakly, in great agony and leaving a broad smear of gore behind him. Portos doubted the guardsman would make it far. He stooped, wiped his blade clean on the fancy cape of the dead one, sheathed it, then pushed open the door to the suite and entered.

Ilios was sitting on the edge of a bed, dark eyes still heavy-lidded, when Portos stalked in. "Wha . . . what are you doing here, and unannounced, Captain Portos? Those damned slothful guards will be well striped for this."

Portos grinned coldly. "No they won't, boy. One of them lies dead out there and the other will be dead soon enough. If it's protection you want, you should put scarred, ugly warriors on guard, not pretty popinjays."

Ilios paled, put one hand to a cheek, his eyes wide. "You mean you *killed* them, both of them? Pahvlos will likely see you hang for such . . ."

Coldly, contemptuously, Portos stepped closer to the bedside and slapped the boy on the other cheek. "Pahvlos will never again do anything for or to another living soul. He's dead too. I drove a dagger into him less than three hours agone. The new *strahteegos* is *Thoheeks* Tomos Gonsalos, and he's a lost cause for such as you, boy; he and his wife live together in this camp and are, I am informed, most congenial and contented, one to the other."

Seating himself unbidden beside the shocked boy, he gripped one of the bare, dimpled knees with a big, hard hand and said, "On the other hand, boy, there is me. I am now sub-*strahteegos*, and I always have been most susceptible to such treasures as you."

Ilios realized that, objectively speaking, he had no other options there and then. Turning his head to look up into the hard, black eyes of Pahvlos' admitted murderer, the boy smiled shyly, then puckered his lips for a kiss, letting the merest trace of a tongue-tip show behind those lips, enticingly. Such had always worked well on Pahvlos, Ilios' first and only lover. . . .

Ilios gasped when he saw Portos' body stripped of his weapons, armor and clothing—extremely hairy, seamed with scars from head to feet, tall, of a darker than Ehleen average and muscle-corded—but those features were not what brought the gasp. Nature had endowed the man hugely.

Portos padded over to an opened chest of toiletries, rooting through it, then turning with a flagonette of sweet-scented oil. Rubbing a small measure of the stuff onto both hands, he sat back down on the rumpled satin sheets and drew the boy's slight body nearer.

Ilios gasped when the big, oily hand commenced to work in his crotch. Later, lying in the glowing aftermath of his blissful fulfillment, it took him a good minute to realize that the man, his new protector and lover, was speaking to him.

"What did my love say?" he purred.

"Your body is incredibly small and narrow, I said," declared Portos, adding, "But then, as I recall, Pahvlos never was able to effect penetration of me."

To the boy's look of astonished surprise, the man nodded. "Oh, yes. Did you think to be the first? I, too, was one of Pahvlos' boys, when I was but a new ensign of barely fourteen years of age and he was a fortyish brigade commander, a sub-*strahteegos* already. But I seriously doubt that he remembered me in more recent years, for he had so many like me, keeping precious few around for any great length of time.

"But enough of reminiscing now, Ilios. I am not yet done with you."

Ilios quickly assumed a sitting posture, shaking his head with vehemence and saying firmly, "No. Oh, no.

I can't . . . won't let you do that, not yet, no. You're
so . . . so *huge*, love. You . . . you'll hurt me terribly,
probably injure me. No, I . . ."

And that was as far as he got before Portos' big,
hard, oily palm smashed against the side of his small
head, stunning him for a moment. However, he recovered enough to try to resist when he felt those horny
hands begin to start rearranging his body and legs. He
discovered to his immediate sorrow that such resistance was not only in vain, it was a serious mistake.

Portos' fist struck his hairless chest like the kick of a
warhorse, forcing all the air from Ilios' lungs, and
before he could once more breathe normally, if painfully, the brutal man had shredded a sheet, tied him to
the bedstead by wrists and ankles and was returning to
the bedside with a waist-belt in one hand and a look of
grim anticipation on his face.

"I understand that you enjoy watching men flogged,
Ilios. I've heard that it excites you. If so, your own
flogging should arouse you even more. And even if it
doesn't, it will be a salutary lesson to you that you
must never deny me my desires . . . ever."

"No . . . oh, please, *please*, no. Don't do it to me,
oh, don't!" Ilios whimpered, straining at his bonds,
tears of terror streaking his pretty face. "I . . . I can't
. . . cannot *abide* pain, don't you see? It . . . it . . . I
. . . my heart will . . . *NONONO!*"

Ilios had never gained any real friends among Pahvlos'
officers, guardsmen and servants, having always been
sullen, aloof, demanding and often downright bitchy,
tolerated and catered to only through the underlings'
fear of Pahvlos. As the loud whacks of hard-swung
leather impacting upon flesh and the shrieks of pain
and shrill pleas for surcease, for mercy, penetrated
easily out beyond dead Pahvlos' private suite, all of
the assembled officers and lesser men exchanged grins
and nods. The spoiled, overindulged little piece of pig

dung was finally getting part of what was, in his case, long overdue.

Portos was no novice at delivering beatings of all sorts, and he tried not to draw blood from the tender, pampered flesh, but he did not stop, to stand, panting, until the entire expanse from Ilios' neck to his knees was but a single, raised welt and shrieks and pleas and shouts were become moaning sobs.

He left his victim long enough to track down a ewer of wine, splash out a cupful and drink it off before going back to the bed, loosing the ankles momentarily, then retying them to the ornate posts at the foot of the overwide bed, thus splaying the slender legs widely.

Portos took his time, knowing his victim to be completely helpless, enjoying himself to the fullest and beginning to half wonder if, after all, he might not be well advised to keep the boy about until he had had the pleasure of completely breaking him . . . or he found a wife with a fat dowry, whichever came first. But, as he spent finally within the boy's quivering, agonized body, he came back to his senses. It was most imperative to Council that this Ilios be "persuaded" to immediately quit the environs of Mehseepolis, for Pahvlos, in his bemused dotage, had named his lover his heir, and such as Ilios was not at all what the Council envisioned as a fitting *thoheeks* and member of the ruling nobility.

After scrubbing himself well with the sponge and toweling dry, he went to his pile of clothes and gear and began to dress while whistling the tune of a merry harvest-dance popular when he had been a boy, more than forty years now past, virtually unmindful of the steady, low moan and occasional gasps, sobs and whimpers from the brutalized boy still secured to the bed with strips of satin sheet, his small hands and feet beginning to discolor from the biting tightness of the makeshift bonds.

Ilios lay in certainty that he had been injured, possibly fatally injured, in the course of the rape, and he wondered if his wounded body could stay alive for long enough to reach an outpost of his people, far to the south, in time. Moreover, he was almost as certain that he had one or more cracked ribs, thinking that the sharp stabs that breathing spawned in his chest could come from no other source.

But terror took over his thoughts again when he saw the redressed, armored man approaching the bed with a slender, sharp-glittering dagger in his hand. The very dagger with which old Pahvlos had been slain . . . ?

"No, please," the boy croaked weakly, his tear-filled eyes unable seemingly to leave those six inches of bluish steel blade. "Haven't you hurt me enough?"

Portos smiled icily. "Oh, no, little Ilios. Today was only our beginning, yours and mine."

Extending the dagger, he sliced through the strips of satin that held Ilios' wrists to the headboard, did the same for the ankles, then said, conversationally, "When once you've washed and dressed, pack up your things and come to my quarters. You'll not be welcome at any other place in the camp, city or *thoheekseeahn*, you know. Tonight, I'll fit you with a nice, thick peg and start stretching you to my size and tastes, eh?"

Then he turned on his heel and left the suite, stepping over the two dead guardsmen as he strolled up the corridor, his weapons and armor clanking, clashing and ringing.

Chapter IX

"You must understand, Tomos," said *Thoheeks* Grahvos bluntly, "that I consider myself to be only a figurehead *strahteegos*, holding a rank-of-honor, as it were; you and only you will command, save for those functions you choose to delegate to your sub-*strahteegohee*. I accepted in Council only because I thought it just then impolitic to further upset those few who might've been leery of a foreigner taking over command of our army. As you surely know, things might've been much stickier than they really were in the wake of old Pahvlos' . . . ahh, demise.

"Have you made any decision as to who will take over the training command?"

Tomos nodded once. "Sub-*strahteegohee* Portos and Guhsz Hehluh will share that function, for once we get the army built up again it will be just too much for one man to handle alone—believe me, my lord, I know of hard experience. Hehluh will also, however, command all of the unmounted troops, and Portos all of the mounted."

"How of Hehluh's Keebai mercenaries—will he be expected to wear three hats, then?" asked Grahvos dubiously.

"Oh, no," replied Tomos, with a chuckle. "He was the first to point out that did I want anything done right, I had best not give him too many jobs to do at once. No, one of his senior lieutenants, a man named Steev Stuhbz, will be taking over field command of the

178

mercenary foot, although for contract purposes, it will still be Hehluh's unit, of course."

"And the heavy horse that Portos has led for so long?" demanded Grahvos.

Tomos shook his head. "Now that presented me something of a problem, my lord. The man I wanted to captain the heavy horse, Captain Bralos, refused the posting, preferring to stay with his own light horse. He recommended Captain Ehrrikos, however. I talked with Ehrrikos, but he declined, saying that he'd take it only if I couldn't get another qualified officer to command it, strongly urging me to approach Captain Bralos. And I did, not quite knowing just what else to do under the circumstances, reapproach Captain Bralos, but he was most adamant in his refusal. However, he did point out a something to me that I had forgotten: Captain Ehrrikos has held his squadron command longer than any other officer still with the army. When I flatly ordered him to assume command of the heavy horse squadron, giving him no other option but to leave the army, he obeyed. Yes, it was a risky gamble, for we can ill afford to lose even one more experienced man or officer, at this sad juncture, but Bralos was certain that the gambit would work on Ehrrikos, and he was proven right, it did."

Noting the low level of wine in *Thoheeks* Grahvos' goblet, Tomos refilled it and his own. "I take it then that my lord will continue to make his residence in the city?" At Grahvos' wordless nod, he went on to say, "Then I must resolve another problem of a sort, my lord. You see, Hehluh is going to take over my old bachelor quarters in the training-command headquarters, Portos is planning to move into the other senior officer house near to mine, I mean to stay just where my wife and I are now, so that will leave Pahvlos' suite completely untenanted, vacant."

"You can't have it converted to other uses?" asked Grahvos.

"Certainly, my lord, I could, but it would be a damned shame, in my way of thinking, to do it over. In the years that he lived in that suite, Pahvlos invested thousands—maybe tens of thousands—of *thrahkmehee* in renovations and furnishings. It covers the whole northeast quarter of the main headquarters building, my lord, on the ground level, with a commodious wine cellar under that.

"There's a long, narrow foyer that opens from the central hallway, a large sitting-room with a hearth for heating, a short corridor from there to the master bedroom with an attiring-room on one side of it and a combination closet and personal armory on the other; beyond that bedroom, the corridor runs on to let to several guest bedrooms. On the other side of the foyer are a very spacious bathing-room with a small pool and piping to a roof tank for sun-warmed water in good weather, as well as to the detached kitchen for heated water in cold seasons. The remainder of the space is taken up by servants' cubbies and storage rooms."

Thoheeks Grahvos shrugged, then suddenly brightened. "I know, Tomos, just lock up those rooms and keep them as is for housing very important guests, heh? That suite sounds to be far more comfortable than anything Council can provide visitors of rank in that crowded city, up there. Also, there's the incontrovertible and unvarnished fact that anyone would be far safer from assassins in the middle of this army's camp than lodged up there in that unhealthy warren behind the walls of Mehseepolis."

"Too," added Tomos, "in a suite so capacious, a large retinue can mostly stay hard by their lord, rather than being lodged here and there, wherever they can be squeezed into the palace complex. I tell you, my lord, sometimes when I'm walking those endless, twisting and turning corridors of the palace, I would not be at all surprised to round a corner and find myself face to face with a snorting, man-eating minotaur."

Thoheeks Grahvos smiled. "Yes, I too know that feeling, my friend, and I freely admit that the additions to the onetime ducal palace were done in a rather slipshod manner, but it was at the time a crashing necessity to provide more room yesterday, if not sooner. Apropos that, are you aware that for some time Mahvros and I have been looking over architectural and layout plans for a new capital city, a roomy city with acreage allotted for eventual expansion at every hand?"

Tomos shook his head, and Grahvos went on, "Well, we have, down there on the plain, just the other side of the river."

Tomos wrinkled up his brows, visualizing the announced location, then commented dubiously, "Even if you moat it, my lord, you'll play hell and pay high to make a city there in any way really defensible. And, if moat it you choose to do, it will end as the centerpiece of a lake or a bog during flood season, you know. That is, unless you build so far from the present rivercourse as to make it easy for a besieger to interdict the canal that will have to supply your moat."

Grahvos smiled again, nodding. "There speaks the trained military mind. Man, have faith in the beautiful world that your own new High Lord envisions: a world wherein cities need not be built primarily with defense in mind, all cramped into too-small areas and basically unhealthy places in which to live. A world wherein country nobility may exchange their strong but cold and draughty and devilishly uncomfortable holds for spacious, luxurious halls set amongst their croplands and pastures. Have faith that your children and theirs will live happily in a sunny, productive land of peace and law and order, with no single bandit lurking along the roads and no armed bands riding about to trample crops and steal livestock and burn villages.

"Have faith in this glorious dream, man; I do. I know that I will scarce live to see it, but you most likely will, and Mahvros, too. This is the dream, included in the High Lord's first letter to me, that has sustained me through all the vicissitudes of the last few years, that when I am only a handful of ashes and no living man can even recall what I looked like, I still will be remembered for being one of the men who helped to finally bring peace and prosperity to the land wherein I was born, a land that I saw suffer so much and for so long."

To *Thoheeks* Sitheeros—who, save for the rare hunt or hell-ride or the rarer mountain interlude to visit with Chief Ritchud or others of his barbarian friends, had been virtually deskbound for years—it was akin in many ways to his early years as a young *thoheeks*, riding out with his picked guards or warband, this riding along sun-dappled roadways beside Captain *Vahrohnos* Bralos, trailed by their two bannermen, bodyguards and the twenty-four lancers, these led by a young lieutenant, one Pülos of Aptahpolis, with the small pack-train and spare horses and single cart trailing behind in charge of the handful of military and civilian servants and a brace of muleskinners.

As they usually camped near villages or holds, they made scant inroads on their supplies, instead buying fresh foods and grain from farmers and petty nobles along the way, folk who were overjoyed to see and accept and who gave good value for hard silver *thrahkmehee* and bright copper *pehnahee* with their sheaves of barley on their one side and the stylized head of a ram which the Council of these new Consolidated *Thoheekseeahnee* had adopted as its symbol on the other.

As almost all of the once extensive olive orchards had been destroyed by the roving combatants during the long years of revolt and counterrevolt and minor skirmishings and settlements of personal vendettas by the nobility, the bread they bought—fresh and hot from village ovens—was perforce topped with slathers of new-churned butter or savory, oniony goose grease. Most vineyards had met the same sad fates as the olive groves, so they bought and drank barley beer, ciders of apple and pear, fermented juices of peach and apricot, honey meads or ales flavored with wild herbs.

The land was good and under the hands of caring man was once more producing the riches it had for all of the centuries that had preceded the awful two decades so recently past. Herds and flocks once more grazed upon the meadows and leas and uplands. Fields of green, immature grains rippled to soft breezes that also set rows of tall maize arustle.

Small boys came running to roadsides to watch the lines of riders all ajingle on their tall chargers, the pennons fluttering at the sparkling steel tips of the long, polished lances of ashwood, sunbeams flashing from plumed helmets, cuirasses and hilts of sabers and dirks. Their elders might still feel the urge to hurriedly gather up small valuables and then run to hide in the woods, but these children had not in their short lifetimes learned to equate soldiers and riders of Council's army with death and destruction, with lootings, rapine and burnings. The passage of the small column of lancers was, to the young, simply a welcome break in their own, endless, wearisome war fought with sticks and stones against the vermin—insect, animal and avian—that haunted the fields of melons, squashes, aubergines and cabbages.

In one domain that did not yet have a full-time

resident lord to hunt out the larger, more dangerous beasts, Sitheeros, Bralos, Lieutenant Pülos and a few carefully picked lancers exchanged their troop horses for hunters and spent the best part of two days in the destruction of a sounder of feral swine which had been despoiling the country around and about, then spent another two days at helping the farm-villagers butcher and cook and eat the rich, fresh pork, it being a very rare treat in summer for their hosts.

In another domain, *Thoheeks* Sitheeros earned great and universal admiration when he rode his blooded hunter in at the gallop and, with his long, heavy Pitzburk sword, hamstrung a ferocious wild bull, so that lancers could finish it off in far less danger to man or horse. Everyone gorged that night on fresh, spicy, spit-broiled beef, a bit tough and stringy, but still satisfying with black bread, brown ale, sweet maize and boiled cabbage.

When he had wiped the grease and sauce from his lips and beard, then swallowed a good half-*leetrah* of the fine country ale, Bralos remarked to his noble dining companion, "My lord, that was indeed a beautiful piece of work you did out there today, and I will for long remember it and tell of it. But, please, my lord, you must think of me if not yourself and not so risk your life. Has my lord any idea just how much trouble it would cause me if I had to deliver back his ashes to Council at Mehseepolis?"

Sitheeros chuckled. "Not half the trouble you're going to be in with me, here and now, if you don't cut out that disgustingly formal military manner of speaking and address me as I have advised you to address me, Bralos.

"As regards the bull, well, chances are that had it been any one of a hundred or so other bulls, I'd've just sat back with the rest of the party and tried to hold him where he was until someone had got back with that crossbow, or at least some dogs. But, hell, man, you know how hunting is. I just *knew* that I could do it with that particular beast, for all that it's been a good twenty years or more since last I did anything similar on a hunt. I just *knew* that I could cripple him without serious injury to either me or my horse.

"Don't you worry about me taking insane risks, Bralos, for I mean to make old bones. My days of active warring are over and done. I intend to die at the age of one hundred years or more, in a soft bed of overexertions with a young and willing doxie, not with a gutful of sharp steel or on the horns of some wild bull, thank you."

On the next day's march, Sitheeros remarked, "You know, Bralos, this ride has been a tonic for me in more than one way, but I also think that it has given me an idea for killing several birds with but a single stone. No army can be allowed to just sit in camp, drilling ceaselessly and doing make-work chores, without suffering for it; any man who has commanded knows that. But neither is the army or Council or our people to be properly served by marching that army hither and yon to no real purpose or with the announced purpose of picking fights along the borders, as old Pahvlos did and tried to do.

"Yes, light and medium cavalry can be put to good use chasing stray bands of outlaw bandit raiders, but what of infantry, eh? Due to their survival necessity to move fast, bandits are always mounted, and even our light foot would play merry hell trying to catch them were any featherbrained senior officer to order them to it. So, must it be the fate of all our foot to sit and vegetate between drilling and endlessly repolishing unused weapons? No, there is better work for them and for the good folk of our Consolidated *Thoheekseeahnee*, I think.

"As of the time that we two left Mehseepolis, all save one of the *thoheekseeahnee* had *thoheeksee* and all of the border marches had an *opokomees*, but as we have seen on this march, right many of these interior lands are totally lacking minor nobility—*komeesee* and *vahrohnoee*—and the common people are working the land without the help or the supervision of any resident lord, given what little aid or advice as they do receive by agents of the *thoheeks* when they ride through each year to collect taxes or to gather men for seasonal work on river levees and other civic projects of a local nature.

"Moreover, many of these lands are quite likely to stay devoid of petty lords until such a time as there is more hard money about for purchase of the titles and holdings of extinct houses, for no one can expect a *thoheeks* who is himself often living on gruel and wild herbs and spring water between harvests to just give valuable assets away to the first promising landless nobleman-born who chances down the road; our world just does not work that way nor will it ever.

"Therefore, we have the current problem: willing, striving folk who could produce far more from lands that even now are showing traces of their old fruitfulness did they but have steady, intelligent guidance and set goals toward which to labor, did they but have access to extra hands during those seasons when they most are needful, did they but have men armed and trained to arms to keep large, baneful wild beasts in check, until these lands each have again their own resident lord with his family and retainers to do all these needful things for them. And this is where our idle soldiery comes into the scenario, Bralos. This is the plan that I mean to put to the High Lord of the Confederation on our ride back with him."

"And what, my lor . . . ahh, Sitheeros," said Bralos

uneasily, "if this great ruler has other plans for our and now his army?"

Thoheeks Sitheeros just smiled. "My boy, we will just have to see how best to cross that stream when we are up on its banks."

"From all that I have been told and the little that I have seen," said the High Lord, "you have done a stupendous job in so short an amount of time, *Thoheeksee.*"

Despite the best efforts of Grahvos, Mahvros, Bahos, Vikos and several others, they had been able to assemble only twenty-two of the thirty-three in Mehseepolis by the time Sitheeros and the escort came riding in from the east with the notable visitor and the new squadron of Horseclansmen.

"We sincerely thank our High Lord Milos of Morai," said *Thoheeks* Grahvos with grave solemnity. "We regret that many of those who have strived so hard for and contributed so much to the rebirth of what was, and not too long since, a smitten, blighted land of chaos and disorder could not be on hand to welcome our overlord and to hear his generous words of praise; but few of the lands are even as yet on a firm, paying basis—be they *thoheekseeahnee, komeeseeahnee, vahrohnohseeahnee* or *opokomeeseeahnee*—and some of our peers simply could not absent themselves from their lands and still be assured that all their folk will be able to eat through the winter coming."

Which was, thought Grahvos to himself, as good a way as any other of which he could think of putting the powerful man on notice that affairs within these Consolidated *Thoheekseeahnee* were just not as yet to a point at which any meaningful amounts of reparations could be paid to the sometime Kingdom of Karaleenos or to anyone else.

He had, of course, heard that Milo was telepathic, as

too were a good many Horseclansmen, but even so he was shocked when the tall man nodded his head of black hair stippled with grey and said, "*Thoheeks* Grahvos, gentlemen, I fully realize that that which you all have so valiantly set out to do will assuredly take time, much more time than has thus far passed. My reasons for making this initial visit to your land has nothing to do with the collection of any monies. I am come to offer help rather than hindrance, you see.

"That which I have learned from the regular reports of *Thoheeks* Tomos Gonsalos, added to the information freely imparted me by your own *Thoheeks* Sitheeros and *Vahrohnos* Bralos of Yohyültönpolis, has confirmed my earlier thoughts of just where I and the might of our Confederation of Eastern Peoples can best be of aid to you, our newest member-state.

"Your northern marches are, I am assured by all, secure and at peace. Your southern marches are as secure as ever they will be with the Witch Kingdom abutting them—and I'll be speaking more of them at a later date.

"Your eastern marches, too, are about as safe and as peaceful as anyone who knows the fen-men could expect them to be. These fen-men are treacherous killers, all seemingly at a never-ending war with all the world and all peoples. They make precious few treaties and they keep or abide by the terms of even fewer. If human vermin truly exist, they are of the race of the fen-men. The one good thing that I can say about them is that, at least in Kehnooryohs Ehlahs and northern Karaleenos, they appear to be a gradually dying race. It is to be hoped—and I sincerely do so hope!—that these scum dwelling on the periphery of your lands will register similar declines in numbers, for only thus can you, will you, ever be free of their unsavory ilk.

"In the west, however, you have a very real problem confronting fledgling naval forces. Considering the degree of destruction that the available seaborne effectives of the late High King Zastros suffered at the hands of Lord Alexandros and his fleet, some years back, it is indubitably to your credit that you have managed to raise any naval force at all within so short a space of time, and that they have proven ineffective in dealing successfully with the existing menace of these marauders is perhaps to be expected.

"Nonetheless, herein is a place and time that the Confederation can prove its worth to you and your people. Even as I speak to you all here, elements of Lord Alexandros' fleet are assembling in and around one of the rivermouth ports of southern Karaleenos, awaiting only the word from one of my gallopers to set sail for Neos Kolpos. If he and his pack of recently reformed pirates cannot catch and put paid to these sea-raiders afflicting your western *thoheekseeahnee*, then be certain that no mortal man can do so, gentlemen.

"During this first part of my stay in your land, I would prefer to bide in your army camp, for I must quickly learn of that army's best and worst features, that I may choose wisely those who will set out with me for the west, those who will make up the landward jaw of the nutcracker with which we will strive to crush and crumble those who now so sorely plague this land of the Consolidated *Thoheekseeahnee*.

"Considering the pressing need, I think that the civil side of affairs here must await the outcome of the military—the naval, to speak with more exactitude. But never you fear, any of you gentlemen; before I depart again for the north, I will appoint a surrogate, a *satrapos* whose title will be *priehkips* or, in the Merikan tongue, prince. This man will have four subordinates immediately under him and their title will be *ahrkeethoheeks*. My surrogate may or may not be one of you gathered here today, but all four of the *ahrkeethoheeksee* will, I solemnly assure you, be one of your own."

Milo's first private meeting with Tomos Gonsalos was conducted in the spacious, comfortably furnished and tastefully appointed parlor of those quarters that had been Pahvlos the Warlike's. Immediately Tomos had spoken his latest and highly candid report to the High Lord, he arose and said, "Lord Milo, please come with me to the other side of this suite's foyer. We found while inventorying the contents of this suite that one of the storerooms had a false rear wall, and behind it was found something I think will interest your High Lordship."

When the section of wall shelving had swung aside and a lamp had been positioned properly, Milo hissed between his teeth at sight of what lay revealed within the secret recess. But he kept a blank face nonetheless and asked Tomos calmly, "What made you suppose that these artifacts would be of interest to me, in particular?"

"Because, Lord Milo," was the reply, "they so resemble those somewhat larger and more ornate ones that were in the compartment of High King Zastros' great mobile yurt, using which, you spoke to the king of the Witchmen."

Milo smiled. "Yes, I had clean forgotten, you were there that day up on the Lumbuh, weren't you, Tomos? All right, who lived in this suite besides the now-dead Grand *Strahteegos*? Never mind, just see that every one of them on whom you can lay hands is put under lock and key until I can get around to examining and questioning them. For now, let's see if this devilish device is working."

When he had connected the male plugs of a thick insulated cable to the matching female receptacles on the two metal boxes, he raised the lid of the smaller of them, then searched vainly for something, before noticing that on this particular model, something was built into one front corner. Slowly, various things in the metal chest started to glow and a humming sound—first very low-pitched, but gradually getting louder—emanated from it.

After he had fingered a switch to a different position from that in which he had found it, he located a large silvery knob and began to turn it slowly and carefully, at the same time saying what sounded to Tomos vaguely like Merikan words, but in an incomprehensible dialect of that tongue that he only had heard once before—up on the Lumbuh River in southern Karaleenos, years ago, when this same lord had used that larger but similar device to talk with the Witch King, who had spoken that same obscure dialect, too.

"Is anyone receiving my transmission?" asked Milo yet again, hoping that he was, after so long, speaking a twentieth-century brand of English. Move the dial another tiny incremental distance. "Is anyone receiving my transmission?"

When he was just about to pack it in for that day, had decided to try later, a distant voice replied, ". . . is the . . . dy Center Base Communications. Who is calling, please?"

"Where's Sternheimer?" demanded Milo coldly.

"I say again," said the voice, "who is calling? I cannot summon Dr. Sternheimer without telling him who is calling."

"All right, boyo, tell him it's Milo Moray. Tell him I've fallen heir to another of his infernal transceivers, and with any luck, I'll shortly have the vampire that goes with it, too."

Placing the flat of his palm over the face of the condenser microphone, he said in current Merikan,

"Tomos, be a good lad and fetch our wine in here. This may take a while, and talking is often dry work."

But by the time he had the goblet in his hand, the same voice came back on, saying, "Mr. Moray? Mr. Moray, are you still on the air?"

"I'm here," growled Milo. "Where's Sternheimer?"

"Dr. Sternheimer is at . . . another location, just now, but he will be back within the week. Dr. von Sandlandt, his deputy, is on hand here, however; would you speak with her?"

Milo shrugged. "Why not? Put the lady on."

Dr. Ingebord von Sandlandt proved, once Milo had shrewdly brought her to a sufficient pitch of anger, a virtual gold mine of information. Hundreds of years of dealing with men and woman had imparted to him the skills necessary to play her like a game fish and extract nugget after precious nugget before he was done. After refusing her offer of "hospitality" as flatly and profanely as he had refused Sternheimer's similar offer years before, he had promised imminent destruction of the transceiver and power unit, then had abruptly broken off the connection, turned off the radio and disconnected the power cable for fear that the Center might be still in possession of arcane equipment capable of tracking back along the beam and locating his position, about which he had been both nebulous and misleading.

"Tomos," he said to his companion, "please send a rider into the city to summon Grahvos and Mahvros . . . oh, and Sitheeros, too. And send for Portos, as well. I have learned some things from that woman down in the so-called Witch Kingdom that I think you all should hear."

"Gentlemen," said Milo to the assembled *thoheeksee* he had had summoned, "that which the folk of this land and others call the Witch Kingdom is no such thing. It is, rather, an unnatural survival of a group of men and women from the world of more than seven centuries ago. Men and women who, just prior to the death of that elder world, had learned how to transfer their minds from their own, aging bodies to younger, vibrant, healthy bodies and thus prolong their minds' lives through what is, in essence, human sacrifice. In a very real sense, they are an aggregation of vampires.

"Armed with devices and knowledge of that older, much more sophisticated civilization, they have for long centuries preyed upon the descendants of true survivors of the long-ago holocausts and plagues that so nearly wiped the races of mankind from off the face of this earth, but there is nothing of the occult or of true magic in their bags of tricks, only mechanical devices and knowledge of how to make use of those devices and use some of them to help in making more of them.

"It is their aspiration to own and strictly rule all of the continent of which their swamps and this land are parts, and they are aware that in order to fulfill this aspiration, they must somehow, in some manner, keep the land divided into tiny, weak, warring states. What you have done in your homeland and what I am doing frustrates their sinister plans. Therefore, something over two years ago, one of these creatures forced her ancient, evil mind into the body of a very attractive young Ehleen and, using the name of Ilios, formed an attachment with your Grand *Strahteegos Thoheeks* Pahvlos, who then, as you know, was one of the most powerful men in all of your Consolidated *Thoheekseeahnee*, both in a civil and a military sense.

"Being fully aware that, was she to destroy the adhesion of the *thoheekseeahnee* and thus the state, she first must wreck the strong army, she set to work with her centuries of wiles upon an aged man in the beginning of his dotage. And you all know far better than could I just what horrors she used him to accomplish. It was a truly devilish scheme, and had he not died when he did, she might well have gained a complete success. Also, she might just have managed to latch on to some other relatively powerful man and tried to continue her dangerous mischief, had she not chanced to be so injured as to feel that she must abruptly leave Mehseepolis and hurriedly seek out things like herself, lest the body she inhabited die and she with it."

That had not been exactly how Dr. Inge von Sandlandt had said it to Milo, of course. "That damned motherfucker of a Greek bastard, that one called Portos, he's a monster, an animal—big as a frigging house, strong as an ox and hairy as a goddam ape! Mr. Moray, that boy was fourteen when I took over, and though the body was nearly seventeen when all this happened, I doubt that it weighed more than fifty-five kilos. There was absolutely no reason for that pig to beat that little body so badly that he knocked loose teeth, cracked the left ramus, broke three ribs and penetrated a lung, and lashed it so ferociously with a fucking sword-belt that it could hardly walk.

"Had it not been for my radio, that body would have been dead with me still trapped within it long before I could have reached our most northerly permanent outpost. Even as it was, with one of the copters waiting for me at a rendezvous point at the limit of its round-trip range, it was a very near thing. Bare seconds after I had transferred into a new body, that of that boy was dead of peritonitis resulting from a ruptured rectum.

"Mr. Moray, I was . . . am . . . a medical doctor, but in my more than seven centuries of life and training and practice, I never before had seen a natural endowment like that bastard has. Penises that size should, in the natural course of things, be hung on horses' bellies, not the crotches of humans."

"Portos buggered your then-body, eh?" said Milo, laughter clear in his voice.

"*Gefühlloser idiot!*" the woman had raged at him. "You think it amusing, do you, *du Zotig?*"

"Well," Milo had chuckled then, "within that body, you had been playing the part of a *pooeesos*, a *Schwuler*, for two years, by that time, had you not?" He had chuckled again and, with laughter clear in his voice, had added, "You knew that Portos was an Ehleen, you vampire bitch, yet you chose to turn your back on him. Now you know precisely why it is bad policy to turn your back on an Ehleen.

"You did at least remember to relax and enjoy it, I hope?"

And then, her scream of pure rage had nearly deafened him.

Chapter X

Rikos Laskos was ushered into the main room of the suite by one of Milo's personal guardsmen. When the door had closed firmly behind him, he said aloud, "*Guten Tag*, Milo Moray. I parted from you last in Nebraska . . . or was it Kansas? *Ach, das ist schon lang her*! Were my notebooks of any value to you and our people, then?"

Milo arose, then, to just stand for a long moment, wide-eyed. "Is it really you, then, Dr. Clarence Bookerman?" he asked in English of seven centuries before. "Where have you been all these hundreds of years?"

Laskos walked across to the sideboard and, after sniffing of the contents of several decanters, chose and poured for himself a small goblet of a powerful brandy. Warming the goblet between his two palms and sniffing appreciatively at the bouquet of the liquor thus freed, he answered, "Why, where our kind are for too much of the time: on the move, of course, putting as much distance as possible between the spot wherein we dwelt happily for a few, short years and the spot wherein we next will try to carve ourselves out a new, hopefully happy, niche for a few more years . . . until people begin to take too much notice of the bald fact that we do not age as do normal folk."

"Where did you go when you left us there in central Kansas?" Milo demanded. "Most of the people who had been yours finally decided that you had felt death approaching and either had ridden off to die alone or to die near to the grave of your wife."

"It surprises me that you remember so much and so clearly from so very long ago, my friend," said Laskos-Bookerman, taking a seat, still cradling his brandy goblet. "My own recall is no longer so good; too many, many newer memories superimposed over the older ones must tend to cloud them, block them, make them of difficulty to drag up from the depths into which they have been pushed and immured.

"I cannot remember just where I went after I left you and those would-be nomads. I do remember that at some time during that period I dwelt for a long time alone in a well-preserved, well-stocked and still eminently livable complex I found carved into a mountain, out there in the Rockies. So long did I there remain that all of my beasts either died of old age or wandered off, and when to move on and find the humans for whose living companionship I hungered I did, it had to be on foot until at last I was able to acquire a scrubby little mount.

"Across the continent, slowly I wandered for years, seeing the natural increase of the survivors of near extirpation, Milo, and also observing the genesis of new societies, civilizations, cultures arising, phoenix-like, out of the dust and ashes of the old. Then, at last, I arrived upon the shore of the Atlantic Ocean. Through great good fortune, the rare kindness of fickle fate, I found a beautiful and incredibly well-preserved miniature version of a sleek ocean-racing boat. She was so beautifully designed and fitted that but a single man, if knowledgeable and active and strong, could easily sail her. In addition to her sails, she was equipped with an auxiliary diesel engine, one of sufficient power to give her decent headway in almost any circumstance.

"I now disrecall what her previous owner had called her, but I rechristened her *Woge Stute* after I had completely refurbished her for a long voyage. I cherished a desire to once more, after so very many long years, see again my *Heimat*, the land of my long-ago birth, and I had faith that this fine, friendly vessel would safely bear me to my longed-for destination.

"Of course, in those times, it took me actual years to hunt out or make all that was needful, but then the one thing for which our rare kind never lacks is time. *Nicht wahr?* Let it suffice to say that at last I felt everything to be in readiness and I put my treasure of a boat back into the water. But of course, contemplating a voyage of such length, the mere fact that she floated and seemed sound could not be enough, so I undertook several trial voyages of lesser and greater distances, each of them teaching and reteaching me things which I had forgotten over the years and centuries I had been almost landbound.

"Finally, on a late-April day, I left the coast of what had once been called the State of Maine behind me and pointed my darling's prow northeast, toward the continent of Europe. At last I was bound for *heiligen Deutschland, mein Heimatland.*"

"My God, Clarence," exclaimed Milo, "weren't you at least daunted to consider such a risk? You can drown, you know. My original coruler of Kehnooryos Ehlahs, Demetrios, died in just that way some years back; was pushed off a bridge in the middle of a battle, in full armor, and with a death-wounded war-horse on top of him, to boot. We found his helm on the bed of the river and nearby a cracked skull that might or might not've been his, too. But no man has ever seen or heard of him, since."

"Naturally, I was afraid, Milo," replied the guest, "just as I was always afraid when the air raids took place during the Second World War, in Berlin. There is at least that much of true, normal humanity in my makeup. But just as beasts and birds and eels and salmon must return to their natal grounds or waters, regardless of obstacles or distances or swarming predators, I was consumed with an irresistible urge to once more see as many of the sights of my ancient youth as still remained in the hills and deep, silent valleys and dark forests that nurtured me of old. Cannot you understand that, my old friend, Milo?"

The High Lord of the Confederation of Eastern Peoples sighed. "Of course I do, Clarence. I know the feeling, believe me. Although I've never been able to remember any of my life prior to about 1937 A.D., still do I often desire to return to places where once I was happy for some years. For instance, although I have been only something like a century removed from the plains and prairies, I often must suppress an itching urge to just saddle a horse and ride west until I once more am where I lived for so very long. So, yes, I do understand, fully, just what drove you to take such hellish risks on the open sea, alone."

"It was a terrible voyage, Milo," said Bookerman-Laskos. "I had, I discovered, chosen a bad time of year for that northerly route, for it was spawning-time for icebergs. After not a few very near-disasters, I reset my course farther south, only to suffer through storm after storm, raising waves that often overtopped my masthead and cost me much of my precious diesel fuel to maintain headway and to keep the bilge pumps going that I not be swamped.

"Those storms it was drove me so far south that my first landfall was not Ireland or England as I had expected but, rather, France, in the Bay of Biscay I was standing in to some tiny, nameless Gascon port, when three craft about the size of whaleboats came rowing out toward me, fast as the crews could row.

"Some sixth or seventh sense gave me warning, and I fixed my set of big binoculars upon those boats while still they were fairly far distant. What I saw through the glasses was not at all reassuring to a sea-weary mariner. All of the men were armed to the teeth, though mostly with a vast assortment of edge-weapons. Nor were their physical appearances an improvement—all looking to be hairy, dirty and most brutish, though strong. So I threw over the rudder and retrimmed the sails, determined to put as many nautical miles as was possible between me and such an aggregation, and I was doing just that when, abruptly, the wind died to almost nothing and, with a hoarse, bellowing chorus of triumph, the rowers came onward, increasing their already-fast beat.

"That was when I repaired briefly belowdeck and returned with my Mannlicher rifle and its carefully hoarded store of cartridges, a *Maschinenpistole* for closer-range work, and two pistols, a saber and a hefty dirk for hand-to-hand, if it came to that.

"I was lucky enough to drop all three steersmen with five shots of the rifle. The next five dropped two replacement steersmen and two oarsmen, these last from out the lead boat, but the boat with still a steersman came on nonetheless, despite my deadly marksmanship, until it was less than twenty-five meters distant. At that, I laid aside the Mannlicher, took up the *Automatisch* and slew them all—rowers, steersman and passengers, alike. At the sound of the weapon, the sight of what I had done to the men in the lead boat, the other two swung about as one and rowed back toward their distant port at some speed.

"I kept watch lest they return until, just a little before sunset, I was blessed with a fresh breeze and was able to sail far upon it before heaving out the anchors and going below for badly needed sleep.

"While searching for other things, mostly things of a nautical nature in Maine, I had lucked across a store of smokeless powders, primers and even some boxes of unprimed brass cases and factory-cast bullets in the exact caliber of my Mannlicher—8×57mm. In late morning of the next day, once more becalmed off the southern coast of Brittany, I was engaged in reloading the rifle cartridges that I had had to fire at the Gascons when I once more heard the distinctive creak and thump of oarlocks approaching.

"I emerged, well armed you must believe, Milo, onto the deck to see with surprise that a double-masted schooner lay rocking in the swell some two hundred meters out from my vessel, and between us, a small boat was being rowed toward me—six oarsmen and a steersman, plus two other men. The glasses showed me that none of the men, neither in the boat nor on the deck of the schooner, looked so scruffy as had the lot off the coast of Gascony. Their clothing looked to be at least clean, and their dress was close enough alike that it might be a uniform of some type, I thought.

"Two of the men in the boat wore sidearms—heavy cutlasses and short daggers or dirks—but none of the others bore anything of a more threatening nature than belt knives of fifteen centimeters or so in the blades. Looking at the schooner, I could see at least a dozen of what looked amazingly like swivel-guns mounted along her rails, men standing beside them with coils of smoking slowmatch in their hands. Her flag was unclear, despite my binoculars, being mostly of a faded red and rusty black, insofar as I could determine.

"Some thirty meters off my port bow, the small boat

heaved to and one of the men stood up in the stern and began to bespeak me through a leather trumpet! I was expecting the Breton dialect of French, and it took me a moment to realize that the language he was using was a very atrocious and thoroughly ungrammatical form of *Russian*. Recognizing his thick accent after a few seconds, I took up my own trumpet and asked him how long he was out from Hamburg. He was obviously startled to hear the good, Frisian dialect, but he became much friendlier, and, after exchanging a few more words, I agreed to allow him and one more to come aboard, but the boat to stand well out from my vessel when once those two had been put aboard, and they all complied with my orders.

"Milo, my friend, fortune assuredly was sailing with me on that day. The schooner, *Erika*, was an armed merchantman out of the Independent Aristocratic Republic of Hamburg. Hamburg was, I was soon to learn, one of the very few large German cities not seriously damaged in the brief exchange of missiles or the drive of Russian forces across Western Europe which followed.

"After breaking a few fangs on Switzerland, the forces of the Bear had bypassed it to sweep on into and through the vaunted but not at all effective French forces, then up through the Low Countries, whose tiny armies did not even try to resist. The German Federal Republic, however, though beset on every hand, still was not only holding its own but had, in certain sectors, begun to actually push the Russians and their satellite armies back, when the Great Dyings began to more than decimate both aggressors and defenders, impartially. The sole missile that came down in Hamburg was launched, surely from beneath the North Sea, very late in the game and in any case failed to explode, *Gott sei dank*.

"The great Russian-led invasion had ebbed as it had flowed, but if any of them returned to Russia, it must have been a miracle, so fast did they drop along the way to die. For some reason, a goodly number of Russians remained in the coastal departments of France, eventually taking Frenchwomen as spouses or concubines, and, therefore, France had become, by the time of my arrival in its coastal waters, a bilingual land, for all that it was as splintered and politically fragmented as any other European nation of that period, perhaps a little more than most, though, really, since the French have never had a stable, central government for any long period since they murdered their king and butchered their nobility at the close of the eighteenth century.

"By the time of my arrival, Milo, a few generations of breeding had brought the population of Western Europe back up to a fraction of its earlier size, but at least such progress had encouraged the people, had made them to think that perhaps mankind was not irrevocably doomed as a species. As the largest remaining port city in all of northwestern Europe, Hamburg was becoming something of a power, and its ships sailed out in every direction, just as its land merchants traveled the roads and byways of the continent with their heavily armed and pugnacious escorts.

"Of course, in times of such uncertainty, ships needs must sail well armed and, often, in convoy, shipping along larger crews than would have been necessary simply for working the vessel. *Erika* was such a ship, standing up from one of the Basque kingdoms with a mixed cargo and bound for home, Hamburg.

"My greatest good fortune was to be able to sail to Hamburg under *Erika*'s strong protection through the waters of the Dutch and English pirates, as well as up the Elbe, where had I not been in company with her I would likely have been blown out of the water by the

line of powerful cannon-and catapult-armed forts or
boarded in force by the river patrols and either killed
or enslaved.

"After so many long years of either total solitude or
companionship of only a few, pitiful survivors of all of
mankind's disasters, I found that new Hamburg to be
most stimulating in all conceivable ways, Milo. It was,
of course, as always, a booming, bustling center of
commerce, but now much, much more than just that.

"Some twenty *thousands* of men and women and
children were resident within the earth-and-wooden
perimeter walls that were fast being replaced with
dressed stone. Protected by well-armed guard ships,
the fishers sailed out and came back up the Elbe,
bearing heavy catches of stockfish to be smoked or
salted or pickled; others of them brought in barrel on
precious barrel of whale oil. Other ships brought in
lumber for the flourishing shipbuilders, or sailed in
laden with broken pieces of old statuary, bells and
other bronze or brass scrap, copper, tin and zinc for
the cannon foundry, sulphur and niter and charcoal
for the powder mills. All of the rest of the world might
be sinking into a slough of despair and barbarism, but
Hamburg was keeping lit the lamp of true culture and
civilization.

"The master of *Erika, Kapitan* Klaus Hauer, and his
son and first mate—the fine young man who had rowed
over to my vessel—Fritz Hauer, escorted me to the
new seat of government and introduced me to him
who just then was serving as *Präsident* of the *Aristo-
kratisch Sammlung* of *Hamburgerstadt, Herr* Hubert
Klapp-Panzertöt, whose surname was derived of his
grandfather, who had been a great hero of the stand
against the Eastern European hordes that had invaded
Germany.

"When once Hubert learned just how much I in my

mind held of the old, near-forgotten technologies of
the world of almost, by then, three full generations
before, he saw me declared an aristocrat and we two
worked together for years until his death, at which
time I moved on, traveling with merchants as far as
Westphalia. I lived there for some years, a client of
the Graf, to whose retainers I taught refinements of
swordplay and oriental martial arts. After some years
there, I moved on; of course, you know how and why
it must be so, Milo.

"For longer or shorter times, I lived all over the
German lands, in France, Switzerland, Spain, Italy,
Hungary, Poland, Slovakia, Rumania, the Baltic States,
the Russian princedoms, all of Scandinavia, the King-
dom of Ukrainia, Bulgaria, Serbia, Croatia, Albania,
Macedonia and, finally the Peloponnese.

"By then, nearly two hundred years after the Great
Dyings, the Greeks were once more getting a bit crowded
on their poor and rocky holdings; despite their idio-
syncratic perversions, no one ever has been able to
fault Greeks at the act of breeding. Unable to feed
themselves by way of farming or fishing, many of the
men of Greece were become pirates of shipping and
consummate raiders of other lands, and my own fleet
was one of the largest, strongest and most feared,
incorporating as it did techniques and relics of times
past which gave it a distinctive edge over its opponents.

"However, as the fleets got larger and more numerous, not just Greek but Italian, Sicilian, Turkish, Syr-
ian, Spanish, southern French and others too numerous
to recount, we too often found ourselves fighting
each other, bleeding and dying and losing ships to no
real account or gain. The field was becoming over-
crowded, you see, friend Milo. That was when the
great idea occurred to me.

"Following actual years of careful plannings and

negotiations, I was able to organize a relatively peace-ful meeting of all the leaders of all the larger fleets of Mediterranean pirates and shore-raiders. So successful in many ways were our parleys that some began to take to heart my contention that were they to not all die by way of bloody violence and find as their only grave the belly of some sea-beast, then they had best find arable land somewhere, that they could hold and which would easily nurture them and their get.

"All knew that such was simply not available in most of the seacoast Mediterranean lands, and what little still was would be so hotly defended by present inhabitants as to demand a cost far greater than any possible gain, could it be taken at all. So I told them of the vast, almost-empty spaces of the sparsely inhab-ited North America that I recalled from before I had sailed back to Europe. I spoke of the fertility of the earth there, of the rich ruins to be stripped, of the thick forests, the abundance of clear water, the sad, huddled, all but helpless knots of survivors, the plentitudes of wild and feral beasts to be eaten and skinned or captured and retamed to the uses of man.

"Two decades of my sermons they heard, and fol-lowing two deadly calamities that struck almost as one—a very powerful man ascended to the sultancy of the Turks and began to not only put down pirates with his numerous and intrepid fleet, but actually to mount bloody seaborne raids on the bases of the raiders, then a succession of terrible earthquakes and resultant tsu-namis devastated the Peloponnese, Crete and many other islands—a large percentage of the sea-robbers of Greece, southern Italy, Syria, Sicily and even far-off Spain made indication that they would favorably con-sider setting sail across the ocean to a new land where the Turks could not so easily hunt them out."

Milo just stared. "*You*? It is you who was responsi-

ble for the conquest of most of the East Coast by the
ancestors of the Ehleenohee, Clarence?"

Bookerman-Laskos shrugged, self-deprecatingly. "It
wasn't all that easy, Milo. Ships that were fine for
sailing or rowing on the tideless Mediterranean would
never have made it across the Atlantic, and I knew
this fact even if others did not know it or think of it. I
had all of the bases moved from Crete and Cyprus,
Sicily and Malta, Sardinia and Corsica and the Balearics
to a single point, a huge, sprawling base, on the coast
of Portugal, a bit south of the vast ruins of Lisbon. We
were compelled to conquer the people of that land in a
succession of wars. Only then could we go about utiliz-
ing their labor, their wood and their shipyards to build
for us an oceangoing fleet.

"I like to think that we were good rulers and protec-
tors of the people, Milo. We drove off countless raids
by sea-rovers, defeated utterly two in-force raiding
fleets of Moors and one of Basques. In answer to
repeated provocations, we sailed up to Bilbao, scut-
tled or burnt all of their ships and even boats, went
ashore and defeated their forces, then looted and fired
the town that squatted among the ancient ruins. No, I
had forgotten, we did not destroy all of their ships;
those that looked usable to our purposes, we sailed or
towed back to our base to add to our burgeoning
flotilla, and, having learned from this episode, we
began to do the same to other Atlantic-coast Spanish,
French, English, Irish and other ports. We carefully
scouted out objectives, struck with overpowering forces,
fought hard, but then most often sailed away with only
usable ships and easily come-by bits of loot, ships'
stores and perhaps a few new women.

"Even so, doing the best that we could, doing it as
carefully but still as fast as we could, it took us the
best part of eight years to make ready for the great
adventure. Using ancient maps and charts, I laid out

our course for North America, and, late in August of that year, we set sail out of our jam-packed harbor—nearly twelve thousand men aboard seventy-eight ships, leaving almost as many men to follow in a second wave whenever enough bottoms were built or taken from others to bear them. And even as we sailed out into the Atlantic, more of our kind were sailing in from the Mediterranean, fleeing the wrath of the savage Turks.

"The voyage, unlike my terrifying solitary one two centuries past, was relatively easy and almost serene. We did not begin to lose ships until we had sailed into the coastal waters and begun to run up against unmarked shoals and other dangers that were not, of course, shown on the two-hundred-year-old charts. But, recall, please, Milo, this all occurred more than two and a half centuries prior to that horrible spate of seismic disturbances, volcanism, tsunamis and land subsidences, so the coast was basically unchanged, with few swamps worthy of the name along them, so landings were effected with a fair degree of ease and we began to acquire a few mounts and send out some parties of scouts to see what lay before us and allow us to carefully choose initial objectives, for it was plain that the lands were not deserted as I had recalled them from so long in the past, but that certain numbers of folk were living on them, exploiting them in various ways.

"We had landed on the Atlantic coast of that area once known as the State of Georgia. There were many ruined places, yes, but there were also quite a few agricultural settlements, two of these large enough to be considered small cities, by then-current Mediterranean standards, and these were called Savannah and Brunswick. We knew that both must fall quickly were we to gain uncontested possession of the rich croplands between them; also, we needed harborage for

our fleet, lest the autumnal and winter storms wreck
it.

"I decided to first attack the larger, stronger of
these little cities. I personally reconnoitered, lying hidden and still in many places for days, but finally emerg-
ing with a sound plan of action.

"With the weapons and equipment then available to
us, Savannah sat impregnable atop its bluff, impregnable by river, that is. But still I sent elements of the
fleet up the river, where they created a noisy disturbance just beyond the ranges of the defensive engines
mounted atop the bluffs. All but a handful of the
foolish, painfully naive Savannanans rushed to the walls
atop the bluffs, and that was when I led my men
against the landward walls. We swarmed up them on
our assault-ladders, flung open the gates and let the
rest of our men in to begin a bloody massacre of the
inhabitants. Understand, Milo, I did try to control my
men, but a single man cannot be everywhere at the
one time, you see. Some few escaped the city, naturally, such things happen in warfare, so we well knew
that the other city, to the south, Brunswick, would be
warned and very watchful.

"The river harbor below Savannah was roomy enough
for our fleethaven for the season of storms, so we
moored the most of the ships therein and let Brunswick
wait and watch and worry while we spent the autumn
and winter and early spring in consolidating our gains
and moving by both land and water against the smaller
centers between us and the other city. I had managed
to convince my bloodthirsty minions that live slaves
were far to be preferred to decomposing bodies, so we
oversaw our new-won lands planted in the spring, then
the most of us marched off southward and westward to
win more land and slaves and loot.

"With all of the countrysides surrounding it in our

hands and all of its vessels sunk or driven off sea and river, besieged Brunswick fell to our arms a year almost to the day after Savannah had fallen. Therefore, with a firm foothold established on that coast, I took four ships and set sail back to the east to fetch back the second wave of Mediterraneans to conquer yet another part of the lands.

"On my return from Portugal, Milo, my starting fleet of some fifty-three ships was storm-scattered, and only forty-one still were with me when we laid over, briefly, on the coast of New England. We were bound for the lands just north of the originally invaded area, but another terrible storm drove us into the southern end of the Bay of Chesapeake, and so we made our base among the shattered ruins of that huge complex of ancient cities and commenced to fan out south, west and north.

"However, after two signal defeats of my Mediterraneans in the north and northwest, I ordered that all expansion head south and southwest, directions in which the indigeneous resistance seemed both weaker and less well organized, while I took thirty-two ships and set sail for Portugal and more men.

"I arrived back at the Portuguese base to find that thousands more folk, both pirate-raiders and more peaceful ones, had come to the base just in time to swell the ranks of the defenders in a war against invading Spaniards from the southeast and swarms of sea-raiders sailing up from Morocco and other points along the west coast of Africa.

"Leaving my fleet and that of the base to combat the Moors, I led out the army and, after a lengthy campaign of maneuver, caught, cornered and virtually exterminated the Spaniards, for all that their force was larger and stronger than my own. My victorious forces came back just in time to meet and drive back into the sea an invading army of Moors whose fleet had cunningly led mine off on a wild goose chase and thus left the base vulnerable and thinly defended. The one fortunate result of all this was, however, that we managed to capture a good two-thirds of the Moors' ships, more or less undamaged, so some ten months after I had returned to Portugal for the second time, I sailed back toward North America with almost a hundred ships.

"The Chesapeake base lay empty of life, and through the tales of the survivors, by then holding lands along the coast of what is now called Karaleenos, I learned that a huge, well-armed army had marched down from central Virginia to join with another army of indigenes in southern Virginia and move against the base, crushing it and slaying all who were unable to crowd aboard the few ships I had left behind.

"The hearing of these tales bred a rage of vengeance in the men I just had brought over the sea. Therefore, deciding that such combative rage should not be wasted, I once more passed over the more southerly lands and led all of my fleet and forces up the rivers and into the heart of the Commonwealth and Kingdom of Virginia.

"Milo, that was a long, grueling war, the conquest of Virginia. Yes, we had cannon, but then so, too, did they. As you no doubt recall, small arms had become very rare by then, repeating firearms almost nonexistent, because of the lack of self-contained cartridges. Most guns as did exist by then were flintlock-muzzle-loaders. The King of Virginia had a corps of two hundred gunmen, perhaps eight hundred bowmen and crossbowmen, a thousand horsemen—about half of whom had at least one flintlock horsepistol—and several thousands more infantry armed with pikes, spears, swords, poleaxes and suchlike. A strong army, well and innovatively led, good morale in the beginning, hard fighters, most of them. But we defeated them, in the end. We took very few male slaves, though, for those men were of the sort who will fight to the very death rather than surrender while still a drop of blood remains within their veins; you have to admire such men . . . but, also, you have to kill them, all of them, are you to retain that which you have won from them.

"As in all of the other lands we conquered, the few units that did run fled to the mountains or took refuge in states not yet conquered by our arms, to the north or the western parts of the south. Again leaving men employed at cleaning out pockets of resistance and otherwise consolidating their conquest, I took some ships and bore back to Europe for yet another wave of my new-style immigrants.

"The base in Portugal was filled to overflowing; so crowded was it become in the three years I had been absent that folk were living perforce in tents and hovels outside the walls on every hand or aboard ships in the harbor.

"The Turkish sultan, stung to the point of malicious rage by Greek coastal-raiding, had first taken most of the islands, one at the time, then had launched an invasion of the mainland of Greece itself, and refugees—whole families of them—were pouring into any place or land that might give them permission to make landfall.

"Aware as I was that, even by that time, the states that had been known collectively as New England still owned only sparse populations and so would likely not be long or difficult in the conquering, I assembled the leaders of the Greek horde and, after extolling the beauty and richness of the lands, put forth my plans for helping them acquire a new home over the sea. Their straits in Portugal were no less than desperate, and so I had no difficulty in filling all of my then-available ships with displaced Greek families."

"Hmmph!" grunted Milo. "So that's why Kehnooryos Mahkehdonya has not only a different culture but even a different dialect, a Greek purer than the tongues of all the other Ehleenohee-settled lands.

"Since you were mostly responsible for settling the distant ancestors of these Ehleenohee here, Clarence, do you have any sense of . . . say, paternity, of being *pater familias* toward these, their very distant descendants?"

Bookerman-Laskos smiled lazily. "Why, of course I do, Milo. Just which of your schemes are you trying to lure me into, eh?"

"Refill your goblet and I'll tell you, Clarence," Milo replied.

Epilogue

Perforce, the one time pirates of the Pirate Isles knew every inch of the still-sinking coastlines of the former kingdoms of Karaleenos and that now of the Consolidated *Thoheekseeahnee* in some detail, so locating safe anchorages in which to lie up and await the summons of the High Lord had presented no slightest difficulty to Lord Alexandros or any of the captains.

Referring to the maps and charts they and their predecessors had drawn over the recent years, they had decided in advance just how many of their ships each place could comfortably hold, assigned certain vessels to each of the ones farthest south, then worked out methods of staying in good contact, that none might be left behind when the time came to sail.

Of a day, a half-dozen of the long, low, lean raiders, lashed one to the other at port and stern boards, their masts all unstepped, were rocking gently in a sheltered cove well hidden behind treacherous shoals and a spit of swampy, much overgrown land, more than a fathom of brackish water beneath their keels and a steady seabreeze sweeping most of the noxious insects inland, as well as helping to dispel the muggy heat.

Aboard the flagship, some seamen-raiders performed necessary cleaning and maintenance tasks—one detail being hard at work roving fresh ropes into the small but powerful catapult mounted just behind the fore-peak of the vessel, another using a small boat to ferry garbage and sewage ashore to be dumped for the delectation of the huge crocodilians and other, lesser scavengers, lest dumping it in the waters of the cove attract the unwelcome company of sharks. With a deafening din of metal on metal, a muscular smith worked at a small forge on deck, straightening blades of swords, cutlasses, boarding pikes and the like, restoring proper curve to the hooks of grapnels and boathooks and speedily fashioning odds and ends of needed hardware from bits of scrap metal.

Nearby to the smith, using the heat of his forge-fire to keep fluid a pot of reeking fishglue, a fletcher with a sack of feathers, a number of small and very sharp knives and a stack of dowels went about his task of feathering new shafts for arrow and hand-dart, ignoring the bright, hot sparks that often flew around him from the blows of the smith's hammers. Within easy reach of the fishglue pot, a pointer fitted carefully chosen and smoothed sharks' teeth of a range of sizes to the dart or arrow shafts; with practiced skill, he wrapped the threads of soaked sinew just tightly enough about shafts and glued heads to dry to optimum tightness without cracking or warping the wood. Those destined to become fire-arrows he mounted with minuscule chips of shark tooth sunk into tiny slits in the wood just behind the heads and secured them with droplets of the fishglue.

Also sharing the heat of the forge-fire was another seaman-specialist who squatted with a long-handled ladle, a set of molds, a small axe and a couple of big ingots of lead; his task was that of melting the soft metal and casting sling-bullets.

Underlying the clang-clang-clanging of the activities of the smith, a constant soft rasping, were the sounds of edges of steel and bronze blades being whetted. And, in the lee of the steersman's deck, under a scrap of awning that stopped the rays of the torrid sun, two persons sharpened their personal armaments with handstones and light oil.

One of these was a slender but very wiry man of early middle years, clearly a *kath'ahrohs* Ehleen of pure or reasonably pure lineage—his skin much darkened by sun and weather, seamed with the cicatrices of old wounds. A faded strip of cotton cloth was lapped around his head to keep the salt sweat from out his dark eyes; otherwise—like the most of the ships' crews—he was naked save for his rings, armlets and a blob of amber—encasing a fly—set in ruddy gold that hung from the lobe of his one intact ear. Squatting with his back leaned against the wooden bulkhead behind him, he was using a very fine stone to bring the blade of a heavy dirk to razor keenness.

Beside him, using a coarser stone to smooth out nicks along the cursive edge of a heavy-bladed two-foot cutlass, lounged a woman bearing an unmistakable racial resemblance to him, though their two sets of features were dissimilar in numerous other ways. To see her long, lithe, flat-muscled body with its proud, upthrusting breasts, flat belly and unlined face, one unknowing would have taken her to be a young woman of certainly less than twenty-five years; in actuality, Aldora Linsee Treeah-Potohmahs Pahpahs, wife of the Lord of the Sea Isles, was easily old enough to have been her husband's grandmother.

Of a sudden, she stopped her whetting of the blade, closed her dark eyes and just sat, motionless. Then she opened her lids again, turned to her companion and said, "Lehkos, Milo is farcalling me. This may be our call to action. I'm going back to our cabin and lie down, relax enough to more easily receive his beamings fully."

In far-distant Mehseepolis, relaxed on the bed in his suite, two long-fanged prairiecats flanking him, his hands in contact with their furry heads in order that their powerful telepathic abilities might meld with and strengthen the range of his own, lay Milo Morai, High Lord of the Confederation of Eastern Peoples. He looked to be asleep, but he was actually in silent converse with the High Lady Aldora, who at that moment was lying on a bed aboard her husband's warship, *Pard*, some four hundred miles distant.

"Aldora," he beamed, "the present fleet anchorage of what navy the *thoheeksee* have been able to patch together in the past few years is at the mouth of the river they call Ahrbahkootchee and is capacious enough for all of Alexandros' ships as well as theirs. Tell him that I said to sail through the Florida Straits . . . no, he'd call that the Dragon Passage. Tell him to maintain a tight formation and maximum safe speed and not to let his corsairs go gallivanting off on any side forays. He should keep his eyes peeled for one or more small fleets of low, rakish, felucca-rigged ships, with permanently fixed masts, most of them painted a dull brownish grey with random patterns of dull green.

"He is not to fight them unless attacked, but if push comes to shove, I'd like to have a few prisoners in relatively sound condition. Stay well clear of the coasts of that long island to the south of the Dragon Passage, the one called Koobah; I've learned that the Witchmen have several stations there with offshore defenses that not even the Ehleen pirates could overcome without losses of more ships and lives than I'd care to see."

"How much time do we have to get there, Milo?" the woman beamed, her unbelievably powerful telepathy never having needed bolstering of any kind for either receiving or sending, no matter how great the distances involved. "The ships are scattered in a number of coves stretching southward along the Atlantic coast, and it will no doubt take a little time to collect them all."

"Don't worry, my dear," Milo assured her, "there's little rush involved, here. I'm setting out with selected units of their army on the morrow, leaving others to follow after. Those who know the country that lies between here and the western *thoheekseeahnee* estimate that it will require two or, more likely, three weeks for cavalry to get there and as much as six weeks for the slower units to arrive in place."

"Then why in hell did you call me so soon?" she demanded.

"Because, Aldora," he patiently beamed, well familiar with her impatience and intemperance, "I want to be certain that our fleet is within quick sailing-time of the Neos Kolpos. The last thing I want to see is the bastards getting out of the little trap I'm setting for them and us having to assault their bases in order to put paid to them, once and for all. Besides, knowing Alexandros and his captains as I do, I am certain that they'll want to sneak in and take soundings in the areas of intended combat well ahead of having to sail their fleet in, so time must be allowed for that, you see."

"All right, Milo," the woman replied. "I'm sorry, I should have known after all these years that you had it all planned out. We'll set sail as soon as the tide rises enough to allow us deep water over the bar and the shoals. How far is it from the southern coast of Karaleenos to where you want us to be, do you know?"

"Roughly twelve hundred nautical miles," he answered. "Unless you follow the coast, which I'd prefer you not do."

"Well, Milo, with favorable winds, we should be standing into this fleet-anchorage in six or seven days . . . maybe even less. Will that be good enough to your purposes? And we wouldn't coast-hug, anyway, not as frequently as sand shoals form and disappear along that coast."

"Fine," was Milo's reply beaming. "In seven days, wherever I am on the march, I'll try to farspeak you, probably in late afternoon or early evening."

* * *

At an informal meeting held later that day in the headquarters of the army, Milo told his audience, "I ride at dawn, gentlemen, along with my guards, two hundred Horseclansmen and Captain Bralos' squadron of lancers. *Thoheeksee* Grahvos, Sitheeros and Vikos have all indicated a desire to ride with me, as well, and they and their guards are more than welcome . . . just so long as they all understand that I make it a usual practice to travel light—no wheeled transport, nothing that a mule's back can't carry easily. Everything else will have to follow with the army and baggage-trains.

"The army will march west in three or four days under command of *Strahteegos Thoheeks* Tomos Gonsalos. It will consist of the scouts, the remainder of the brigade of cavalry under sub-*strahteegos Thoheeks* Portos, the Keebai pikemen, the light infantry, the foot-bowmen, the dart-men and the slingers, the artificiers and all other specialists that the commander thinks will be of need."

"How many elephants, my lords?" asked Captain Nathos respectfully.

"What point in taking along any?" asked Captain Ahzprinos, adding, "After all, we'll be marching into the very Land of Elephants."

"Quite so," agreed Nathos, "but you still had best have a few of mine on the march for emergencies. Else, how are you going to get a wagonload of grain out of a mudhole without unloading it, eh?"

Tomos Gonsalos nodded. "There is that, of course; you've a good head, Nathos. How many would you recommend?"

"For the projected numbers of troops and baggage, my lord *Strahteegos*," replied the elephant-captain, "a minimum of four, but six would be better, that there always be one available in need and that they none of them be worked too hard or for too long."

Gonsalos nodded again. "So be it, Nathos. Six elephants will go with me and the army. Will you command, or will one of your lieutenants?"

Captain Nathos grinned. "Turn down a free visit home? Not me. Yes, I'll command the contingent that accompanies your force, my lord."

"All right, gentlemen," said Milo, "now that that is all settled, we come back down to another reason we are met here this day. Soon, your army will be melding with the Army of the Confederation. Before it can, we must standardize your systems of ranks—which is archaic, clumsy, repetitive and most unwieldy in practice.

"The lowest and the highest and two median ranks in your current usage will be retained, but others will be added between them. Your lowest rank of officer, ensign, will stay just where it is and keep its present meaning and function. Junior and senior grades of the rank of lieutenant will be eliminated and the one rank of simply lieutenant substituted for them; furthermore, lieutenants will no longer command troops of horse or companies of foot, only platoons or sections. Captain will henceforth be the rank of commanders of troop or company.

"Above that, there will be no more senior captains, captains-of-squadron, captains-of-battalion, captains-of regiment, captains-of-brigade and the like. Commanders of squadrons of horse and battalions of foot will bear the rank of major, and regimental commanders will bear that of colonel. Brigade commanders will be called brigadiers. As I earlier said, the two grades of *strahteegos* will stay in both name and responsibility.

"When once a complete blending of the armies has been accomplished, there will never again be any selling of ranks within it. Promotions, thenceforth, will be predicated upon each officer's ability, not upon his individual or family wealth and aspirations, nor even upon his civil rank. Thus, you will not be burdened with the risk of valuable troops to the command of some wellborn, wealthy, titled ninny who looks very good on parade but who lacks the brains that God gave a boar-hog and cannot find his arse with both hands and a pack of dogs.

"Amongst what you now call the common soldiers, you are going to witness and hear of even more changes, gentlemen. In this army of yours, your rankers are designated only as soldier or trooper, sergeant and a few ambiguous specialist titles. Within the Army of the Confederation, on the other hand, there are no less than some fourteen gradations of soldiers' ranks, running from recruit up to army sergeant-major, each higher one denoting increased responsibilities, increased privileges and higher pay. This is what the future holds for your army, too, like it or not. It has worked well for me, since I reorganized the army of Kehnooryos Ehlahs, half a century ago, and it will work just as well for you.

"You see, gentlemen, when well and properly led, after being well and thoroughly trained, your so-called common Ehleen soldier is easily the match of any Middle Kingdoms professional soldier extant, as I discovered a half-century and more ago in the north. The two main reasons that he has served you and other Ehleen states so poorly in times past have not been his fault in any way. One of these has been a stubborn application of hidebound, pigheaded traditional practices—crowded, inflexible battle formations; officers' reflexive assumption that all common soldiers are thickheaded and childish and respect only raw force; an almost total lack of care for the common soldiers, as illustrated best by failure to provide more than the bare rudiments of protective clothing or armor for them or to provide them and to train them in the use of auxiliary weapons. The other principal reason has been their leadership, their officers, notably on the level of junior officers.

"Gentlemen, simply because a man happens to be nobly born, trained from boyhood in arms and the hunt, has never meant that he is therefore automatically a born leader of fighting men, tactician and strategist all rolled into one. Such men have existed, do exist at present, but they are and always have been exceedingly rare. An army cannot expect to have good units without good officers, and in order to have good officers, candidates must be very carefully selected, well trained in the beginning and subjected to continual training and periodic quality evaluation throughout their active careers with the army.

"Immediately this current campaign is done, all of these changes will gradually be put into effect in your army. You know, many of the changes I have outlined were also thought of and seriously contemplated by your late Grand *Strahteegos* Pahvlos, too."

"*Pahvlos the Warlike*?" chorused Grahvos, Portos and not a few more.

Milo nodded. "I've read that old man's journals, you see. Shortly after he took over your army and saw the strengths of Guhsz Hehluh's pikemen, the Confederation-style cavalry of Portos and Pawl Vawn's Horseclansmen, he began to first question, then stringently criticize blind Ehleen traditionalism in his own mind, think things through, then set down conclusions and work out solutions to existing problems. Had he gone further along those lines of thought, had that satanic Witchmen's agent Ilíos not appeared and begun to twist his mind, then you might be very much farther along the way to a truly effective, well-organized, really modern army. It's a pity."

ABOUT THE AUTHOR

ROBERT ADAMS lives in Seminole County, Florida. Like the characters in his books, he is partial to fencing and fancy swordplay, hunting and riding, good food and drink. At one time Robert could be found slaving over a hot forge, making a new sword or busily reconstructing a historically accurate military costume, but, unfortunately, he no longer has time for this as he's far too busy writing.

HORSECLANS FANS PLEASE NOTE:

For more information about Milo Morai, Horseclans, and forthcoming Robert Adams books contact the NATIONAL HORSECLANS SOCIETY, P.O. Box 1770, Apopka, FL 32704-1770.